THE LIES BENEATH

ANN EICHENMULLER

HighTide
Publications, Inc.

Deltaville, Virginia

Published by High Tide Publications, Inc.
1000 Bland Point Road
Deltaville, Virginia 23043
www.hightidepublications.com

Thank you for purchasing an authorized edition of *The Lies Beneath*. High Tide's mission is to find, encourage, promote, and publish the work of authors. We are a small, woman-owned enterprise that is dedicated to the author over 50. When you buy an authorized copy, you help us to bring their work to you. When you honor copyright law by not reproducing or scanning any part (in any form) without our written permission, you enable us to support authors, publish their work, and bring it to you to enjoy. We thank you for supporting our authors.

Edited by Cindy L. Freeman
Book Design by Jeanne M. Johansen

ISBN: 978-1-945990-29-8

To my husband Eric,
whose love and support
made this book possible.

Prologue

THE WOMAN WATCHES THE sun edge over a bare horizon, the stark lines of the Chesapeake Bay Bridge Tunnel caught in its golden light. She has made this trip every morning for three years, save the few days last winter when ice formed a skin on the water and her kayak remained chained to a post on the beach. She slips out each day before dawn, leaving her husband lying in their bed, and paddles to the deep water of the channel, watching as with each stroke the shore recedes until she knows she is over the tunnel. The woman is still then, aware of the cars moving beneath her, millions of gallons of water filling the space between the air that surrounds them and the air she breathes. She cannot say why, but this ritual makes her feel young and alive.

It is November. She wears a thick wetsuit and a life jacket, not because she needs either one–the water is not yet cold, and she is a strong swimmer—but her husband is afraid for her. Though he never says it, she knows, and so she makes this small concession for him. And perhaps he has reason to worry. She is sixty-six years old. On these fall mornings she is often the only one here to watch the day come in.

A low bank of clouds slides eastward, blocking the dawn, and the golden liquid around her turns to ink.

It is a mark of her previous profession that she senses the shape in the darkness beside her before she can see it. Instinctively she raises the paddle from her lap, lifts it to strike downward, but she is a second too slow. The shape rises from the water, all black, and latches onto the aluminum shaft. Sunlight punches out from the space between clouds, and for an instant they are frozen by brightness. The woman stares at the masked face of a diver.

The man leaps up and puts his full weight on the shaft, jerking it downward. The woman releases her grip too late, and she is pulled forward, plunging face first into the water. She struggles to right herself and kick upward, but the shape below has her ankle, pulls her down. Something slams against her back, hands tearing at her life jacket. She punches at it, but the heavy water slows her movements, and then the jacket is gone. There are hands around her legs, around her chest, dragging her deeper, and she cannot get free.

The woman weighs a hundred and thirty pounds, and it takes three strong men to hold her down.

Her lungs burn, and she thrashes wildly, but the pull is inexorable. Already the light above her grows pale, and she is pressed on all sides by the liquid darkness. She knows this is her last conscious thought, the last emotion she will feel before her body takes over, against her will and against her training, forcing her to breathe in the water that will choke her.

It is not love or regret for the husband she leaves behind, nor is it rage against the faceless men who are taking her life. Though she cannot see them, she knows them just the same.

No. It is surprise.

What took you so long?

Then her mouth opens, and the coldness fills her heart.

Chapter 1

IT WAS LATE AFTERNOON on day one of my resurrected life.

The breeze picked up, and I felt *Serenity*'s sails catch the wind, felt the moment when her heavy hull became almost weightless, lifting me up and over the waves. I wanted to make Norfolk before sunset. It had been nine long hours since I untied the lines and left the dock. I had travelled more than fifty miles since morning.

My friends, even the ones who knew me well, thought I was crazy. Just when it seemed I was getting past my husband's death, when it looked like I might be ready to live a so-called "normal" life, I suddenly announced I was taking off for the Caribbean in my own boat—me, the woman who had never sailed past Stingray Point alone.

I could understand their concern. Sometimes I wondered if I were crazy myself.

I checked the chart. The northwest wind and an outgoing flow had pushed me east of the channel, nearly even with the inlet at Little Creek. This area was home to several military bases, but even so I was surprised by the activity I saw—two choppers skimming the water and a dozen small boats at least, civilian, Navy, Coast Guard, all combing the mouth of the bay. A drill perhaps, though it looked more like an emergency response. I felt a little frisson of fear–they were directly over the Chesapeake Bay Bridge Tunnel, the only link between Norfolk and Virginia's Eastern Shore. Officials had been warning since 9/11 the structure was vulnerable to a terrorist attack, and though a new tunnel had been started, it was years from being finished. Had their predictions been correct?

This is our new normal in the twenty-first century, to wake to televised reports of blood on streets, shrapnel in subway corridors, children's bodies on restaurant floors. Would we wake tomorrow to see footage of a gaping hole and a flooded tunnel?

I turned down the squelch on the VHF and listened to Channel 16. The Coast Guard was asking boaters to keep watch for a missing kayaker in the vicinity of the mouth of the Chesapeake Bay between the Little Creek channel and Cape Henry. I breathed a sigh of relief, and at the same time, I felt a pang of guilt.

A heart might have stopped beating, and I had been grateful it was only one.

Saddened by the thought, I lifted my binoculars dutifully and scanned the surface in every direction. There was nothing to see except other searchers. According to my gauge, the water here was still close to 65 degrees, making survival possible. Still, there was not much sunlight left, and with the current rushing into the Atlantic, the chances of finding a living survivor were probably slim. I murmured a quick prayer for the kayaker, whomever he might be, and turned my attention back to sailing.

According to the GPS, I was less than an hour from the dock at Waterside…an hour from seeing Josh Culliver. I sent him a quick text with my position as a knot formed in my stomach, part anticipation, part fear. What if he changed his mind?

It was like being sixteen all over again—and I was far from that. Back then, I might have called him my boyfriend. At thirty-five, it seemed a silly thing to say.

The truth was we never really dated, never even shared a kiss. I first met Josh less than a month ago when he tied up to the dock beside me, an ex-soldier with amazing green eyes, an unflappable smile, and a head full of bad memories. He was bound for the islands, though he never said which ones. I liked him from the beginning—his easy manner, the way he looked at me when I talked, his enthusiasm for the future—but not enough to follow him south when he asked.

He untied *Andromeda*'s lines from the post beside me one morning and left, and that's where the story should have ended. Then a client I was working for turned a gun on me, and that unexpected brush with death led me to re-evaluate my priorities. A week ago, I called Josh Culliver to see if his offer still stood. The next day I paid up my storage unit for a year in advance, sent pleasant but firm farewell emails to my clients, and canceled my slip agreement with the marina.

My mother the psychiatrist diagnosed this as a knee-jerk reaction to being faced with my own mortality. She was probably right—she is very good at what she does. I didn't care. I just knew it was time to move on. I had no idea what might happen next, but for the first time since Ryan's death, I wanted to find out.

The phone chimed, Josh's text lighting up the screen. *Already at the dock. Can't wait to see you.*

Excitement tugged at me. I started the engine, pulled in the jib, and doused the main. The shore moved by more quickly as I entered the channel, and I passed behind the naval ships in port just as the last rays of sun dipped below the horizon. Ahead in the distance, I saw the lights of Waterside.

The knot in my stomach grew as I closed the distance between us. I could make out the docks now, set against the backdrop of restaurants, shops, and hotels. This late in the season the slips were only half-full—a few fishing boats, back after a day chasing rockfish, two larger trawlers, and a smattering of sailboats. Just across the channel was mile marker zero, the beginning of the Intracoastal Waterway, an inland patchwork of rivers, canals, and locks that stretched to South Florida. It was the fluid highway the snowbirds used to escape winter, chasing seventy degrees south.

I hailed the Waterside dockmaster on the radio. He answered almost at once, and I could hear laughter in the background, a deep, rich sound I recognized as Josh. That meant he had already made friends with the marina staff—not a surprise, since he got to know more locals in his first week in Irvington than I met in three years. He had a gift for closeness that seemed strangely at odds with the decade he spent as an Army sniper. Then again, perhaps it was a necessary skill for the job.

The dockmaster gave me my slip assignment and promised he'd be outside waiting to help me tie up. There was no traffic on the water, so I ducked below to look in the mirror. My face was red from the sun and wind, my short, streaked blonde hair tousled, but there wasn't time to do anything with either one. I went back up on deck and eased the throttle as I maneuvered *Serenity* toward the docks. A few minutes later a squat gray-haired man ran down the pier, waving, a tall figure jogging effortlessly beside him. Despite the baseball cap pulled low over his forehead and the scraggly beard, I knew it was Josh.

I put the engine in neutral and glided toward the slip, tossing a bow line to each man.

"I knew you'd make it," Josh said with a smile, pulling *Serenity* against the finger pier and tying her loosely to a cleat.

"I almost didn't recognize you," I teased.

"What do you think? I was going for that pirate look," he said, rubbing a hand across his face.

"Then you nailed it," I joked, leaning toward him. He put one foot up on the rail of the boat, reached across the bowsprit, and crushed me in a hug. I buried my face in the warmth of his neck and felt an unexpected rush of happiness. Then the dockmaster tightened the starboard line, pulling *Serenity* away to the other side of the slip, and Josh jumped back, narrowly escaping a chilly plunge in the harbor. We both laughed.

"How was your sail?" the dockmaster asked, unaware he had nearly dumped Josh in the water. He was perhaps fifty, wiry and weathered, wearing a blue marina work shirt that bore the name Phil.

"Not bad," I answered. "Mostly light winds, but at least it was sunny, and nothing broke." I stepped onto the dock and extended my hand. "Sandi Beck."

He grasped it firmly. "Phil Scott. Nice to meet you. If I can get you to come fill out a dock card, that'll be all I need today."

"I appreciate your staying open," I said, glancing at my watch. "I know you usually close at five."

Phil smiled. "Well, your friend here was tellin' me stories, and once we got to talkin', I lost track of time."

I glanced at Josh, who had come up behind him.

"Why doesn't that surprise me?" I said, and Josh grinned.

"No matter, though," Phil went on, leading us up the dock. "Only one waitin' for me at home is my dog, and J.D. doesn't mind so long as he's fed by seven."

I followed the dockmaster to the office and registered *Serenity* for three nights. That would give Josh a chance to get familiar with my boat and for us to get reacquainted before we shoved off. *Andromeda*, his Irwin, was docked in North Carolina. Our plan was to sail the first hundred miles to the Outer Banks together on my boat, then continue solo from there. By then, I should be comfortable enough to handle *Serenity* alone, regardless of the conditions, and *Andromeda* would never be more than a radio call away.

"Hungry?" Josh asked as we left the office.

I realized then my last meal had been half a peanut butter sandwich at 10 a.m.

"I'm starving," I admitted. "Have you had a chance to look around?"

We had the same taste in restaurants—small, casual, and off the beaten path. There were plenty of places to eat at Waterside, but in this favorite after-work hangout they were already busy and loud. Following hours of solitude, I didn't feel ready to be hemmed in by noise and crowds.

"Yep. I found a place a few blocks away. After being at the wheel all day, I thought you could probably use a walk."

Cooler air was coming in off the ocean, so I grabbed a jacket to throw over my sweatshirt. We cut through the Waterside complex in the falling light, crossed Waterside Drive, and caught the sidewalk on Granby Street. As we walked, I heard about Josh's drive up from Manteo with the salty charter captain who had offered him a ride, and I filled him in on some of the cast of characters we both knew back in Irvington. We chatted comfortably all the way to Brew Haha, a little bar and grill in an alley off Granby which, at least according to its sign, was known for its burgers and craft beers.

Several blocks from the hustle and bustle of the waterfront, the restaurant was empty but for the two of us and a bartender named Anthony, who looked about fifteen despite his occupation. We picked a spot by the window and had menus in our hands and two bottles of pumpkin ale on the table in less than two minutes.

Being the sole customers is a double-edged sword; the service is superb, but you are also a captive audience for lonely servers. Anthony was clearly eager for conversation, and before I could even open a menu, I learned he was a junior at Old Dominion University, had already met Josh at lunchtime, and was considering a career in the Navy if he didn't get into grad school (though his girlfriend didn't think the military was a good idea). He also played drums on the side and thought it would be cool to start a band. I would have liked to be politely aloof, but Josh listened with rapt attention and nodded in all the right places, seeming to genuinely care about our bartender's future. When Anthony finally left to put in our order, I rolled my eyes at him.

"Is there anybody you won't talk to?"

He was about to answer when something behind me caught his attention. I looked over my shoulder and saw he was focused on the TV at the end of the bar. The sound was muted, but I could see it was a video clip of the scene I witnessed on the water earlier. According to the headline, there was an unsubstantiated report the kayaker had been found, though search and rescue operations continued.

"I saw that," I said. "It was right near the Bay Bridge tunnel."

"With the current there, I'm surprised they were able to find a body this soon."

I noticed he did not say "survivor." According to the tickertape at the bottom of screen, the kayaker had been reported missing at 9 a.m. this morning. Hypothermia would have set in hours ago, even given the moderate fall water temperature. No matter what it looked like or what they said to reporters, the searchers had known all afternoon this was not a rescue operation. All they were looking for now was someone to bury.

We both sat in silence. When you spend so much of your life on a boat, it is easy to forget the water can be a hostile environment. The lost kayaker was a sobering reminder of what could happen if you became complacent.

Our mood was lifted by Anthony, who returned with a bowl of complimentary trail mix and proceeded to pull up a chair. If there is such a thing as taking all the oxygen from a conversation, Anthony mastered it. The only break in his personal monologue came when the cook stuck his head out from the kitchen and shouted for Anthony to pick up our order. I have no doubt he would have talked through our entire dinner, too, but another couple came in and sat at the bar, forcing him to get back to work.

Josh and I chatted about the next day's schedule for a few minutes when I saw his eyes flash back up to the screen. There was a live shot of a body being lifted ashore from the deck of a Coast Guard vessel, bright camera lights glaring against the darkness. The caption identified the victim as the missing kayaker, though no name was given pending notification of next of kin.

"At least now they'll know," Josh said, eyes sad, and I nodded.

Then Anthony was back, two more drafts in hand. He collected our empty plates and cast a longing look at the chair, but just then the front door opened, and three uniformed sailors came in. He hustled off, and we were alone again.

"San, I know we've got a lot to do tomorrow, but I have a favor to ask," Josh said.

"Sure, of course. What do you need?"

"My Aunt Maggie and Uncle Alan live in Virginia Beach, pretty near here, just off Shore Drive. If it's okay with you, I'd like to swing by there this evening. They were out of town when I docked in Norfolk on the way south, and I haven't seen them since the last time I deployed. They retired here a few years ago," he explained.

"I'd love to," I assured him.

"Alan is my father's brother," Josh went on. "He and my aunt lived right next door when I was growing up. They didn't have any kids, so they kind of adopted my sister and me. I don't know if they'll be home—I tried Aunt Maggie's and Uncle Alan's cell phones, but they went right to voicemail. I left a message for both of them, but I haven't gotten anything back. If you're sure you don't mind…"

"I don't."

He gave me an appreciative smile. "Thanks. Let me pay the bill, and then we'll walk back to the hotel and grab my rental."

I started to argue about paying my own way, but he rose and pointed his finger at me.

"No ma'am. Not open for debate," he grinned. "But don't get too excited. You can catch the next one."

"Let me guess—a five-star meal," I kidded.

Josh laughed. "You're quick."

I watched him walk up to the bar, aware of a pleasant warmth that might or might not have been related to the beer.

On the walk back to the hotel, Josh filled me in on the relatives I would meet. Maggie Culliver had been in Army intelligence and became a CIA analyst after she married Alan. Later Josh's dad, who was a senior FBI official, helped her move over to a job with Homeland Security. The two often worked together on interagency task forces.

"Whatever they did, it must have been highly classified," Josh said.

"No matter how many questions I asked, neither one of them would ever say a word. It drove me crazy as a kid."

Alan was the opposite, according to Josh. The co-founder of a company that produced marine and aerial drones for the Pentagon, he loved sharing his work with his nephew and never seemed the least concerned about security clearances. It was he who inspired Josh's love for boats.

"He let me go to the lab with him whenever they were doing hull speed tests on the experimental unmanned vessels. It was incredible–this huge tank, high speed jets, slow motion cameras—and I was maybe twelve at the time. It was the coolest thing I'd ever seen."

I smiled as I watched his animated face. There was a childlike quality about Josh that contrasted sharply with his military bearing. He wore an aura of confidence and competence like a second skin, yet there was a vulnerability about him, too, one he did not even pretend to hide.

It was a seductive combination. I found myself hoping there was more to his interest in me than a shared need to escape.

"What?" he asked, stopping in mid-sentence to look at me curiously.

I blushed.

"I didn't say anything."

"I know. But you got this look on your face, like you had an idea."

"False alarm," I said, shrugging, but I avoided his eyes.

We cut through to the Hilton's parking garage and Josh stopped beside the Jeep Renegade he had rented earlier.

"You sure you're up to this? You look really beat," he said, searching my face in the fluorescent light.

"That bad?" I asked lightly, but even to my ears my voice sounded tired.

"Don't get me wrong, you're a beautiful woman," he said, causing my face to redden again. "But you've got these dark circles under your eyes. I'm pretty sure you fell asleep while we were walking, though I guess maybe that was my fault for boring you."

"Very funny. You were completely fascinating, I swear."

He ignored me as if I hadn't spoken. "You've been up since, what four-thirty, five o'clock? That's sixteen hours without a break," he said seriously. "If you want to put this off till tomorrow…"

"No. I'm good. I couldn't sleep right now anyway. Let's go see your aunt and uncle."

Josh had their address, though he had never been to the new house.

The GPS led us to a tree-lined street bordering a bayfront beach just before 8:30 p.m. Number 5986 was an expensive-looking, whitewashed cedar and glass cottage on stilts, its steeply pitched metal roof rising to a widow's walk at the peak. All the windows were lit, and there were several cars at the curb.

"Looks like they have company," I observed.

"If they're busy, we won't stay," Josh said.

As we walked past the cars to the front porch, I noticed a dark sedan with lights on the dash and in the rear window. One of the guests was in law enforcement.

The inner door was open, and through the glass we could see two men and a woman standing in the foyer, talking in low voices. Josh wrapped his knuckles lightly against the frame, catching the woman's attention.

"Can I help you?" she asked, opening the door.

"Yes ma'am. I'm Josh Culliver, Alan's nephew," he said. "This is my friend, Sandi Beck."

She nodded, her mouth drawing down at the corners. "Of course. I've seen your picture. I'm Sallie Hathaway, Maggie's friend. I live across the street. I'll take you to Alan."

We exchanged quick glances. Something seemed off—the voices were too quiet, the mood too somber for a party.

Josh and I followed Sallie Hathaway down the hallway to a large, open kitchen. A man stood with his back to us, head bowed, in deep conversation with two uniformed officers. Worry creased Josh's forehead. Something was off.

The police officers looked toward us. The man turned, following their gaze.

"Josh, my God!" he cried. "What are you doing here?"

He was as tall or taller than Josh, and he had the same hair and face. Alan Culliver.

The man was beside me in two steps, his arms around his nephew. When he finally stepped back, there were tears on his cheeks.

"I'm so glad you're here," Josh's uncle choked out.

"Uncle Alan," Josh said softly, and I could hear the fear. "What's going on?"

Alan Culliver stared at Josh, looking confused. The officers shuffled their feet, their eyes on the floor. I had seen those looks before. I knew before I heard the words.

"I'm so sorry," Alan stammered. "I thought...I thought that's why you came."

He took Josh's hand.

"Your Aunt Maggie is dead."

Chapter 2

JOSH SAT IN A chair on the Cullivers' wide back deck, staring out at the moonlit water. I stood beside him awkwardly, unsure of what comfort to offer. I was still trying to wrap my mind around the fact that the body we had watched lifted ashore on the bar television had been Maggie Culliver's.

Over his shoulder, through the French doors, I could see Alan sitting at the kitchen table, still talking to police. I heard a door open off what must have been the laundry room, and the two men we had seen talking to Sallie Hathaway earlier came outside. One was at least six-and-a-half feet tall, heavy and bald with a gray goatee, the other thin with a bird's nest of coarse blond hair. Both were dressed in jeans and windbreakers, and I caught the smell of sweat and salt spray as they came closer.

"Sallie says you're Alan's nephew," the bald man said, extending his hand to Josh. "Bill Swann. I'm a friend of Alan's and Maggie's. I live just down the beach here. This is Craig Evanson from next door."

Josh started to rise, but Swann waved him back down.

"We wanted to tell you...we're the ones who found Maggie. We took out the boat as soon as we got the word from Alan she was missing," Swann said, looking into Josh's face. "I heard tell you're a soldier, so I thought you might want to know more about it. But it's up to you."

"I do," said Josh, though his voice cracked. "I do want to know."

Bill nodded to his friend, who moved forward.

"Maggie goes out every mornin' she can. She doesn't stick by the shore—she goes out to the channel, where the tunnel is. She usually gets out there a half hour or more before sunrise. Sometimes I'll see her paddlin' in when I let the dog out."

Evanson's voice wavered, and he wiped a hand across his eyes.

"I figured if something happened, it would have been while it was still dark. Low tide was pretty near six a.m., so it was just comin' in, and after sun up we had some chop from the north. We thought waves might have pushed her ashore near the Little Creek inlet...." He looked down at the deck and his voice trailed off.

Bill Swann cleared his throat and picked up where his friend left off.

"We found her in the shallows, close to the point. Maybe four feet of water, with a two-foot swell washing her against the sandbar. Otherwise, I doubt we would have seen her. She was face down, wasn't wearing a life jacket. She'd been...." Swann stopped, swallowed. "She'd been gone some time. There wasn't anything more to do. We radioed the Coast Guard, and they came and got her."

Josh's lip trembled. He looked down, his jaw tightening, and when he raised his head again his face was firm and blank.

"Did you see any other injuries?" he asked, his tone even and emotionless.

The men exchanged glances. "There was a cut on her head, but no blood. We think maybe she was bumped by a boat...after...."

"Nothing else?"

They shook their heads.

"Thank you for telling me," Josh said. "And thank you for finding her."

"Least we could do. Maggie is...was a good woman," Bill said. "This is a close neighborhood. We tend to look out for each other. We're—all of us—gonna' miss her."

Both men laid a hand on Josh's shoulder as they passed. After they went inside, he looked up at me.

"I'm sorry about this."

"You have nothing to apologize for," I responded at once. "I'm sorry you lost your aunt."

He nodded.

Just then the kitchen door opened, and Alan stepped out. Through the glass I could see the room behind him was empty.

"The police just left," he said, as Josh rose. "There's nothing more we can do tonight, but if you're going to be around tomorrow...."

"Sure, Uncle Alan. Whatever you need."

The two men hugged, and I was struck again by how alike they were. As they drew apart, Alan came toward me, his hand outstretched. "I'm sorry. With everything that happened, I didn't even ask your name. Did I understand correctly from my brother you've got a sailboat, too, and you're traveling south with Josh?"

I hadn't known Josh shared that information with his parents.

"Yes, sir. I'm Sandi Beck," I said, taking his hand. "I'm sorry for your loss."

Alan squeezed my hand in his. "I'm sorry Maggie isn't with us. She... she loved Josh, and when she heard from Josh's mother he might be coming to Norfolk to meet you, she was excited at the thought of seeing you both."

He held my hand a minute longer, then let it go and put his arm around Josh.

"Would you go with me tomorrow morning to...to see her? I have to meet with someone at the funeral home and I need to go talk to our pastor," he said with some effort. "Maggie wanted to be buried at Arlington. Your dad said he'd take care of that for me. But we need to have a service here for Maggie's friends. I'd...I'd appreciate your help."

Josh shot me a quick glance, and I nodded. Obviously, our plans would need to change.

"You just tell me what time, and I'll be here."

Alan looked at him with gratitude. "I don't mean to sound selfish, but I'm so glad you're here. We have made some wonderful friends in Virginia Beach, but..."

"It's not the same as family. I know," Josh said.

Alan stood there for a moment, his eyes drifting out to the dark water. He stifled a cry, and I watched as the composure he had so carefully maintained fell from his body. His legs shook, and he fell back into a chair and buried his head in his hands.

"I just can't believe she's gone," he sobbed.

Josh held his uncle, murmuring soft words. I stood there, feeling like a voyeur, then slipped inside quietly. I wandered into the empty living room and paused before a long driftwood shelf lined with framed photos. There was a picture of a small, trim woman with curly black hair standing beside Alan on a rocky overlook, and another of the two of them on a beach somewhere in the Mediterranean. There were photos of the woman alone, holding up a rockfish and riding a mountain bike, and several of the two of them with another couple I took to be Josh's parents. There was a photo of Alan and the woman standing beside a young Josh as he blew out candles on a cake, a little girl sitting on his lap.

The woman had bright blue eyes and a spray of freckles across her nose, and she did not seem to age at all. In every picture she was smiling.

"You would have loved her," Josh said. I had not heard him come up behind me. I looked around him for Alan.

"Where's your uncle?"

"He said he'd like to be alone for now. I'll come back first thing in the morning."

Josh put his arm around me, and we walked slowly out of the silent house. As we reached the car, the lights went out behind us.

Chapter 3

I WOKE TO THE gray of morning, the cabin chilly from the overnight air. I had not bothered to turn on a heater but had simply fallen into bed, pulling the blankets over me, still wearing my clothes from the day before. I stretched, feeling the stiffness in my muscles. It was nine o'clock.

Josh had walked me to the boat before going back to his hotel room. We hadn't said much, but I think we both understood there was not much to say. He hugged me before he left, the way you would a sister or a friend. I was vaguely disappointed, but I knew it was better that way. Loss and grief can drive you into someone's arms, but such things do not last.

Now I had the day to myself. Josh sent a text saying he didn't expect to be back until late afternoon, and there was not much for me to do but wait. I showered and dressed, then walked to a coffee shop we passed last night on Granby, my Kindle under my arm. I spent two hours there, reading a new book by Garth Stein, drinking cappuccino, and nibbling a fabulous bagel with homemade veggie cream cheese, spinach, and sprouts. I became so entranced in the novel I didn't hear my name called until a woman touched my arm. I looked up at her, startled, and it took me a minute to place her as Maggie Culliver's friend from last night.

"It is Sandi, right? You were with Alan and Maggie's nephew? I know, under the circumstances, you might not remember me. I'm Sallie Hathaway."

I nodded. "Hi, how are you?"

She was carrying a large coffee in a to-go cup, but she pulled out the stool beside me.

"Do you mind? I have a little extra time. I work at the Nauticus Museum, but it's a slow day and my next school group isn't for another hour."

I suppressed the urge to tell the truth—it was a really good book, and I was in the middle of a pivotal chapter—but instead I closed the cover of the Kindle and scooted my stool to the left to give her more room.

"I saw Josh pick up Alan this morning," she said. "I'm so glad he's there with his uncle. This sort of thing is never easy, and it's worse when it comes so unexpectedly."

I murmured my agreement. Any talk of a sudden death ultimately brings back what happened to Ryan, though it did not sting as it once had.

"Did you ever meet Maggie?"

"No. Josh and I haven't...we've only known each other a month," I explained.

"Oh?" Sallie gave me a curious look. "You seem so close. Well then, let me be the one to tell you, Maggie was an amazing woman. Smart, talented, independent, and her energy level! I loved her to death, but sometimes I just had to tell her I couldn't keep up. She wanted me to run a 5K with her at Thanksgiving—the Turkey Run. It's a charity thing. Had me out jogging every evening for a week back in September, if you can imagine such a thing. I went to work barely able to walk. I finally told her I'd donate a hundred dollars if I could just meet her at the finish line."

She laughed, remembering, and I laughed with her, though it died in our throats.

"So, what did she say?" I asked.

Sallie paused and sipped her coffee. When she spoke, her voice was no longer light with reminiscence.

"It's funny, you know, that you should ask that. I expected her to be all over me about quitting, but she just shrugged, said she wasn't sure she was going to run after all. I asked her why, and she said she had a lot going on. I thought that was strange because she's retired, and except for volunteering at the shelter, Maggie hasn't gotten involved in much else."

"Was she having any health problems?" I asked.

Sallie shook her head. "I don't think so. She had a physical over the summer, and she said it went great—no issues. The doctor told her she had the bones of a thirty-year-old. To be honest, I thought maybe she and Alan were having troubles."

Her voice dropped a little as she said this, and I drew back uncomfortably. I was not interested in gossip about Josh's aunt. Not that I minded speaking ill of the dead if they deserved it, but I did not know Maggie or Alan Culliver, I was not a blood relative, and by my own code of ethics, I had no reason or right to speculate about their relationship.

Sallie must have caught my reticence.

"I know, you're probably thinking it isn't any of my business. But Maggie and I were close, and she was such an open person...it wasn't like her to be bottled up. Then all of a sudden, she would be gone, one or two days at a time—first she said it was her mother, then she said it had something to do with tying up some loose ends from her old job— but she wouldn't look me in the eye. I wondered if maybe...there was someone else."

She paused as if she expected me to say something. When I didn't, she responded for me. "I know, I'm some friend, telling you this. But the thing is, I am a friend, and it bothers me that she might have died with something...unfinished."

I could not read Sallie Hathaway enough to know how sincere she was. Was she worried there was a man somewhere, waiting at a hotel room or a restaurant table, wondering why Maggie didn't answer his calls? Would he eventually find the nerve to come looking for her? If so, what would it do to Alan Culliver to find out about his wife's infidelity from her lover?

If Maggie never told her husband about the affair in life, she would not want him to find out after her death.

In my experience, when people dig into the past, regardless of their good intentions, someone always gets hurt. I run my own personal advocacy business, a career I created after Ryan's death. Many of the men and women who hire me do so because life is messy, and they don't want to get their hands dirty. My job is a cross between being a legal adviser, a private investigator, and a family counselor, and it has made me somewhat jaded about human relationships.

"If Maggie didn't tell you something, whatever it was, that was her choice," I said, perhaps a little more curtly than I intended. "I think you have to respect people's choices, especially when they are dead."

Sallie flushed, and I knew that was not the response she expected. She rose stiffly.

"You're right. Please forget I said anything."

"I won't say a word," I said, and I meant it.

She was about to turn away when her glance fell at my half-eaten bagel. "Is that spinach?"

I looked at her, puzzled by the shift in conversation.

"Haven't you seen the news? There was a terrible salmonella outbreak down south last week. They've tied it to fresh spinach from some restaurant. You might not want to eat that."

Before I could respond, she was moving toward the door. "I have to go," she said over her back. "Nice seeing you."

I watched through the window as she hurried down Granby, taking long strides, a tight frown on her face.

I considered throwing my bagel in the trash, but it was a really good bagel. I told myself she was probably exaggerating the whole thing to distract me from what she'd said, and that rationalization, along with my new "live life to the fullest" philosophy, allowed me to finish eating with only minor misgivings.

I was not as successful at putting Sallie's accusations out of my mind. Not that I had any reason to believe her, but unfortunately, you can't unhear something, and now the possibility of infidelity was like a song I couldn't get out of my head. I hoped Sallie Hathaway was wrong about Josh's aunt, but if she wasn't, I prayed Maggie Culliver had covered her tracks.

If not, a lot of people would be hurt.

Chapter 4

"DOES IT GET ANY easier?"

Alan Culliver stood beside me on his deck as the last streaks of red faded on the western shore. Josh had gone to pick up sushi, and I sensed he did not want to leave his uncle alone, so I offered to stay behind. I looked up at him, unsure of what he meant.

"Josh told me about your husband. He said it happened three years ago," Alan explained. "Right now, I can't imagine making it three days."

"I know. But you will."

He smiled wanly. "What if I don't want to?"

I reached out and slipped an arm under his.

"Give it time."

He sighed. "I just keep thinking of all the stupid things…. We had some problems, Sandi. I guess all married couples do. I'm so sorry about those petty arguments over nothing…how I wasted those minutes with her. I wish I could tell her that. At least…at least I woke up before she left yesterday. Sometimes I sleep in, but yesterday I got up, started the coffee, and kissed her goodbye. The last thing I said to her was 'I love you'."

"Then remember that," I said.

A silence followed. I could tell Alan needed to talk, but still there was hesitation. I tried not to remember Sallie Hathaway's words.

"We were married thirty-two years," Alan said finally. "We never had children. It wasn't a decision we consciously made, but we were both… so committed to our jobs, I guess, that by the time we started to think about it, it seemed like it was too late. And we had Josh and Dani. They were so close, we felt like they were ours."

His voice broke, and there was a pause while he struggled to master his emotions.

"Then there was all the political mess in D.C., and it seemed like a good time to move on with our lives," Alan went on. "Retirement was a little harder on Maggie than it was on me. She had trouble letting the job go. She had all this pent-up drive, and nothing to do with it. She was fine for the first year or so, you know. We took trips, did our bucket list. But her old boss was always calling her with a question, or asking her opinion about something, and I could see that being out of the game was eating at her."

He looked out toward the bridge.

"Paddling the kayak relaxed her. I offered to get one, too, and go with her, but she knew it wasn't really my kind of thing, and anyway, she liked to go alone. She said it was her meditation," he said softly. "At first, I watched her from the house, until she got so far out she was just a dot on the water...and I made her wear a life jacket. She said she didn't need one. You didn't know Maggie, but she was so strong, a natural swimmer... I just don't understand how...."

His voice drifted off.

Josh had pulled me aside when they first got back that afternoon. The Coast Guard officer writing the report on Maggie's death told Josh the evidence pointed to Maggie's kayak being capsized by the wake of a larger boat. It had been found overturned, the paddle missing. The life jacket was floating some distance away. He said it was possible she took it off because she thought it was hampering her efforts to swim. It was also possible she had not been wearing it in the first place, regardless of her promise to her husband. Either way, the report listed water temperature as the culprit. The officer pointed out that while Maggie could have survived an hour or more in the November water, based on the location of the kayak and the tide, the accident appeared to have happened at least four miles from shore. Even a strong swimmer would have been hard-pressed to make it to dry land in that amount of time under those conditions. To further add to Maggie's difficulty, the deeper water near the tunnel was known for its strong, fast-moving current. With no evidence of other illness or life-threatening injuries, the coroner listed cause of death as drowning, likely resulting from hypothermia. Time of death was between six-thirty and seven a.m.

I shivered.

Alan Culliver had probably still been drinking his coffee when his wife's boat capsized, and she had drowned within sight of the deck on which we now stood. For the first time, I was grateful Ryan had died on a highway, miles from my reach.

I heard the front door open and turned to see Josh emptying Styrofoam containers on the kitchen table. I squeezed Alan's arm.

"Dinner," I said gently.

As we walked inside, Alan shook his head at his nephew apologetically. "Thank you for picking up the food, Josh. You'll both have to forgive me. I'm not being much of a host. I never even offered either of you a drink. Would you like beer or wine or something else?"

"Beer for me," Josh answered, unwrapping chopsticks.

"Me, too," I said. "I'll get it. Just point me in the right direction."

Alan gestured to a side door by the laundry room.

"We keep beer out in the garage. Why don't you help me carry some inside?"

I followed Josh's uncle down a short set of stairs to the rear of a wide two-car garage. A red Corvette and black Cadillac Escalade took up most of the space, but a refrigerator and chest freezer were pressed against the back wall, along with metal shelving and a clothes rack. Several wetsuits of different sizes hung on hangers next to a buoyancy control vest, with tanks, mask cases, and fins sitting on the shelves. A damp circle stained the concrete below the largest wetsuit.

"Did you and Maggie both dive?" I asked.

Alan followed my gaze. "Not Maggie, no. She had some sinus issues, had trouble equalizing. I took one of those one-week vacation classes."

"Oh, in the islands?" I asked, thinking about the Caribbean course Ryan and I had taken.

"I wish," Alan said with a smile. "I got my certification here in Virginia Beach—this extreme diving class run by ex-military guys. I took the course just to get my card, but it was more role-playing, kind of combat diving. What about you?"

"I got my certification in the Bahamas, but I haven't been on a recreational dive for four or five years, not since we dove the Devil's Den in Florida. I dive my boat—clean the prop, check over things—that's about it," I answered.

"Maybe you'll have a chance to pick it up again when you go south," Alan said, rummaging through the fridge and handing me several bottles. He grabbed a few more, and we started back to the kitchen.

"Maybe," I agreed.

The act of eating and drinking together restored some sense of normalcy, and as we ate Alan began to tell stories about growing up with his brother and about Josh as a boy. His face glowed, and he looked truly happy as he escaped, at least for a time, from his present pain. I thought about what Sallie Hathaway had said, and I found myself hoping fervently that she was wrong.

"Do you remember that time—I think I was sixteen—when we all went out on Mr. Jansen's boat?" Josh asked, already laughing.

Alan slapped the kitchen table. "Oh my God, yes! Sandi, you should have seen this sailboat. Out of the box new, must have been fifty feet, and Bart Jansen—he was Maggie's boss—he was so proud of it. He had been telling us he was a born sailor, and my brother had been ragging on him for days, asking him the names of things, you know, and how to tie knots. Well, we sailed out of a marina in Baltimore Harbor, and Bart yells that we're going to put up the mainsail. The boat had one of those in-mast furling systems, and he keeps pushing some button to unfurl it, but nothing's happening. So, he tells Josh to climb up and take a look. Bart asks him if he can see where it's stuck, and Josh says no. Bart's getting aggravated, and he says, 'Well what can you see?' and Josh says, 'Well, sir, I can see you're pushing the wrong button.' Turns out the boat had a remote windlass, and Josh was watching the anchor go up and down on the bow!"

It was the first time I had heard Alan Culliver's laughter.

"Do you still talk to him?" Josh asked when the hilarity subsided.

Alan's expression grew somber. "Your Aunt Maggie did. He'd call to run things by her, and the two of them would talk for hours. He retired last December, moved to the Eastern Shore, but from what I gathered, he was still keeping his hand in now and again because he called Maggie four or five times last winter, all hush, hush, you know how those guys are. You grew up with your father. But then last February he fell off his dock. They had a hard freeze up there. He must have fallen right through the ice."

There was an awkward silence as all of us thought of Maggie.

"Are you doing anything with your company now that you retired?" Josh asked. I could tell he was looking for another topic of conversation.

Alan shook his head. "I still work on designs, but I do that here and then let the engineers work out the bugs. I handed over the reins of the business to my partner when Maggie stopped working. You remember Jack Gardner."

Josh nodded.

"He's doing a fine job. In addition to the military contracts, he's working on a big deal with Atlantic Power. They're putting in some huge solar farms and off-shore wind farms, part of the push for renewable energy. Plus, they have drilling operations and a new gas pipeline. We've repurposed some of our military drones to perform maintenance and monitor operations. It's a real opportunity for expansion," Alan explained.

"That's great."

A shadow crossed Alan's face. "There were some glitches, but Jack said he'd get them all ironed out, and the company's worth has gone up since he took over. But something about it worried Maggie. I still hold a controlling interest and I sit on the board, and she made some hints about my getting out."

He shook his head, looking regretful. "I got a little defensive, told her I built that company from the ground up, and I wasn't about to just walk away from it."

"I'm sure she understood that," Josh said.

"I don't know. She got her back up, said that wasn't what she meant at all, and to forget she'd said anything. So, I dropped it. But the whole thing was kind of left hanging between us...."

Josh reached over and squeezed his arm.

"Aunt Maggie loved you. Nothing would have changed that."

Alan blinked and nodded. "I know."

The phone rang then, and Alan excused himself, moving to a small den off the kitchen to answer it. Josh began clearing away the take-out containers.

"What are the plans for your aunt?" I asked quietly. I had not wanted to bring it up with his uncle in the room.

"Their pastor is doing a memorial service at the funeral home here tomorrow night, closed casket, and then her body will be flown to Arlington. My dad is working on scheduling a military burial at the National Cemetery. There's a waiting list for retired military, but Maggie had a lot of friends in D.C., and he thinks they'll be able to fast track her interment."

"What do you want to do?" I asked. It was Wednesday, and we had originally planned to head south no later than Friday. I didn't mind spending the extra days in Norfolk, but Thanksgiving was eight days away. I had promised my mother we would have dinner with her and my father in Myrtle Beach. It was probably the one thing that kept her from having me committed when I told her what I was doing. If his aunt's funeral was anytime in the next week or so, we would have to come up with an alternative schedule.

Josh must have been thinking the same thing because he gave me a rueful smile.

"I know going to your folks' place is important to you," he said. "I'm sorry about how this is working out."

I felt a rush of guilt. "Don't even think that. Trust me, my mother will make a turkey dinner whenever we show up, even if it's the middle of December."

Which was true. I'd hear about it, of course, but that wouldn't stop her from cooking.

Just then Alan came back in the room.

"I was just talking to your dad on the phone," he said to Josh. "They've scheduled Maggie's interment at Arlington for next Wednesday. I told him there's no point in him and your mom driving all the way down here for the memorial service when we'll be driving up there in a week. He said to tell you he expects all of us–Sandi included—to stay at the house for Thanksgiving."

Josh shot me a quick look.

"I don't know. Sandi promised her parents we'd have Thanksgiving dinner at their house," he began.

Hurt was evident in Alan's face, though he tried to hide it. I broke in.

"But under the circumstances, I'm sure they'll understand completely," I said. "Josh, please tell your parents thank you for the invitation. I'm looking forward to meeting them."

This was a blatant lie. I hadn't even thought about meeting Josh's parents, at least not until I had a better idea where our friendship was headed. I had enough angst about him meeting mine. I thought I caught a hint of amusement playing at the corners of Josh's mouth, but Alan beamed at me with gratitude.

"Thank you, Sandi. I didn't want to have to drive up there alone."

We finished our beers, each thinking about the service and the funeral ahead. After a long silence, Alan excused himself and went upstairs to bed. Josh gave me a ride back to the marina. He had cleared out of his hotel room after Alan insisted he stay at the house, claiming it was ridiculous to be paying for a place to sleep when the house had two empty bedrooms. Josh's uncle offered one to me as well, but I declined. I carried my home with me, and nothing would be as comfortable as my own bed.

It was nearly ten when I finished showering and climbed into the V-berth, too late to inform my mother of the change in plans. Instead, I curled up on my pillow to finish my book and promptly fell asleep. I awoke sometime after midnight, the opened Kindle still in my hand, my face wet with tears. I felt a deep, aching sadness I could not explain, the remnant of a dream I could not remember. All I knew was that I had been speaking to a woman with black hair, and both of us had been crying.

Chapter 5

I STOOD AGAINST THE back wall of the viewing room, watching as men and women shuffled forward, voices hushed, to shake Alan Culliver's hand and pass by the closed coffin and framed photographs of the woman who lay inside. Josh stationed himself on one side of his uncle and Alan's pastor stood on the other, both offering the quiet support of their presence. The service itself was over, but nearly every chair was still filled with people talking about Maggie, tissues in hand.

I did not know Maggie Culliver, so I could not truly mourn her, but after more than two hours listening to the sounds of sorrow and murmured condolences, the thick atmosphere threatened to crush me. I had been to too many of these affairs, and at every one I was haunted by a memory of myself, swathed in black and standing by a casket, shaking hands I could not feel and mouthing words I could not say.

I slipped out the door and walked past the restrooms to the deserted end of the hallway. There I found an empty bench, and I sank down, grateful to have a place to be alone. I leaned my head back and closed my eyes, letting the distant drone of conversation lull me into a half-sleep.

"What are you doing here?"

It was male voice, taut with anger. I opened my eyes but saw no one.

"I came to see Alan," said a second voice.

The bench on which I sat was next to a high table, blocked from view by a long white satin cloth and a vase of flowers. I could not see the men on the other side, and it was obvious they were not aware of my presence.

"It isn't a good idea for you to be here," the first man said sharply. "We don't need any screw-ups. Do you understand that?"

The second man was calm. "I don't screw up. Everything is fine. But I owe this to Maggie. It's about showing respect."

There was a tense silence.

"Do what you need to do and get out," the first man said finally.

"I always do."

Footsteps moved away, their sound fading out on the marble floor, followed by a long sigh and a rustling movement. A door squeaked open slowly, then shut. I eased up from the bench and saw the hall was empty.

One of the men was in the restroom, and the other must have gone to the viewing room. I stepped past the door gingerly, certain that neither party would appreciate knowing I had been an eavesdropper to their conversation. Not that I was sure what I had overheard. It was clear the disagreement between the two men involved one of them coming to Maggie's service. Why shouldn't he be here? How could his presence "screw" it up? I was reminded of what Sallie Hathaway had said. Perhaps the second man was Maggie's lover. If so, the affair and what he might say to Alan in the emotional aftermath of Maggie's death could be the reason for the first man's alarm.

I reached the viewing room and stood in the entrance. Josh was still standing beside his uncle, though they had moved to the back of the room. Alan's shoulders were slumped, his face drawn and tired, and I caught Josh looking at him with a worried expression. Sallie Hathaway was approaching them, and I found myself wondering whether Alan harbored any small, niggling doubts about his wife. As if he read my thoughts, Alan glanced over at me.

I looked away.

This isn't a case. It isn't a challenge or a puzzle to solve, I berated myself. Maggie was Josh's aunt, and what she had or had not done in the past no longer mattered. She was gone, and it was none of my business.

Sallie Hathaway left, followed by several others. The crowd in the room thinned, and the funeral home staff tactfully opened two side doors and brightened the lights to encourage the rest of the mourners to head home. The last few guests moved through, speaking to the bereaved husband as they left. I watched as Alan shook hands with a strongly-built man at least half-a-foot taller than he.

"I'm sorry for your loss," the man said, and I recognized the deep, flat tone of the second voice in the hallway.

"I appreciate your coming, Chris. Thank you."

He must have felt my eyes because Chris's head swiveled around, and he locked in on my face. I was frozen for a moment by cool steel-gray eyes, but then I blinked and he turned away, nodding at Josh and striding out a side door. I heard a throat clear behind me and realized I was blocking the entrance.

"I'm sorry," I said, stepping aside. A thin man with a shaved head brushed past me, walking purposefully toward Josh's uncle. Surprise and something else, some emotion I could not read, played across Alan's face.

"Jack! I didn't expect you to fly up," he said, and the thin man embraced him.

"Don't be foolish. I had to come. You know Maggie meant the world to me," he said.

The anger was gone, but the voice was the same. This was the first man from the hallway. He was forty-five or fifty, slightly built but wiry, with a face and neck too bronzed and flawless to be a real tan and a suit too well-cut to be off the rack.

"Jack, do you remember my nephew?" Alan asked, putting his hand on Josh's shoulder.

"Of course. Josh, right? Army?"

"Not any more, sir. Separated," Josh said, shaking the man's hand.

"And this is Josh's friend, Sandi Beck," Alan said, gesturing to me. "Jack Gardner, my partner and current CEO of I.U.S."

I stepped forward and took the proffered hand. It was cold.

"I.U.S.?" I asked.

"Innovative Unmanned Solutions. That's the company Alan had the foresight to found and the good judgment to hand over to me," Jack Gardner said, taking my hand and shaking it firmly. "Alan, you'll be happy to know we got the Navy contract for the new FJ drone, and it looks like we'll have the agreement with Atlantic Power finalized this week. You're going to be a much richer man."

"That's great," Alan said, forcing a smile.

I was struck by Jack Gardner's lack of sensitivity, but he went on, apparently oblivious to his partner's discomfort or the impropriety of discussing his financial successes at a memorial service.

"We were fortunate. That vote in the North Carolina State Senate could have killed the whole deal, but we had just enough votes to defeat it," Gardner continued, warming to his topic. "I tell you, the environmentalists—"

"Mr. Gardner, could you excuse us?" Josh cut in, his face set. He turned his uncle away and guided him toward where the pastor and Craig Evanson were standing. The movement took Gardner by surprise, and he stared after them, eyes narrowing.

"That is one of the men who found Maggie," I said, feeling a need to offer some explanation.

"Of course. Well, it was nice meeting you…Sandi," he said, but he was looking through me. "I have to be going. I've got the jet standing by at Norfolk International. Tell Alan and his nephew I said goodbye."

"Of course."

He walked out without a backward glance. I was reminded of Reed Steele, a real estate developer who had breezed in and out of my life. The ego and self-centeredness were much the same, but while Steele had a beguiling personal charm, there was something shrewd and unpleasant about Gardner, something distasteful I couldn't quite place.

I wondered why Alan Culliver would choose a man like him to be his partner.

I glanced over at Josh, who was still standing by his uncle's side. This was the first time I had seen him in anything except jeans. He was wearing one of Alan's suits, and it made him feel like a stranger to me, reminding me again how little I knew of this man I was going to be spending the next weeks and perhaps months beside. I wondered for the first time if my impulsive decision to go south with Josh was a mistake.

He looked up and our eyes met. He smiled his lopsided grin, and again I felt the current and the warmth.

I liked him. I liked being with him. This trip was about moving on with my life, and if that was all that ever came of it, I told myself I would be satisfied.

Josh bent his head to murmur something to Alan and walked over to me.

"I'm sorry for ditching you like that," he said. "I just can't stand that guy. I can't believe he was talking about money when Aunt Maggie just died."

"I know," I agreed. "I can't imagine him as your uncle's partner. They are complete opposites."

"My mom says the same thing. But Alan was so into the technical, engineering side, and he really hated the political part of it—negotiating contracts, lobbying Congress to fund projects, that kind of thing. He just didn't have the patience for people who couldn't understand physics. He needed somebody with a totally different skill set to take the company where it needed to go. He could never have expanded it the way Jack has," Josh admitted. "The guy's got talent, but I still don't like him."

"Who was the other man your uncle was talking to when I came in? Chris somebody?"

"I don't know. Why?"

Josh was watching me with renewed interest. He told me once whatever I was thinking or feeling was written all over my face, and I wondered what he read there now. More intriguing, I thought I caught a twinge of jealousy in Josh's expression.

I explained I had overheard Jack Gardner and Chris arguing in the hallway. "They didn't sound very happy with each other. I was just wondering how they're connected."

"Not happy how?"

I replayed the dialogue as I remembered it. Josh shook his head.

"Hard to say without knowing more. It sounds like Chris might be working for Gardner. If he's connected to I.U.S., maybe he wasn't supposed to take time off. Or maybe things aren't going as well as Jack made them out to be, and he was afraid Chris would say something to Alan."

That was a possibility, though based on my conversation with Sallie I thought the romantic connection to Maggie was a stronger one. Either way, it was not a topic I needed to broach at her memorial service—or anywhere else, for that matter.

"Maybe," I said.

Josh looked at me curiously, but Alan came up and Josh's attention was diverted before he could question me further. The last of the guests had gone, and only the three of us stood in the room.

"Thank you again, both of you," Alan said. "I can't tell you how much it means to have you here."

Josh hugged his uncle, and the two of them went to the casket at the front. I watched as Alan rested his hand on the wooden box holding his wife's remains.

"Time to go," he said.

Simple words, spoken as if Maggie could hear. I felt the tears burn behind my eyes.

Chapter 6

JOSH SPENT THE NEXT few days helping his uncle pack up Maggie's clothes to donate to the local women's shelter. She had been a volunteer in their job-coaching program, mentoring abuse victims and assisting them with resumes and interview skills. Alan saw it as a continuance of Maggie's wishes, but he could not face the task by himself. I understood—people deal with grief in different ways. Some refuse to accept death, leaving rooms as untouched museums for a past they cannot release. I was the opposite. I sold or gave away everything, including the house Ryan and I shared, keeping only *Serenity* and one of my husband's flannel shirts. Our possessions were imbued with memories, and I feared the weight of them would suffocate me.

With time on my hands and nothing to do, I rearranged every storage locker on the boat and then took to exploring the city's streets. I missed my exercise classes and regular gym workouts, but I made up for them with brisk walks across town, enjoying the cool fall air. I fell in love with downtown Norfolk, its quaint buildings, southern charm, and brash young energy. It was a bustling mix of new and old, and I explored all of it. Phil, the dockmaster, saw me on one of these excursions out beyond MacArthur Center and pulled over to give me a lift back to the marina. I declined, still eager for exercise, but when I walked past the office on my way to the boat, he called me inside.

"You know, this ain't a small town," he warned. "Don't get me wrong, I love Norfolk, it's a pretty place, but there are sections a woman shouldn't be walkin' through by herself. The marina truck's out front, keys are always on the wall. I don't much use it. You just help yourself if you get an itch to go somewhere."

I thought about the empty dive tank stored in one of the rear lockers. I used it to clean the boat bottom before I left Irvington, and I liked to keep it filled in case a line or some other debris fouled the prop when I was motoring. I originally planned to find a dive shop when we got to the Outer Banks, but it might not be a bad idea to get it done before we started down the Intracoastal Waterway.

"Do you know of any dive shops nearby?" I asked, explaining I was looking for an air fill.

Phil shook his head. "Not familiar with 'em myself, but I know there are some. We got a diver we call when we have an emergency, and he gets his tanks filled somewhere 'round here. You'd have to look it up on the internet."

I pulled out my phone and Googled shops in the downtown area. The closest was Adventure Dive in Little Creek, just a few miles away.

"If you don't mind, I'll take you up on the truck," I said.

"Help yourself. She's got a half-tank of gas."

"Thanks. I won't go far."

The marina truck turned out to be an old Ford 150 with equal amounts of paint and rust. I loaded my tank and its rack in the back and climbed in. The driver's seat springs were shot, leaving my head barely even with the steering wheel—a situation that made city traffic somewhat disconcerting. I drove slowly, prompting several of my fellow drivers to pass me with irritated looks (and one universally recognizable hand gesture), but I found the dive shop without sustaining any damage. It was a small concrete block building on Little Creek inlet across from the Naval base dock, its floor space crowded with racks of wetsuits and equipment. I made my way to the back counter where I was greeted by a pale, thin woman with frizzy mouse-brown hair, reading glasses perched on her nose, combing through an inventory printout. She looked to be about forty.

"Welcome to Adventure Diving. How can I help you?" she asked in a monotone, never raising her eyes from the pages.

"I need a tank fill," I answered.

"Ten bucks. Bring it in, sit it over there by the back door," she said, gesturing with a quick movement of her head, still focused on her work.

I went out to the truck and grabbed the tank, then stood it beside a collection of at least a dozen others against the wall. I noticed they all had tags with names and dates. I went back to the counter and stood there for a good three minutes, watching the woman read, before I finally cleared my throat. She looked at me over the top of her glasses without expression.

"Don't you need me to fill out something?" I suggested.

She put down the pages, slid off her glasses and pointed them at me.

"Has Kenny done your tank before?"

I said no and explained I was just passing through Norfolk by boat on my way south. She warmed at this information and laid her glasses and pencil on the counter, extending her hand.

"Lucky you. I'd do anything to get out of here," she said. "I'm Laurie Anderson. Nice to meet you."

"Thanks. I'm Sandi Beck."

Laurie rummaged in a drawer and pulled out an orange ticket and a Sharpie. "Fill that out. Kenny—that's my husband—is out on a certification trip in Morehead City. He won't be back till tomorrow. He's the only one who can fill tanks."

I wrote my name, the date, and my cell number on the tag. As I handed it back, I gestured to a set of smaller, thinner canisters stacked apart from the others next to three high-pressure steel 120 tanks.

"What are those little tanks?"

She followed my hand. "They're for rebreathers. We have one on display over there. One of my husband's partner's ideas. He demonstrates it in the Commando Course, but we haven't sold one yet. I told Kenny, they're just too expensive. Chip and a couple of his Navy buddies have them. Those are their tanks. They brought 'em in yesterday for a fill."

I walked over to the display, locked in a heavy glass case. It contained a thin, lightweight backpack with space for two of the small canisters. The marketing information touted the semi-closed-circuit rebreather as a cutting-edge system for serious divers, allowing them to recycle air and make the diving experience virtually "bubble-free."

"What's the Commando Course?" I asked.

Laurie pointed behind her to a chalkboard on the wall, listing the shop's classes and prices. The Commando Course was by far the most expensive, though it was only five days in length.

The woman snorted. "It's grown men playing dress-up if you ask me, but what do I know? It's our most popular class. You get your basic PADI card, plus you learn survival and self-defense skills, knife and speargun training, and diving in overhead environments. They run it like a boot camp."

I thought about the course Josh's uncle said he took. "Do you know Alan Culliver? I think he may have been one of your students."

She nodded. "He sure was. He's in that picture over there. First time they ran the course. Maybe two, three years back."

I moved nearer the framed photograph on the wall. It showed a dozen men, mostly average-looking and middle-aged, wearing full wetsuits and posing on a sandy beach. Alan was in the back row, but what stood out were the three men in the front center. They were younger, taller, and better built than the others, and though their faces were shadowed, there was something familiar about one of them I couldn't place. I leaned in, looked more closely, and drew in a surprised breath.

It was the man I overheard arguing with Jack Gardner in the funeral home.

"Who are these three guys in the middle?" I asked.

"You mean the real soldiers," she said with a laugh. "The one with the blond hair is my husband, Kenny. The other two guys are his partners, Chip Holland and Chris Holtz."

"They were all military?"

"Navy SEALS. Chris and Kenny got out at their twenty and opened this shop. Chip bought in last year. Chris and Chip are mostly silent partners. They do security for some big-bucks military contractor, but they come back in town to teach the Commando Course. Kenny's the one who runs the place. And me," she added. "Not exactly my dream job, but the store doesn't make enough to hire someone else when he's doing certification dives. So here I am. And to think I married Kenny to get out of Virginia Beach, and I'm right back where I started."

That explained why Chris Holtz had been at the funeral. If he worked for a military contractor, it might be I.U.S. That would support Josh's theory about the conversation I'd overheard.

"How's his wife doing?" Laurie asked.

I started. "Who?"

"Maggie Culliver, Alan's wife," she repeated.

"I…I'm sorry," I stammered. "I thought you would have heard. Maggie passed away. She died in a boating accident a few days ago. It was on the news."

"Oh, God, I'm so sorry," the woman said fervently. "I didn't know. I don't pay much attention to the television. We have three boys, and it's all I can do to get them to do their homework and take a shower every night. That's—that's just awful. I really liked her—she had spirit."

"You were a friend of Maggie's?" I asked.

"Not really. I just knew her from the shop. Last summer Alan paid for private lessons for Maggie, over in the pool," Laurie said, gesturing out the window to the marina next door. "Most of our stuff is done out in the Bay or at the Y, but Alan knew somebody over at the yacht club, so he got permission. Anyway, she tried as hard as anyone I've ever seen, but it was no good. She had a deviated septum from years back, just couldn't equalize. Chris told her the first day it wasn't going to work, but she came back day after day and tried again. She didn't quit till she ruptured her eardrum, and even then, it was Chris who stopped the lessons."

The realization hit me.

"So, Chris Holtz was her instructor."

"Yeah. He doesn't usually teach anything but the Commando Course, but I think he did it as a favor to Alan. Man, he's going to be upset when he hears."

I opened my mouth without thinking. "He already knows."

Laurie raised her brows in surprise. "You're friends with Chris?"

"No. I saw him at the memorial service. I mean, I didn't know his name until just now…when I asked about the photo."

"I can't believe he didn't call to tell us," she said, shaking her head. "Well, anyway, do me a favor. Tell Alan Laurie and Kenny are sorry for his loss."

I promised I would. We stood there awkwardly for a moment, then Laurie glanced down at her inventory.

"I'll be back tomorrow for my tank," I said, taking the hint.

"Not till after noon," she reminded me. Then the glasses were on and she was back at work. I said goodbye on my way out the door, and she mumbled something from behind the pages that might have been "Have a nice day."

Out in the truck I mulled over what Laurie had said. It sounded like Chris Holtz was more than just an acquaintance or an employee. If Sallie Hathaway was correct in her suspicions of an affair, then Chris Holtz was a potential contender for the role of Maggie Culliver's lover.

I started the truck when my phone rang. I dumped out my purse, spilling my phone, mascara, and a dozen receipts to the floor. I managed to grab the cell just before it went to voicemail.

"Hello," I said breathlessly.

"So, you're still alive."

The sardonic tone was pure Wayne. I was immediately awash in guilt.

"I know I told you I'd check in when I got to Norfolk," I groaned. "I totally forgot."

"Nice to know I rate high on your list of priorities," he said. "So, where the hell are you now?"

"Still in Norfolk."

"Why? What happened?" he asked, his voice at once full of concern. "Didn't that guy show up?"

I smiled. Wayne had purposely avoided calling Josh by name since I told him about my plan to sail south. He was officially "that guy" in all our conversations. I understood it was Wayne's way of showing protectiveness. Brash, blunt, and unabashedly sexist, he had nonetheless been my closest friend and my only real confidant since Ryan's death. A journalist for the Washington Post, he was competitive and cutthroat in his profession, but that was a side of him I seldom saw. It was true there were three women who could tell you what a lousy husband he was, but then again, he would willingly tell you all that himself. I knew he wasn't a saint, but neither was I. We both understood our flaws didn't define us.

"That guy is Josh Culliver, and nothing happened with him. It was his Aunt Maggie. She passed away the day we got here," I explained.

"Are you talking about Maggie Culliver?" he asked. "She was your boyfriend's aunt?"

I ignored the label he'd applied to Josh. "Yes. I take it you knew her?"

"Yeah, we went way back," Wayne replied. "I met her when I was a new reporter, right out of Northwestern. She was a class act—professional, by the book, but friendly, at least for a spook."

"Spook?"

"Spy," he clarified. "She was an Army intelligence officer, but from what I heard she was really a CIA operative in East Germany before the Berlin Wall came down. By the time I met her, she was working as an analyst, and then she moved over to Homeland Security after 9/11. She oversaw some important terrorist task forces, stopped a lot of attacks most of us would rather not know about. I guess she's been out of the game a couple of years now, but we all noticed when the news about her death came across the wire."

"I don't know about being out of the game," I mused, thinking about what Alan had said. "It sounds like with that kind of job you never really get to walk away. Her husband told me she still got calls from people she worked with asking for help."

"That's typical of D.C. Most of them keep their security clearances for life. You never know when some old threat is going to rear its ugly head, and then you need people with first-hand experience," Wayne said. "Do you remember who her husband said she heard from and what they needed?"

You'd think by now I'd know I had to watch myself when talking to a reporter.

"Don't start," I warned him. "There's no story here, and I will personally kill you if you bother Josh's family."

"C'mon, San, what do you take me for? I wasn't going to bother anyone," Wayne protested, then added, "I just wondered if you knew who called her. If they were asking for help, there had to be a reason. I haven't had a real lead in months, and I could use a story. No one wants to hear about Congress right now."

"You're impossible, you know that?" I grumbled. "Anyway, it won't do you any good. This happened almost a year ago. The only name I got was Bart somebody, and he died last winter."

There was a sharp intake of breath.

"Did you say Bart? Bart Jansen?"

"Yes. Why?"

No answer.

"What's going on, Wayne? Who is Bart Jansen?"

"He was the Assistant Director of National Intelligence. He and Maggie Culliver worked together for five years on a terrorism threat assessment task force."

"So, what does that mean?"

"Nothing," he said after a long pause. "It probably means nothing. But it is noteworthy."

"Noteworthy how?" I asked, thinking about my conversation with Sallie Hathaway. Maybe I had been looking in the wrong direction. "They weren't…involved with each other, were they?"

"It's conceivable. They were close, spent a lot of time together," he said, sounding intrigued by the possibility. "I heard a few rumors, but I figured it was just sour grapes, somebody who got passed over for a promotion or something. That's not what I meant."

"Then what's so noteworthy about him calling?"

"If Jansen contacted Maggie, it could be related to national security. Maybe some threat we haven't heard about," he answered. "Just out of curiosity, what made you ask if they were involved? Do you think she was having an affair?"

I considered lying, but Wayne knew me too well. I told him about Sallie Hathaway's insinuations and the conversation I'd overheard between Chris Holtz and Jack Gardner.

"I don't know, San. I never figured Maggie as the type to skulk around behind closed doors, if you know what I mean. My guess is her nephew was right. It's more likely that what you heard was related to I.U.S."

"It sounded more personal than that to me. Like Chris Holtz really cared about her."

"My advice? Just forget it. This is a bad idea," Wayne observed.

"What's a bad idea?"

"You poking around in Maggie Culliver's private life. Does your boyfriend know about this supposed affair?"

"He's not my boyfriend," I snapped, "so you can stop calling him that. His name is Josh. And I'm not poking around in Maggie's past. I'm just telling you what I heard."

He was unconvinced. "I know how your mind works. You can't stand a secret. You'll turn this whole thing over and over until you find something out."

"I will not. And you have no room to talk. How many secrets have you splashed all over the front page of the Post?"

"Oh, so now it's my fault," he said with a mixture of annoyance and amusement. "Look, I didn't call you to debate ethics. I called to see if you were okay, which clearly you are. So—"

"I appreciate your calling. You know I do," I broke in. "Suppose there wasn't anything going on between Jansen and Maggie, and his calls did have something to do with national security. Any idea what? Josh's Uncle Alan said the calls were last winter, right up until he died."

"You never give up, do you?" Wayne said. "I don't know, but like I said, it's interesting. Could be a terrorism threat that hasn't been publicly disclosed, one Jansen was read in on. There's something from around the same time, I just can't remember—"

He was interrupted by noise in the background. I heard a quick, muffled conversation, and then Wayne was back.

"Breaking news, San. Gotta' go. Didn't I see the funeral is in Arlington? Are you coming up?"

"Yes. We'll be there Tuesday evening, and I'm not sure when we're driving back down."

"Turkey Day dinner with the in-laws, huh?" he smirked. "That's great! Call me. We can do lunch on Friday—I'll pay."

Before I could think of an appropriate comeback, the line went dead. Wayne had to have the last word.

I sat there in the dive shop parking lot, listening to the rough hum of the Ford's engine. I knew Wayne was right. Whether Maggie Culliver was having an affair with her diving instructor or her old boss, it didn't matter now. Her secrets, whatever they were, had drowned with her.

I should have known better, of course. Secrets always find their way to the surface.

Chapter 7

WE WERE SWIMMING IN a river of dark suits, winding our way through the green fields of Arlington under a sapphire blue November sky. Around us, thousands of white grave markers stood with military precision, silent watchers over the final journey of Margaret Catherine Kennedy Culliver's flag-draped remains. Some two dozen steps behind the open caisson, a military chaplain walked with Alan Culliver, followed by Josh's parents, his sister and her boyfriend, and the two of us. Just beyond us strode powerful men and women whose names I did not know, their importance signified by the medals on their chests or the security details at their heels. Two hundred people, maybe more, all there to walk one small woman to her final resting place.

Many of them had spoken at Fort Myer's Old Post Chapel, mounting the podium to pay tribute to Josh's aunt's remarkable life. They told of her missions in East Germany during the Cold War, of her postings at embassies in unstable countries, of her keen wit and her ability to assess and counteract the threats facing us every day. Listening to their stories, I was struck with a sense of my own insignificance. Like the former soldier beside me, these were people whose actions affected not just one or two individuals, but villages, cities, nations. Any pride I felt in taking on unjust landlords and small-time hustlers was swallowed by the realization that someone like Maggie Culliver had placed her life in jeopardy day in and day out for much of her career. I watched her husband sitting in the pew in front of us and wondered if he felt any bitterness for what

Maggie's job must have cost them. Even if she had been unfaithful, it was a storm they would have weathered. I felt a deep sadness for him that just when they might have had a chance at a different life, hers was taken away.

Now Alan walked solemnly, his face set, his eyes blank. If he felt anything at all, it was buried within.

The caisson stopped at the curb. Up on the green, a small tent stood over an open grave. Josh slowly released my hand, his fingers brushing against my palm. He was wearing his dress uniform, his face clean-shaven, and it was like looking at a stranger.

"Be right back," he whispered.

And then he winked, transformed again into the scruffy, lovable gypsy I met at the marina on Carter's Creek. I gave him a brief, grateful smile.

He joined his father and several other men, many in uniform, as pall bearers. They carried the casket up the gentle slope and placed it on the pedestal within the tent. There were no chairs set here, a signal that we would not be staying long. Arlington did thirty funerals a day, sometimes more, keeping up with unending demand as veterans of Korea and Vietnam passed away and service members in Iraq and Afghanistan continued to die in the slow drip, drip, drip of casualties that no longer made the evening news.

Graveside honors were limited to ten minutes, regardless of sacrifice. There were just too many bodies to bury.

We walked up the hill behind the pall bearers, the closest relatives standing nearest the casket. I hung back on the fringe, and Josh seemed to understand, because after the casket was in place he stayed beside his mother and father, head bowed.

The chaplain said a few words, read a passage from Scripture, and we recited The Lord's Prayer. After a military salute, a man in his sixties wearing a U.S. Marine uniform played "Taps." The flag was lifted from the casket and folded ceremoniously, then presented to Alan Culliver.

He stared down at it as if unable to place what it was, or how it came to be in his hands.

With that, it was over. The crowd moved away, each mourner touching Alan's shoulder or back, leaning in to say a few soft words upon leaving. Josh and his father stood together, shaking the hands of guests, while his mother separated herself from the family and walked over to me.

"I need you and Josh to stop and get a bag of ice. I'm not sure we have enough."

I had known Mrs. Culliver less than twenty-four hours, and I already understood she never asked, she told. She was no more than five feet tall, with brunette hair shorter than mine and a stocky build suggesting hard muscle rather than fat. She looked directly at you when she spoke, and there was nothing frivolous about her. She had a way of sharing her opinion with raised eyebrows and a stiff jaw, and I could see from the moment we met she thought I was wrong for her son.

"Of course," I said.

She nodded and moved on quickly, reaching out to grasp the hand of someone she knew. I wondered what it would take to make her like me, but I knew that wasn't the real problem. No matter how much Joanne Culliver might warm to me as a person, she was looking for someone to entice Josh to come home, back to the real world of fenced yards and nine-to-five jobs. I had not lived in that world for years, and I was too old and had too much baggage of my own to be anyone's savior. I couldn't argue with her logic.

Especially since I thought the same thing myself.

The Cullivers were having people back to their house in Bethesda for what we used to call a wake and now called a life celebration. Josh's mother and his sister Dani were making hors d'oeuvres for the reception last night when we arrived, the kitchen counters covered with an assortment of cutting boards and baking sheets. Dani hugged her brother and then threw her arms around me in an exuberant welcome, leaving flour on both of us, but Joanne merely nodded and continued chopping vegetables. She did stop what she was doing long enough for Josh to kiss her on her cheek and introduce me. Feeling vaguely unwelcome from the beginning, I tried to win points by offering to help with the food. Joanne Culliver shook her head.

"Unnecessary. Dani and I have a system," she said dismissively. "Besides, I'm sure you're exhausted from the drive. Have a glass of wine and relax. Josh, Sandi's going in the sewing room. Your father put up the cot in there. Tell Alan he'll be in the guest room."

I followed Josh through the family room and up the hall, past a formal living room on one side and a large dining room on the other. The Cullivers' house was a 1950s brick colonial nestled in an older neighborhood of sidewalks, manicured yards, and towering oaks. They had lived there since Josh was three, and the furniture and décor had the worn, comfortable look of home. We passed a wall with hand-printed lines dating from the late eighties showing heights for Josh and his sister. He followed my gaze and grinned.

"My mom. She measured us every Easter and Thanksgiving and wrote it up there—that is, until I was fourteen," he said, pointing to a measurement of 6'1" that was written in a different script. "Then she couldn't reach it anymore and my dad had to do it."

I was reminded of that now as I watched Joanne work her way through the crowd toward her husband. Josh's father looked much like his son and brother, tall, broad-shouldered, and dark-haired, but while Alan and Josh were open and friendly, Andrew Culliver was quiet and reserved. A learned behavior, perhaps, from living with the forceful Joanne.

"That was nice. I mean, like, for a funeral."

This was Keith, Dani's boyfriend, a junior at the University of Maryland. He had black hair hanging nearly to his shoulders and was cultivating a sparse moustache and even sparser beard. Keith was studying environmental tourism, another of those twenty-first century majors I suspected was designed to bolster college enrollment rather than fulfill a demonstrated need in the job marketplace. No doubt you needed a master's degree for that.

"It was very nice," I agreed.

Dani bounced up beside him. Cute rather than pretty, she had her mother's expressive face and plain-spokenness and her brother's puppy-like good nature. It was impossible not to like her.

"Wasn't that so beautiful? When the old guy played the trumpet, I thought I was going to lose it. It was just so perfect. Aunt Maggie would've loved it," she said, putting her hand to her heart dramatically.

"I think it was a bugle," Keith corrected, but he did not say it with much conviction.

"Bugle, trumpet, same thing," Dani responded. "Sandi, did Mom ask you about getting ice? We were going to do it, but she wants us to rush home and put the scallops and the quiche in the oven to heat up."

No, she didn't ask, I thought, but I bit back that reply.

"Yes. We'll take care of it."

"Don't you just love riding in Josh's car? It's the coolest thing ever," she gushed. "I wanted to borrow it after he left—I mean, what does he need a Mustang for if he's living on a boat? But Mom said no, it was still his, and he could come back anytime. Ha—I guess she was right!"

I didn't say anything.

"Shouldn't we be going?" asked Keith, gesturing to the group of mourners making their way up the road to their cars.

"Yep, you're right. We'll see you back at the house," said Dani, giving me a spontaneous hug. Then she grabbed Keith's arm and pulled him down the hill toward the cars.

At least one of the Culliver women was happy I was there.

Josh walked toward me, holding out a piece of paper.

"Do you mind? I'd like to visit these graves before we go."

I saw it was a list of three soldiers' names, directions next to each.

"Not at all. Your mother did ask us to stop for ice on the way home."

"She'll be fine until we get there."

He took my hand and we walked down to his car, a baby blue restored '68 Mustang convertible. He and his uncle Alan worked on it from the time Josh was thirteen, completing it for his sixteenth birthday. I understood why Joanne Culliver wouldn't part with it—the car was important to Josh, and while it was parked in their Bethesda garage, she believed he would always come back.

Maybe she was right.

"You okay?" he asked as we got in the car.

I assured him I was fine. His look said he knew I was lying, but he let it go, starting the car and turning on the radio. He grabbed a blanket from the back seat and threw it over my legs.

"Top down," he announced with a wide smile, and a few minutes later we were driving slowly through the cemetery with the cold wind on our faces.

All three of the graves Josh wanted to visit were close together. He told me about each of the men as we found our way through the maze of roads. The first was a staff sergeant who served under him, the second a lieutenant who had been a close friend. The former had been killed by a roadside IED, the second in a firefight during the rescue of young Iraqi women taken by terrorists. The third was another sniper who committed suicide just last summer. I could see he was the one who bothered Josh the most.

We parked and found their names. Josh squatted by the stones and talked to each man as if he were there, genial conversations filling them in on soldiers they served with and on his own life. His eyes were bright with tears, but he did not cry, and when he finished, he took my hand again and we walked back to the car.

"Beautiful day," he said. It made me wish I could protect him, keep anyone or anything from hurting him ever again.

But wishes are for children, and even if I had tried, I don't think I could have prevented what was to come. Those wheels had been set in motion a long time ago.

Chapter 8

ALCOHOL IS A KIND of truth serum. If you are angry, or jealous, or prone to violence, a few drinks will release the beast within. If you harbor guilt, you will be driven to confess; if you hide bitterness, it will seep from you like a poison. Joanne Culliver sat across from me on the screened porch, her face hidden by darkness, her reserve weakened by remorse and five glasses of pinot noir.

"I just think I should have done something. I know it was none of my business, but I should have asked. And I didn't. I didn't," she said.

I had no idea what she was talking about. We sat alone, Josh and his father having taken over kitchen duty. Thanksgiving dinner was over, Alan off visiting Maggie's mother in a nearby nursing home, Dani and her boyfriend deserting the family as soon as the dishes were cleared for a party given by one of her high school friends. This left only Josh's mother and me.

I had switched to sparkling water hours ago, unwilling to guess which truth would work its way from my lips.

"I loved Maggie. I did," Joanne said adamantly, though I hadn't disagreed. "I missed her when they moved. Twenty years—that's how long they lived next door to us. But we got together once or twice a month, when she'd come to see her mother and stay here overnight. When Alan called, at first I thought she'd just forgotten to tell me. I mean, how was I to know?"

She took a swallow from her glass and waved it precariously.

"But then she didn't come, and she didn't call. I called her, she didn't answer. I texted. I was about to tell Andy when she sent me a message. Do you know what it said?"

She waited, and I gathered it was not a rhetorical question.

"No. What did it say?"

She made a shushing noise. "She said I can't tell anyone. Not Alan, not Andy. I have to lie and say she was here. And she can't tell me why. Well, what was I supposed to do? It was after eleven o'clock. Andy was in bed. So, I went to bed. This was a Friday night. Andy slept in the next day, and when he got up, I told him Maggie already left."

I listened in stunned silence. It sounded very much like Joanne Culliver was admitting she covered for Maggie's infidelity.

"This happened last winter, and she never said another word about it. Then she did it again last summer, and I lied right from the beginning when Alan called. I sent her a text, and she thanked me. That's it. No explanation. And I never asked," she added, emphasis on each word. "What kind of a friend does that make me?"

"A loyal one," I said.

She made a snuffling noise that might have been crying.

"I don't even know why I'm telling you this. You must think I'm crazy. Josh's crazy mother. I'm sorry, you know—sorry I've been a bitch. It's just Josh is fragile. If you had seen him when I flew to Germany...I thought he was going to die."

I was glad she couldn't see the surprise on my face. Josh had never mentioned being injured.

"I didn't realize it was that bad," I said, unwilling to admit he had not shared any of this with me.

"Oh, it was bad. Broken ribs, broken arm, but that wasn't the worst. He had swelling in his brain. They put him in a coma, drained some fluid, and then all we could do was wait. The doctors couldn't tell how much damage had been done.

"I can't tell you what it felt like when he opened his eyes," Joanne went on, her voice choked with tears. "His first words were 'Mom, what are you doing here?' like nothing happened. I just fell apart. He seemed totally fine, and we knew everything was going to be okay. I even thought maybe it was God's will, because he decided to get out of the military. I thought, finally he'll have a normal life. And now look."

Instead he quit his job, got on a boat, and sailed into my life. No wonder Joanne Culliver hadn't welcomed me with open arms.

She must have realized what she said, because she tried to walk it back, however ineffectively. "Not that you aren't normal, Sandi. It's just that we expect more of Josh. Sailing around on a boat isn't a life."

I'd heard that before.

"I don't think this is permanent, Mrs. Culliver. Maybe it's just something Josh has to get out of his system."

She must have decided I included myself in this observation. "I'm so glad you feel that way," she said, rising unsteadily. "As long as you understand it's just a temporary thing. It's not like he'll marry you."

She stumbled past me, nearly crashing into the sliding glass door of the family room. I briefly considered letting her fall—well, more like I briefly fantasized about letting her fall, all the while knowing I wouldn't let it happen—and then I supported her with one arm and opened the door.

"Thank you," she said. "I've got it now."

She flopped onto the sofa and started snoring.

I stood for a moment, torn between injured feelings and an unwanted impulse of compassion for the woman lying before me. She was no different from my own mother, who waited still for me to return to normal after Ryan's death. Neither one of them could accept their children were forever damaged by what had happened to them.

Perhaps no mother could.

I walked toward the kitchen. As I did, I thought again about Maggie Culliver, about the kinds of experiences she had survived.

Who knew what damage she had been hiding? Or what she had done to find peace?

Chapter 9

"HOW WAS THE FUNERAL?"

I looked up from my menu to see if he was being sarcastic, but Wayne's face was bland.

"Beautiful. Sad. Listening to all those people talk about Maggie…she had an amazing life. She was a true heroine," I said.

He nodded his agreement as he sipped his coffee. We were sitting in a café in Bethesda's arts district having an early Friday brunch. Aware the streets would be crowded with Black Friday shoppers, we had chosen a spot close to Josh's parents' house. Josh, his father, and uncle were out at a local shooting range, demolishing clay pigeons in what was a Culliver after-Thanksgiving tradition. Josh's mother was in bed with "the flu," by which I mean a hangover. At least that kept her from raising any eyebrows when Wayne picked me up.

"And what about your boyfriend's family? How did that go?" Wayne asked, reading my mind.

I grimaced. "I feel like a pariah. I am definitely not what his mother had in mind."

"That's what happens when you rob the cradle, cougar," he teased, but his eyes were sympathetic.

"Thanks. I appreciate your support," I said, and he laughed.

We stared at our menus for a few more minutes, but our waiter failed to materialize. The restaurant consisted of several small rooms, and as far as I could tell, it was staffed by only two servers.

"You know, after I talked to you the other day, I remembered something about Bart Jansen's death," Wayne said. "I didn't take it seriously at the time, thought it was just some crazy conspiracy bullshit, but when you told me about the phone calls, it got me thinking."

"About what?"

He lowered his voice. "There was a leak last January about a suspected bioterrorism incident. Nothing specific, just that something had happened. But it was vapor—I couldn't find anything concrete. I contacted Jansen, thinking maybe he'd heard something. Sometimes these retired guys are more willing to talk, and I knew he had plenty of contacts inside the department. But no one picked up the phone. I tried a few more times, even left a message, but I never got him. Then he died a few weeks later."

"Are you trying to make a point?" I asked. "Because you've lost me."

"I'm not finished. Have a little patience," Wayne scolded. "A couple of days go by, and my editor passes off this anonymous caller to me. The guy says he has proof Jansen was murdered, says he heard Jansen and another guy arguing on Jansen's dock. He didn't see the whole thing, but he was sure the guy pushed Jansen off."

"Why didn't he call the police?"

"He did. Said they wouldn't listen and that's why he notified the Post. I called the police to check it out. Turns out they knew exactly who I meant. The source was Jansen's next-door neighbor, and he'd been calling 911 at least once a week since Jansen moved in."

He took a long swallow of coffee, probably just to aggravate me.

"About what?" I asked finally.

His eyes twinkled. "I was getting to that. I looked back at my notes last night. The guy's name was Mortimer Gundy. The first time he called police, he said he had proof his new neighbor was a spy. The police went out to the house, and Jansen told them who he was and explained he'd had a Russian history professor from Georgetown spend a few nights. Jansen even went to Gundy to clear up any misunderstanding, but it had the opposite effect. Mortimer got paranoid. After that, he was convinced he was the target of illegal surveillance, told the police he was being followed, his phones were bugged. They said he was a real whack job."

There was another long pause while Wayne finished off his coffee and looked around for our waiter.

"But now you're not so sure," I prompted.

"No. The phone calls to Maggie suggest one of two things—either they had some kind of relationship, which fits your gossipy neighbor's scenario, or he needed her help on an issue related to national security. Let's just suppose it wasn't an affair. Then maybe Jansen knew something, and it put him in danger."

"Was there any evidence Jansen's death wasn't an accident?"

Wayne sighed. "No. On the other hand, I didn't really look. Normally I'd go around the neighborhood, knock on a few doors, see if I could corroborate any part of Gundy's story. But the detective I talked to said it was a waste of time. Jansen fell through the ice, but there's no way it was murder. The water wasn't deep there, so even if somebody pushed him in, it wouldn't have killed him."

"Then how did he die?"

"They figure his heart gave out. I mean, he basically went through the ice and drowned in three feet of water. There was no indication of a struggle, no defensive wounds, no tracks on the shoreline, no evidence of more than one person present."

I considered this. "If that's all true, what's bothering you now?"

"This Mortimer, his description of the attacker was pretty vague—tall, wearing a knit cap, so no hair color. Most he could give me was he got the impression the guy was military. But the car was a different story. He said the murderer was driving a red Corvette. That doesn't fit the usual conspiracy scenario. No one drives a red Corvette unless they want to be noticed. It didn't sound like something Gundy would invent."

I felt a cold chill on the back of my neck. "Did you say a red Corvette?"

"Yeah. Why?"

I didn't answer. I wasn't about to tell him I had seen a red Corvette in Alan Culliver's garage.

"What's the matter?"

"Nothing," I said. "There's just...I felt a draft, that's all. Isn't that our waiter?"

Wayne waved his arms at the man, successfully sidetracked. While he ordered, I struggled to calm my fears. Suppose Alan had gone to see Jansen. It didn't mean anything. And besides, there were plenty of red Corvettes in the United States. But he was tall, and he had what could be described as military bearing, and he might have believed Jansen was having an affair with his wife.

"Miss? Did you want to order?"

I looked up to see Wayne and the waiter both staring at me.

"Um, the salad with crabmeat, vinaigrette dressing."

"Everything okay?" Wayne asked as our server walked away.

"Fine."

He didn't look convinced, but he let it go. "Anyway, I thought I'd have my staff dig around a little, see if there's anything more about the bioterrorism rumor from last winter, maybe go back and talk to Jansen's neighbors about the red Corvette."

"It sounds like a dead end to me," I said, not meeting his eyes.

"Sometimes the best stories start with a dead end," Wayne responded. "If it leads somewhere, I'll let you know."

I already knew where it could lead—to Alan Culliver.

"I don't think that's a good idea, Wayne. Suppose you're wrong, and it turns out there was some romance between Bart Jansen and Maggie? That's nobody's business but theirs. I don't want to see her name dragged through the papers."

"Trust me, I'm not interested in ruining her reputation. But I have a hunch there's a story here, San, and you know me," he said with a shrug and a smile.

I did. That was what worried me.

"So, what about you? What are your plans?" he asked, and I was grateful for the change in subject.

"We're heading back to Norfolk tomorrow. We plan to leave the dock Monday morning and make it to Manteo to pick up Josh's boat on Tuesday. We'll probably lay over a night or two there and then head on to Ocracoke."

"You're really going to take two boats? Wouldn't it be easier to go together in one?"

It was a question I'd gotten from my mother and everyone I knew back in Irvington, but I thought at least Wayne would understand.

"I'm not going on this trip to be with Josh. I'm going because I want to go myself," I said. "I barely know him. It's not like we're ready to move in together."

"People crew on boats all the time without being romantically involved," he pointed out. "Not that I would know, of course. That's just what I've heard."

"Stop. This topic is not up for discussion."

"Okay," he agreed, waving his napkin in surrender. "Just do me a favor—keep in touch. I worry about you."

"I'll be fine. The ICW is an inland waterway. It's not dangerous."

Our salads came, and our conversation moved on to other things, but a feeling of unease niggled at the back of my mind. It wasn't my uncertain relationship with Josh or even the journey that bothered me.

It was Alan Culliver's red Corvette.

Chapter 10

THE DIESEL ENGINE CHUGGED along, its heavy rhythm the only sound in the thick fog. On either side of us, branches reached up and over the water, long limbs disappearing in the whiteness. I checked my watch and then the chart on the seat beside me. We were in the Great Dismal Swamp Canal, a narrow channel of water dug by slaves more than two centuries ago at great human cost. A recent storm left debris floating just below the surface, and with our limited visibility, Josh was stationed at the bow to warn me of anything in our path.

We had pulled away from the dock in Norfolk at 7 o'clock on a day that dawned unseasonably cold and damp. It was November thirtieth, the Monday after Thanksgiving, and temperatures hovered in the upper thirties, twenty degrees below normal. Low clouds obscured the tops of buildings, and bridges stretched up into nothingness, lost in an icy mist. Both of us wore our foul weather gear, lone bright patches of yellow against the grayness.

This leg of the journey had no space for sailing, and at first we made a steady six knots under power, putting us through the Deep Creek lock at its eight-thirty a.m. opening. Now we were pushing to make the one-thirty p.m. opening at South Mills, a task complicated by the many times I had to slow to make my way around submerged logs.

"Do you want to switch?" Josh called out from the bow.

We were in a fairly wide section of the canal, so I took the engine out of gear and waved him back. There were no other boats to be seen. I ducked below to heat up a pot of coffee on the stove, and he followed me down, grabbing a towel to wipe the rain from his face.

"This place is living up to its name today," he said.

"If I'd known there was this much debris, I would have taken the Albemarle Canal instead."

"And miss this once-in-a-lifetime opportunity? No way," Josh grinned.

The Great Dismal had been his idea. He had taken the other canal on his way south, but every boater he met told him he had to try the ICW to Elizabeth City at least once. The fall foliage in coastal North Carolina was just past peak, and I'm sure it would have been beautiful—if we could see it.

"If we don't make the next lock opening, we won't get to Elizabeth City before dark," I said. "I don't want to motor through this mess if we can't even see in front of us."

"Agreed. There's an anchorage about ten miles past the lock. We should be able to make that even if we don't get through until the three-thirty opening. Either way will work," he said, then seeing my glum expression added, "Hey, at least it stopped raining."

I didn't answer. I tended to think of myself as relatively optimistic, but I found Josh's cheery disposition mildly irritating. My clothes were clammy all the way down to my underwear. If there were a positive side to this little adventure thus far, I wasn't seeing it.

As I reached for the coffee cups, he circled my wrist with his hand and tugged me gently around to face him.

"It'll be fine, San. Don't sweat the small stuff."

He looked so concerned that I felt a pang of guilt. Since Joanne Culliver's midnight confession, I had kept my distance from Josh. It wasn't intentional, but I felt at odds with myself, and it manifested in a detached reserve. I manufactured a wan smile.

"Sorry. I'm just cold and cranky."

"And wondering what you're doing here." He looked down at me, his expression serious. I started to protest, but he put his finger to my lips.

"It's okay. I get it. But let's not throw in the towel yet. We've only gone twenty-six miles, and I promise, it will get better. Okay?"

His green eyes locked on mine, the warm skin of his hand touching my lips. The air between us slowed, and the blood rushed to my face.

I jerked backward, and he dropped his hand.

"You'd better get up on deck. I'll bring you your coffee," I said, turning my back to him and reaching for the insulated mugs. I heard him sigh, then make his way back to the helm.

I spent the next hour on the bow with plenty of time to consider what was wrong with me. Why couldn't I just relax and appreciate the moment? Why did I pull back? Did it matter if his mother was right, and this time with me was nothing but a temporary phase? After all, I was the one who had avoided getting or staying involved with anyone. How was this relationship any different than the brief romances I had in the past year?

That little voice in my head, the one that reminded me of inconvenient truths, piped up at once.

Because you knew from the beginning those relationships wouldn't work. You thought this one just might.

At that moment the fog cleared, and the sky brightened, a good omen if you believed in that sort of thing. With better visibility I was able to see obstacles in the distance, allowing Josh to increase our speed to six knots again. We made the lock a half-hour early, giving us time to tie up and have lunch while we waited. I put a container of frozen crab soup on the stove and started the oven to warm a loaf of bread. The cabin grew comfortably cozy from the added heat.

"The soup smells incredible," Josh said, opening a soda and taking a seat at the table.

"I wish I could take credit. I froze four quarts from Willaby's Café before I left Irvington," I admitted, opening a bottle of iced tea and sliding in beside him.

"So, you're feeling better?" he asked.

"Relieved. We should get to the dock with time to spare."

"Anything else on your mind?"

I met his eyes and looked away quickly, but it was long enough.

"That's what I thought. You want to talk about it?"

I tried to play it off. "Oh, you know, the usual—what am I doing here, what do I plan to do with my life?"

"Well, right now, we're waiting for the lock to open," he said, smiling. "So that's one down."

I didn't smile back at him. "That only covers the next twenty-five minutes."

"So, are you looking for a one-year plan, a five-year plan, or are you thinking long-term, like fifty years?"

His tone was teasing, and I felt like he was mocking me.

"I'm looking for someone who will mention he had a traumatic brain injury before he decided to quit his job and throw his life away."

It came out more harshly than I intended.

"Ouch," he said, and my face colored.

"I'm sorry," I said quickly. "You have no obligation to tell me anything. I just...I'm not sure if this was a mistake."

Josh sat back in his seat, his expression serious, and drummed his fingers on the table for a minute.

"Okay," he said, as if in answer to some inner dialogue. "I wanted to do this in Norfolk before we left, but with everything that happened, the timing just wasn't right. I thought maybe when we got to Manteo—but this is better. So, okay."

He leaned forward, his eyes fastened on mine. "I'm assuming my mother talked to you. I'm sorry about that. She means well, but she has spent most of her life ignoring any facts she doesn't like.

"Yes," he continued, "I was wounded. Yes, I had a pretty wicked concussion. But I made up my mind to resign from the Army for the reasons I gave you. I saw who I was becoming, and it wasn't who I wanted to be. I made the decision a month before my Humvee was blown up. I have the paperwork to prove it."

"But what about the rest of it—quitting your job, buying the boat?" I persisted. "Don't you think it could be a result of your injuries?"

Josh smiled. "Contrary to what my mother believes, this was my plan all along. Do you know how many real vacations I had in ten years of service? One. I thought I deserved a year."

"Then why did you take a job to begin with?" I asked, but I could already guess the answer.

"Because my mother freaked out when I told her. She said I was overreacting, that I was going to ruin my life. She convinced my father to get me an interview with a contractor he knew, and they all seemed so relieved I was home...I didn't want to disappoint them. You know, I hadn't really considered how hard it was for them, me being deployed. But I wasn't in the office five minutes before I knew it wasn't going to work for me. It's like the walls were closing in. I knew I had to get out of there if I didn't want to end up with a white tombstone over my head."

"Josh, what you've done…what you've seen…there's no way I can understand what you've been through."

"No," he agreed, "but I can't understand what you've been through, either. I never loved anyone the way you loved your husband. With the things I had to do, how much I was gone…it just didn't seem fair to another person. Do you know what I mean?"

I nodded.

"Okay, then, I'm glad we got that cleared up." Rather than looking discouraged he sounded upbeat.

"So where does that leave us?" I asked.

Because it didn't sound like it left us anywhere it all.

He must have read my face. "It leaves us exactly where most people are. Working it out. Everybody's got baggage. It's what you choose to do with it."

"But you're so much younger than I am," I began.

Josh shook his head. "You'll need a better argument than that. I've spent ten years in the military, almost nine deployed in some pretty scary places. Who do you think is older in real years, me or the guy who got out of college and has been sitting behind a desk for the past fifteen or twenty years? Trust me, Sandi, I've got an old soul."

What he said made perfect sense. I looked at him—the damp brown curls falling on his forehead, the light shadow of a three-day beard again softening his face—and I imagined his long arms wrapping around me. I didn't want to believe Joanne Culliver, but I was afraid to take the chance.

"You're right," I said carefully. "Everything you've said. But I'm not exactly sure what you want, and we might not want the same things."

His eyes crinkled in amusement. "Oh, so you want me to go first? I get it. Okay, what I want. I want to get to know you better. I want to make you laugh. I like to imagine a future with you in it. I'd really like to kiss you. What about you?"

My head felt fuzzy, and I knew I was blushing.

"Ditto," I said.

He grinned. "Great. We've got thirteen minutes till the lock opens. Let's eat."

I don't know what I expected, but that wasn't it. I felt a twinge of disappointment, but I forced a smile and got the bowls of soup. My stomach was jumpy with confused emotions, but then again, maybe I was just hungry. Still, I liked what he had said—a future with me in it.

I might be ready for that, after all.

I half-expected there to be awkwardness the rest of the day, but Josh kept the conversation going, sharing stories from other cruisers he'd met, and by the time we had finished lunch I felt almost at ease. The lock opened and we continued the eighteen miles to Elizabeth City, tying up to the free town dock just before five. We were greeted almost at once by an elderly gentleman carrying a rose.

"Welcome to the Harbor of Hospitality," he said, handing me the stem. "I'm Ed Hutzel."

I had read about this tradition in the Waterway Guide. Started by a resident named Joe Kramer, the practice of greeting transient boaters with roses from his garden continued after his death, perpetuated by a group called the Rose Buddy volunteers. Several of Kramer's rose bushes had been transplanted to the area around the wharf, and judging from the clippers in Ed's jacket pocket, mine had just been cut from one of them.

We introduced ourselves and explained we would be spending the night before heading to Manteo the following day.

"You had some right nasty weather up north there this morning, I hear. Fella' up the dock from you got here two hours ago and said it was thick as pea soup," Ed said, gesturing to a small trawler, the only other boat in a slip. "Usually I expect a few more snowbirds this time of year, but I guess they held out for a nicer day. Do y'all need a lift anywhere?"

"We appreciate the offer, but we're fully provisioned," Josh said. "We just needed a place to tie up for the night."

Ed nodded. "Well then, I'll leave you and your pretty wife to get some rest. Gwen's already sent me two texts telling me dinner's ready, and I'm sure I don't need to tell you, son, you don't keep a woman waiting."

I colored, and Josh laughed.

That night Josh barbequed steaks and asparagus on the stern rail grill. There was no electricity at the dock, but we started the generator long enough to microwave potatoes, then shut it down and lit the kerosene lantern. I opened a bottle of cabernet, and we had a quiet dinner aboard, our first of the trip. The sky cleared, and afterward we bundled up in blankets and sat out in the cockpit, watching the stars. It had been a long day, and when we both yawned at the same time, Josh suggested we turn in. By 8:30 I was snuggled in my darkened V-berth, eyelids heavy, while Josh crawled into the aft quarter berth and turned off his light.

I fell asleep to the deep, even sound of his breathing and the muted music of water, wishing he had kissed me goodnight.

Chapter 11

THE NEXT MORNING, WE set off early for Manteo, reaching it by mid-afternoon. The cold weather pattern continued, and by the time we were tied beside Josh's boat *Andromeda* at the dock, I felt decidedly glum. My mood improved with dinner at a pub in the waterfront district, but it plummeted again when we went below to check the weather forecast. A complicated cold front was approaching, one expected to intensify and bring rain along the northern end of the Outer Banks and an icy mix to Virginia Beach in forty-eight hours. We would need to head south as far as Ocracoke tomorrow to miss the worst of the system. We agreed to leave the dock as soon as it was light, and I went back to my berth on *Serenity* alone.

Twenty hours later I was eyeing the channel behind Ocracoke Island dubiously, trying to match it with the chart in my hands. It was about four in the afternoon, and the once-steady northwesterly wind had become gusty and variable, creating choppy, confused seas. Aboard *Andromeda*, Josh took the lead. We both dropped sails an hour before, knowing we had to thread the narrow channel under power to make our way into the harbor. From this angle, it was difficult to make out the numbers on the navigational markers, but I could swear they didn't match what I had on the paper in front of me. No wonder it was marked with the warning "Local knowledge only."

"*Serenity*, this is *Andromeda*, over?"

We were monitoring the same open VHF channel and had been

exchanging advice back and forth all day. Coming off a single restless night in Manteo, I felt a kind of jet lag along with a growing sense of despair. I couldn't help it—I missed Josh's presence on my deck. A voice on the radio is not the same as another pair of hands.

"This is *Serenity*. Do these markers match what you have on your chart?"

I heard rueful laughter.

"I was about to ask you the same thing. Looks like the last green is missing. Is that what you see?"

"That's what it looks like. I think the channel goes right next to that sandbar on your port."

Several seagulls were standing on a piece of beach in the direction we needed to go.

"I agree. All right, pull your speed and hang back a minute. If I run aground, at least you'll know what not to do."

I eased back on the throttle and watched as Josh positioned his boat as close as he could to the red marker. He inched by, and I thought for a moment he was stuck, but then *Andromeda* slipped through the entrance and into the channel. I breathed a sigh of relief and increased the speed of the engine. Josh's voice crackled over the radio.

"Come on in. The water's fine."

I followed in his wake, motoring through the winding channel, past the ferry dock, and into the quiet water of Silver Lake. The harbor on Ocracoke is at the southern end of the island, adjoining a village of the same name. Accessible only by boat or small plane, it has managed to escape the rampant development of the rest of the Outer Banks. This late in the fall the large parking lot by the National Parks Service office was nearly deserted, and only a handful of people walked the waterfront street. No one came to greet us as we docked, but a sign on shore informed us the office was only open on Saturdays from twelve to five beginning November first and advised us to place nightly slip fees in the provided envelopes, along with vessel identification information, and drop them in the box by the office door.

"It's a Wednesday night. What are the chances there's any place open for dinner?" I asked, noting CLOSED signs on the poolside bar in front of the nearest hotel. Neither of us had eaten lunch.

"In December? Probably slim. Let's take a walk, see what we can find."

We were still bundled in coats, hats, and gloves from the sail, though the buildings here blocked the wind, making temperatures more pleasant. The sun broke out below a bank of clouds, and I felt my mood lighten. I had made it, after all, sailing in conditions more challenging than any I had faced on my own. I grabbed Josh's hand and squeezed it, and he smiled.

"Good job today, Captain," he said warmly.

"You too, Captain," I responded, and we both laughed.

We strolled to the end of the street, passing several shuttered restaurants, until we came to an open consignment and bike rental shop on the corner. An antique wooden runabout on stands in the yard caught Josh's attention, its varnished sides gleaming in the low sun.

"Man, look at the brightwork. What a gorgeous boat," he said, running a hand along hull.

"I thought you'd come back," a voice behind us said.

We turned to see a bearded elderly man kneeling on the shop's porch, working on a bicycle. He stopped what he was doing, stood, and walked toward us, his eyes on Josh's face. As he got closer, he shook his head.

"Well, I'll be—I thought you were someone else. You are the spittin' image of a guy who was in here a couple of months ago, lookin' at *Lorelai*, but I see now you're a lot younger. He said the same thing. Barry Coxell," he added, proffering a grease-stained hand which Josh shook.

"I'm Josh Culliver, and this is Sandi Beck. We're the two sailboats tied up over there in the harbor," Josh said, gesturing toward *Serenity* and *Andromeda*, then turning his attention back to the runabout. "She's a beautiful little boat, Mr. Coxell."

"I tell you, it sure beats all how much you're like him, down to the voice. Your daddy's name wouldn't happen to be Alan, would it?"

Josh looked at the man in surprise. "No, but my uncle's name is Alan."

"You two are very much alike," I observed.

"Well, that's it, then. Small world," the old man said. "Do me a favor— y'all tell your uncle I'm willing to drop another thousand from the price I gave him back in September. I'd like to get 'er sold before I close up for the winter. We get a little crowd in here for Christmas, but January and February are deader than a doornail."

"I'll tell him," Josh said. I waited for him to ask about a place to eat, but he seemed lost in thought, so I mentioned we were looking for an open restaurant.

"Darlin', not much open on a weekday this time of year besides Howard's Pub," Coxell answered. "That's about three-quarters of a mile up the road. If you're going to be here more than just one night, y'all might want to rent a bike. Best way to see the island."

I looked at Josh, who wore a perplexed expression.

"What do you think?"

"Sure," he said, though it was clear he hadn't been listening. "Sounds like a plan."

Coxell gestured to the rack on the side of the building. "Pick any two you like. You can pay me when you bring 'em back. I close tomorrow at five."

"Don't you want an I.D. or something?" I asked.

He laughed. "Darlin', I trust you. Besides, it's not like y'all can get 'em off the island without someone noticing."

I saw what he meant. Each bike had "Big Barry's" painted in bold letters across the frame.

I thanked him and Josh and I picked out two bikes with baskets. The only vehicles on the road, we peddled side-by-side in the direction of Howard's.

"Is everything okay?" I asked when we had gone four or five blocks without conversation.

"Yeah. Sorry. I'm just kind of confused. I went over our cruising plan with Alan before we left, and we talked about Ocracoke. My folks used to bring my sister and me here a lot, and we rented a house on the sound side with my aunt and uncle once when I was a teenager. He said it was the last time he stayed here."

"Maybe he forgot," I said.

"Maybe."

"Or maybe he was in Hatteras in September and just came over on the ferry for the day."

"Yeah. That's probably it," he agreed, his face clearing. "I think I remember my dad mentioning Uncle Alan was going on a dive trip on the Outer Banks. Remind me to tell him about *Lorelai* the next time I call. Hey—there's Howard's."

A gray clapboard building with multiple wooden decks, the pub was the last structure in town. Beyond it the road stretched into the distance surrounded by nothing but sand, dune grass, and short scrub pines. Its interior was endearingly tacky, the walls decorated with neon beer signs, vanity tags, and a dizzying array of Howard's Pub t-shirts and memorabilia. A few guys sat at the bar and two tables were occupied by a young family with small children and a single woman reading a novel while she ate. We were approached by a twenty-something waitress dressed in black, an impressive dragon tattoo climbing out of her t-shirt and crawling up her neck.

"Hi, I'm Charlotte, and I'll be taking care of you," she said, grabbing menus and leading us to a table in the corner across from the reader. "So are y'all staying on the island?"

"We sailed down from Manteo," Josh explained. "We're staying on our boats."

"Boats? Like, you each have a boat?"

Josh did not give yes or no answers. I, on the other hand, preferred only the most necessary conversations when trying to get fed. In typical fashion, he described every step of the cruise thus far, our plan to make it to the Keys in the New Year, and the potential of spending the remainder of the winter somewhere in the Caribbean. Meanwhile, I counted the number of piercings in Charlotte's ears, lips, and face. I would have looked at a menu, but she still had them cradled in her arms.

"Wow, that is so cool!" she enthused when Josh finished. "Are you guys, like, independently wealthy, or do you telecommute or something?"

"I just got out of the military," Josh said. "I saved up enough to take a year off."

"What about you?" she asked, turning to me.

I wasn't about to get into the insurance settlement from Ryan's death. "It's a vacation," I said.

"What do you do when you're, like, working?" Charlotte persisted.

"Sandi has a really unusual job," Josh began, failing to note my look of exasperation. "She's a personal advocate."

"I've never heard of that. What do you do?"

"I fix problems," I said.

"Like what?"

I sighed. Clearly short answers weren't going to save me any time with Charlotte.

"Sometimes it's investigative, like finding background information on someone, or looking for a missing person. Usually it's more about interpersonal relations—working out deals with exes, that sort of thing."

"So, you're like a lawyer?" Charlotte asked a little dubiously.

I could have told her about Cilla Lewis, who I helped to secure a multi-million-dollar inheritance, or the two women in the past year who tried to kill me. But I didn't.

"Can I get a Chardonnay?" I asked a trifle sharply.

Charlotte, looking slightly offended at being reminded of her role as server, nodded and slapped the menus on the table. Josh hid an amused smile and asked about the beers on tap. While he was ordering, I became aware of the woman at the next table. She was no longer reading but was instead staring at me intently. Her eyes met mine and she dropped them, focusing on the open book, her face scarlet.

Josh was complimenting Charlotte on her recall of the pub's beer selection, flattery which resulted in a return to her former friendliness. She ran through a brief list of specials and promised to return with our drinks. When she was gone, Josh handed me my menu.

"For someone who makes a living working with people, you don't seem to like them very much," he observed.

"I like people just fine," I retorted. "I also like to eat when I'm hungry."

He pretended to write down notes on an imaginary clipboard. "Needs to be fed on time. Got it. See, I told you this was a good opportunity to get to know each other better."

It was impossible to be annoyed with someone that good-natured. I gave up.

"Just don't get in a conversation with the cook until she's brought our food," I warned.

Fortunately, the cook never came out to say hello, and Charlotte served our drinks and dinner without incident. Josh spent the meal telling me about his childhood trips to the Outer Banks, several involving fish of such enormous size that I felt obligated to question the truthfulness of his memories. As engrossed as I was in our conversation, I did notice when the woman who had been watching me left, paying her bill at the bar and then striding quickly to the door without once turning her head.

It was nearly seven when we finished our meal. We rode Big Barry's bikes back under the streetlights, noting how few windows were lit in the houses and hotels we passed. The night was clear, the wind now at our backs, and the temperature dropping rapidly. By the time we parked our bikes in the rack at the end of the dock, I was shivering.

"It's been a long day," Josh said, putting his arm around me as we walked down the dock. "Go take a hot shower and relax."

I didn't put up an argument. As much as I enjoyed his company, I wanted nothing more than to curl up with a hot cup of tea and a book and read myself to sleep.

"I've had fun," I said. "Thank you."

"No problem. It was my turn to pick up the check."

"Not just that. Thank you for inviting me along."

He tightened his arm and kissed my hair.

"You know, you're much nicer when you're full."

I pushed him away, but I was laughing.

That night I snuggled under heavy blankets, the hatch open to the cold air. I knew Josh was just a few feet away, lying in the bow of *Andromeda*, and it made me feel a part of something bigger than myself. I stared into the night sky until my eyelids became heavy, finally falling asleep to the silent movement of stars.

Chapter 12

I SLEPT WELL PAST sunrise and woke to find a note in my cockpit. Josh's freshwater pressure pump had died during the night, and the closest replacement was in a marine parts store on Hatteras. They opened at nine, so he was catching the eight-fifteen ferry. He hoped to be back at the boat by ten.

I checked the clock. It was already eight-thirty. It looked like I was on my own for breakfast.

I had seen an ad for a coffee shop a block from the waterfront on the placemat at Howard's. I checked the outdoor thermometer and saw it was already fifty degrees, so I put on jeans and a heavy sweatshirt and decided to walk.

The air was crisp but not cold, with a strong southerly breeze pushing a few puffy clouds northward in an otherwise clear sky. You would never know a hundred miles to the north a cold front was dumping freezing rain along the coast. I kept a fast pace and the walk warmed me enough that I drank my cappuccino and ate my pumpkin muffin sitting outdoors in one of the wide wooden Adirondack chairs lining the coffeehouse porch. I was not alone—every seat was full, mothers and shopkeepers and retirees, all of us basking in the morning sun.

The leaves were falling along the tree-lined street, their faded yellows and reds fluttering and dancing in the wind. The warm fall had slowed the season at home in Irvington, the leaves falling just as I was preparing *Serenity* for her trip. Now, a few hundred miles south, the cycle was repeating. It was like being a time traveler. I wondered again how it was going to feel to skip winter altogether, to sail through autumn until we reached summer once again. The three winters I had spent on the boat had been, at times, brutally cold and miserable, though I had grown to love the quiet of the marina and the soft hiss of snow as it fell on the surface of Carter's Creek. Perhaps I would love palm trees just as well.

Someone coughed, and I realized a man was standing with his coffee and Danish, waiting for a chair, while my own cup and plate were empty. I surrendered my seat, returned my dirty dishes, and decided to meander down the street while I waited for Josh to return. I had passed an art gallery on my way in, its windows dark, but now a welcome flag was flying from the pole by the door. I entered, setting in motion a wind chime hanging nearby.

"Hello!" a voice called from the back of the shop. A woman wearing a smock splattered with paint worked her way through the maze of displays to greet me. She stopped suddenly halfway across the floor.

"Oh, my," she said, eyes wide.

It was the woman from the restaurant.

"You must think I'm crazy," she said, wiping her hands on her smock and crossing the distance between us. "I overheard you at Howard's Pub. I would have said something to you then, but I just didn't want anyone else to hear."

She reached out and grabbed my hand, pressing it between her own.

"I should have known the Good Lord would take care of things. I'm Kathy Dvorak, and I can't tell you how glad I am you came through that door."

It was an unusual greeting, and instinctively I started to pull away, but something in the woman's expression stopped me. Kathy Dvorak was perhaps sixty-five, of medium height and slightly plump through the waist and hips, with clipped salt-and-pepper hair. She wore dark-rimmed glasses that made her brown eyes look large and perpetually surprised, with a face bare of makeup except for a dusting of flesh-colored powder, a vain attempt to cover the purple shadows beneath her eyes. She continued to grip my hand as if afraid I would disappear.

"I apologize for eavesdropping, but as soon as I heard what you said, I thought, 'I should ask her to help.' But I couldn't do it, not in the pub. I didn't want everyone talking. You know how small towns can be," Kathy

Dvorak said.

I did, but I still didn't see how my visit to her shop could be an answer to prayer.

"Ms. Dvorak—" I began.

"Oh, please, call me Kathy," she broke in.

"Kathy," I said, extricating my hand, "I'm only here one more night. We leave Ocracoke tomorrow. I'm not sure how much help I can be."

Her eyes filled with tears, and I felt a surge of remorse. How much harm could it do to listen?

"Why don't you tell me what the problem is, and I'll see what I can do," I relented.

Her lip quivered.

"I need you...I need you to find my husband."

I had been hoping for something a little less calamitous.

"Is there someplace we can sit down?" I suggested, since a missing spouse did not sound like a case I could clear up in a few minutes of conversation.

Kathy blinked, but it was too late. Tears slid down her cheeks. Embarrassed, she scrubbed them away with the back of her hand.

"Come back to the studio."

I followed her to a room at the rear of the shop which served as her work space. It was crowded with easels, half-finished canvases, art supplies, and a kiln. She pulled out two chairs on either side of a butcher block table.

"You said you needed me to find your husband. How long has he been missing?"

"That's just it. I don't know if he is missing," she said. "That's what I need you to find out. I don't want to call the police if this is all just a... misunderstanding."

I sighed inwardly. Stories that started this way inevitably ended with emptied bank accounts and lovers in roadside motels, and I hated being the bearer of bad news.

"Why don't you start at the beginning," I said.

Kathy straightened her back and took a deep breath. "Right. Everett—that's my husband—worked at Fort Detrick for thirty years."

The name of the place was familiar, but I couldn't place it. I waited for her to continue.

"He retired about four years ago and we moved here. He always loved

Ocracoke, and he's happiest when he's got a fishing rod in his hands. I wasn't too thrilled with the idea, to be honest. I had friends and a support system back in Maryland, but he told me I could open a studio, do my painting and my sculpture, and so I went along with it.

"I'm not complaining," she added quickly. "I love it here, and the gallery has done well, better than either of us expected, but nothing like the salary Everett made when he was working. He has a pension, and he put money aside over the years, but we hadn't counted on the storm."

I knew a destructive Category One had hit the Outer Banks three years ago.

"Weren't you covered by insurance?"

"He couldn't get hurricane coverage on the boat, and that was a total loss. We had two trees come down on the house, and our deductible was twenty percent because it was a named storm. We had to dip into our savings pretty heavily," Kathy explained. "I don't handle the finances—I was a stay-at-home mom, and except for a few art shows after the kids were gone, I never had an income. But I could see Everett was worried about the money. Then he got this job offer, and he seemed so relieved I just couldn't complain about him going back to work."

"What kind of job offer?" I asked. I wasn't sure how any of this related to Everett going missing, but I had learned from experience it was best to let clients talk.

"That's just it—he couldn't say. Understand, that's nothing new. The work he did for the military—well, he couldn't talk about it, and I didn't ask. This was the same sort of thing, classified research for a government contractor. He never told me how much he was making. He wouldn't even tell me the name of the company. All I know is he would take the Cedar Island Ferry once every few months and be gone for two or three weeks. When he'd come back, he'd put a thousand extra dollars in the household account, but they were paying him a lot more than that. He bought me a new car, a convertible BMW, he started looking at new boats, and we took this wonderful Alaskan cruise…." As her voice drifted off, she stared at her hands, folded on the table.

"And then what happened?" I prompted when it seemed like she wasn't going to speak.

"Back at the end of October he left like he always did, said he'd be home in about three weeks," Kathy Dvorak said. "But this time he didn't come back."

"And he never called?"

She moved uncomfortably. "This job—whatever it is—is top secret, and he stays in a dorm at the lab. He has to turn in his cell phone when he gets there, and he can't make a call until he's out of the facility. Sometimes he goes somewhere and he'll sign out his phone and call me or text me, but usually, I don't hear from him until he's on his way home. This time I got a text on the eighteenth of November saying he'd be back on the twentieth. I closed the gallery early Friday, made a nice dinner… but he never came. No call. Nothing. That's not like Everett. If he says he's going to do something, he does it."

"Did you try to call him?"

Kathy flushed. "Not at first. He told me not to call him when he was working, and to be honest, I was a little put out. But when he didn't come home by the Sunday morning—that was the week of Thanksgiving—I tried his cell phone. It went straight to voicemail."

"What were you supposed to do if you had an emergency?" I asked.

"There was another number—he said it was the company's security," she said, rising and getting her purse off the counter by the sink. "Here it is."

Kathy Dvorak handed me a business card. It had no company name, no insignia, but the words Gate Three at the top and a phone number. I didn't recognize the exchange.

"Did you try calling this?"

She nodded. "Three times. The first time a man answered, and when I asked about my husband, he said he would check and to call back in ten minutes. I did, and someone else got on and said he didn't know anyone named Everett Dvorak. I asked for his name and the name of the company, and he hung up. I thought maybe it was just weekend help and it was above his clearance to know names, so I tried again Monday, thinking I might get somebody else. A recording said the number was no longer in service."

I could understand Mrs. Dvorak's concern and why she hadn't called the police. She had nothing to go on—no address, no company name, no contact person. Her husband's absences had followed no set schedule. There was no actual evidence that he was missing. He could be in Aruba with another woman. Or he could call his wife tomorrow morning to say he was on his way home.

"Have you checked your accounts—banking, credit cards—to see if they've been used since he's been gone?"

She flushed. "No. I didn't think of that. As I told you, Everett always handles the finances."

"Is your name on any of the accounts?"

"I know it's on the household account. I'm not sure about the others. And I have credit cards in my name for our VISA and American Express accounts."

This was at least a start. "Then you'll need to look up statements for the past five weeks. I'd also like you to write down anything you think might help me track your husband—a photo, his cell phone number, make and model of his car, license plate number, dates he took the ferry. Also, bank statements for the deposits made in the past two years to all your husband's accounts," I said, fishing my wallet from my back pocket. I handed her my card. "You can email me the information whenever you get it, and I'll see what I can do."

Kathy hesitated. "I just don't know. Everett will be upset when he finds out."

I bit the inside of my cheek. "Kathy, you asked for my help. I'm sure your husband will understand why you were worried about him. And if something has happened to him, it is up to you to get him help."

She swallowed and nodded. "All right. I'll try. It might take a few days."

"Just do the best you can," I said, standing to go. She rose and walked with me to the front door.

"Thank you for listening. I know this is…an odd situation," Kathy said. "I just didn't know where to go for help. Do you need me to write you a check? If you'll just tell me how much…."

I put up a hand to interrupt her. "I haven't done anything yet," I said. "Get me that information and I'll see what I can find. If it looks like I may be able to help, we'll work out payment then."

She was still thanking me when I stepped out the door. A thought occurred to me.

"What was the name of the organization you said Everett worked for before he retired?"

"USAMRIID at Fort Detrick – The United States Army Medical Research Institute of Infectious Disease," Kathy explained. "It was all very hush-hush."

I had some potential resources—Josh's father, who had connections within the intelligence community, and Wayne, whose investigative reporting probably included a few pieces on Fort Detrick. Perhaps one or both might know specifically what Dvorak had done for USAMRIID, which could in turn lead to his current employer.

"Thank you. Send me whatever you find, and we'll go from there."

It was after ten when I left the gallery. I walked straight back to the boat, cutting across a few lawns. As I got to the dock, I saw Josh's open cabin door.

"Hello!" I called.

His head popped up, a smear of grease across his cheek.

"Hey! How was your morning?" he asked.

"Interesting. I'll tell you about it later. Did you get your part?"

"I did," Josh said, holding up a crescent wrench. "I already got the old one off. It shouldn't take more than twenty minutes to put in the new pump. I'll come over when I'm done."

While he was working, I did a computer search on the emergency number Mrs. Dvorak had given me. It was disconnected, and no listing was available, but I was able to glean a general location—Cherry Point, North Carolina, home to a Marine base and numerous military contractors. I tried running a search for labs involved in the study of infectious diseases in the area but turned up nothing. I Googled Everett Dvorak's name and got a few newspaper articles and a list of published works on the National Institute of Health site, all of them involving viruses, parasites, and food-borne bacteria, and none of which I could fully understand. I did find one interesting piece of information—at least some of Dvorak's research revolved around the potential threat of these diseases as biological weapons.

"Worried about something you ate?"

This was Josh, who had come aboard and was standing behind me, peering over my shoulder at an article detailing the potential transmission pathways for E. coli in the U.S. food chain.

"No, it's the writer I'm worried about," I said, sliding around on the seat to face him. I described my chance meeting with Kathy Dvorak. I half-expected Josh to discount her story, having grown up with a family well-versed in government secrets, but instead he agreed with her concerns.

"I've never heard of anything like that. If it is a legitimate contractor, the basic company information must be a matter of public record. I understand they might want to keep the specific research at a facility quiet, especially if it has something to do with biological weapons. Most people don't want that kind of thing in their community. And it's not unusual to collect employee cell phones. But if you do, you have to provide emergency contact information for family members."

"Maybe Dvorak lied. He might not even have a real job. All his wife knows for sure is he was gone for weeks at a time and he came back with money," I said.

"Any history of gambling?"

"Not that she mentioned, and he had to have a top-secret clearance to work at Fort Detrick. If he had a gambling problem, wouldn't that have turned up in a background check?"

"You'd think so," Josh agreed. "The other possibility is that Dvorak isn't working for a legitimate contractor. Possibly whatever he's working on is illegal."

"Like what?" I asked. "He was a biologist."

"I'm sure there's an overseas black market for viruses that can be used as weapons. Or it could be he was working on black market vaccines."

That scenario would explain the secrecy and the lucrative pay, though the possibility was worrisome.

"If you're right, is he missing because he wants to be, or because something bad has happened to him?" I asked.

"It's a good question. What are you going to do next?"

I told him I asked Mrs. Dvorak to email me information about her husband, along with credit card and bank statements. Hopefully, there would be a trail of receipts to follow.

Josh looked at me thoughtfully.

"If you think this guy is really missing, you should talk to my father. The FBI is going to want to know about the disappearance of an expert in biological agents," he said. "This isn't the kind of thing you can handle on your own."

It was a reasonable suggestion. I understood the mechanics of human relationships, but I had no experience with the military-industrial complex, infectious diseases, or classified government intelligence. Still, I was a little irked at being told what I should do.

"Everett Dvorak could be at work or he could be sitting on beach with his lover drinking a Mai Tai," I argued. "Right now, I just don't know, and I promised his wife I'd look into it quietly. I don't think calling the FBI is what she had in mind."

Josh nodded, but his forehead was still creased with concern. "I get it. I understand this is what you do. But if you find out something is really going on...."

"I'll hand it over to the appropriate authorities. I promise."

It was a promise I should have kept.

Chapter 13

I DID NOT HEAR from Kathy that night. I walked by her shop on Friday, but it was closed, and I put Everett Dvorak out of my mind. Josh was intent on getting to Morehead City in time for the beautiful weather forecast for the next week, so we left Silver Lake early Saturday morning. A coastal low brought heavy rain, and standing at the helm, hair dripping and hands numb, I began to seriously question whether I had the stamina or desire to continue captaining *Serenity* alone. We got to Oriental well after dark, and it was all I could do to open cans of beef stew for dinner. We ate in tired silence, even Josh's perpetual good humor failing him, and parted as soon as the dishes were done. I barely kept my eyes open long enough to shower and tumble into bed.

When I woke the next morning, the sun was already pouring through the portholes. I grabbed my watch and groaned. It was nearly nine o'clock.

"Sleep well?" Josh asked when I stepped out in the cockpit. He was drinking coffee and reading a newspaper on his deck.

"You should have woken me up," I chided, climbing over the lifeline and stepping onto the dock.

"Oh, no. You needed the sleep," he said. "There's more coffee in the galley, and I bought donuts."

My stomach growled audibly in response, and he laughed.

I went below, filled a cup, and picked out something cream-filled, chocolate-covered, and decadent. I stuffed the first bite in my mouth before I got back out on the deck.

"Hungry, were you?" Josh teased, sliding over to make room beside him.

"Famished. How soon do you want to get going?"

"I figured around ten-thirty. We've only got about four hours to go today. I called ahead to Dockside. They have us reserved for two slips on the T-pier, but they've got a boat tied up there right now. It came in last night with engine trouble, and it's too big for their lift. They can't tow it to the other boatyard until this afternoon. So, there's no rush."

I digested this information along with the remainder of my donut.

"I went up to the office this morning. The shop is open—that's where I got the donuts—and they have a lounge with computers if you want to check your email. Wi-Fi isn't working."

I remembered Kathy Dvorak. "I should do that. Thanks."

I went back to *Serenity* to grab my cell phone, notepad, and a pen, and walked up the gravel path to the marina office. The lounge was just off the screened porch, a postage-stamp sized room with two computer desks, a copy machine, and a card table with four folding chairs. A small paperback bookrack hung on the wall, stocked with dog-eared romance novels.

I logged into my Gmail account and scanned the inbox. Sure enough, there was something from Kathy Dvorak from late last night. I opened it and saw there were seven attachments, all PDF files, along with a brief email explaining she had scanned the recent credit card and bank statements she found in Everett's desk. She also included several photos and a copy of his car's title and registration, and "something else that might help."

I opened each of the attachments. The photos showed a short bespectacled man, slightly overweight, with thinning pale brown hair and a pasty complexion that spoke of years spent indoors. His thin lips were pressed together in all but one, in which he showed a weak smile.

If it weren't for the money, I would say the chances of Dvorak running off to Aruba with a girlfriend were nonexistent. On the other hand, a fat bank account is a powerful aphrodisiac.

The next document showed that the scientist drove a ten-year-old forest green Subaru, registered to both him and his wife. A gas card statement was also attached, with transactions for the month of October. There were several small fill-ups on Ocracoke, and two larger charges from a gas station in Swansboro, North Carolina. I wrote down the name and address. The next attachment was a VISA statement from November seventh that included three meals at the same restaurant, also in Swansboro, about a week apart. The last of these was the second Saturday in November. I wrote down the name and address of the restaurant as well.

The frequenting of the same establishments suggested wherever Everett Dvorak worked was located near Swansboro. It also pointed to a pattern of behavior, and people who followed routines were much easier to trace than those who were unpredictable. Chances were Dvorak had been buying his gas and food in the same places for the past two years and would continue to do so if he still worked in the area.

The quarterly bank statement was next. It included savings and checking as well as several long-term certificates of deposit and a money market account. Whatever the scientist was involved in, it was paying off. He had more than twelve thousand dollars in his checking account and more than forty-six thousand in his savings, plus another hundred-and-fifty thousand in forty-eight month CDs. But it was the money market account that got my attention. Direct deposits had been made twice in the past three months from an unnamed, numbered account, each for more than seventy-five thousand dollars. This had clearly been going on for a while. Everett Dvorak had a balance of nearly three-quarters of a million dollars.

Someone was paying the retired scientist very handsomely–but for what?

I noted Kathy Dvorak's name was on everything except the money market account. I wondered if she had seen that, and what she thought of the amount of income her husband appeared to be keeping from her.

The last attachment was an ad from a yacht brokerage in Beaufort, North Carolina. This must be the "something else" Kathy had found. It featured a sixty-four foot Garrett Bay custom built convertible sportfish boat with twin diesels and a stunningly beautiful interior for an asking price of more than four hundred thousand dollars. The phone number at the bottom was circled and the name Greg was printed beside it. It seemed Everett Dvorak had been in the market for a new boat. I jotted down the boat's description and the name and number of the brokerage.

I have a gift for finding bits and pieces online and putting them together to solve problems, but this seemed almost too easy. Both Swansboro and Beaufort were near Morehead City, as was Cherry Point, the exchange for Mrs. Dvorak's mysterious disconnected contact number. I was confident someone in the area would remember my client's husband, and one clue would lead to another. It looked like the only thing that could keep me from locating Everett Dvorak was if he went home to his wife first.

I logged off the computer and checked my watch. I had twenty minutes to spare. I stepped out on the marina's screened porch just as my phone rang. It was Wayne Kremm.

"I didn't catch you in the middle of abandoning ship or anything, did I?" he asked in lieu of a hello.

"No, I'm actually on land at the moment. We're in Oriental, but we're heading for Morehead in about a half hour. What's up?"

"Is your boyfriend around?"

"Josh? No, why?"

"Because I don't know if you'll want to share this or not. After I talked to you, I did a little digging on Bart Jansen and Maggie Culliver. Not what you think," he said, before I could protest. "I didn't come up with anything suggesting a romantic involvement, but I have a friend down at the Virginia Pilot, Elsa McCormick, and she has a contact in the police department. Anyway, I asked her if she'd see if there was any more about the investigation into Maggie's death."

"Why would you do that? And what investigation?" I questioned, stunned.

"You have to admit, it's a coincidence, two high-ranking former intelligence officials drowning nine months apart," he pointed out.

"That's exactly what it is—a coincidence," I replied hotly. "The Coast Guard told Alan it was an accident, Wayne. Maggie's kayak was probably capsized by the wake of another boat and she drowned as a result of hypothermia."

"Yeah, that's what my friend said. Except for one thing. There's an eyewitness who claims Maggie was attacked."

I froze. "What do you mean, attacked?"

"There was a waterman on his way across to Kiptopeke. He called 911 at six-twenty-five a.m. and reported seeing a kayaker fighting off a whale or a shark he says came up out of the water. The police notified the Coast Guard, and they put out a bulletin. When Alan Culliver called to say his wife was missing, the Coast Guard used the waterman's information to narrow down where she might have gone in the water."

"I talked with the men who found Maggie's body. She didn't have any bites or injuries that would indicate an attack," I observed.

"Right. That's what the police said. They ruled it out. The guy was at least a mile away, the sun was barely up, so they figured it was just an optical illusion."

Wayne paused.

"But you don't think so," I said.

He let out a long breath. "I don't know."

"But Wayne, suppose Maggie's kayak was attacked by some marine creature. How can that be anyone's fault, much less a crime?"

"It couldn't. But when I was talking to Elsa, she mentioned she was investigating a complaint about Navy exercises infringing on private property. She interviewed a man who claims one morning he was sitting at the table eating his cereal when a Navy diver walked out of the bay and right through his yard, then got in an unmarked van on the street. She checked with the military, and they denied there was any exercise that day or that any Navy personnel had transited civilian property, but this guy swears that's what he saw."

I couldn't make the connection between this information and Maggie's death and said so.

"Okay, think about this a minute. Jansen's death was an accident, but his neighbor swears he was attacked. Now the same thing with Maggie. The waterman saw a black shape come out of the water. He said the kayak was parallel to Chic's Beach at the time. And the guy Elsa interviewed lives on Chic's Beach, and the date of his complaint is the same day Maggie died. Do you get the picture now?"

An image flashed in my head: a man's wetsuit hanging above a damp spot on the garage floor.

"You're saying a diver swam out to the middle of the bay to kill Maggie Culliver? That's crazy," I said.

"I know it sounds crazy, but the more I think about it, the more it makes sense."

"I think you're stretching. Leave it alone, Wayne. Please."

Wayne's tone changed. "Any other time you'd be telling me to run this down. Find the truth. Serve justice. What's going on? What aren't you telling me?"

I didn't answer, but Wayne knew me too well.

"It isn't that you think I'm wrong," he said, suddenly understanding. "It's that you think I could be right."

I looked up to see Josh walking toward me.

"I can't have this conversation right now," I said, and I turned off my phone.

Chapter 14

I TRIED NOT TO meet Josh's eyes as we prepared to leave the dock. I knew I should bring up what Wayne had told me, but what was I going to say? I heard a rumor your aunt was fooling around and just happened to mention it to a reporter? Your mom lied to your father and uncle because she suspected your aunt was having an affair? Oh, and by the way, I think it's possible—unlikely, but possible—your Aunt Maggie was murdered by her own husband?

Everything Wayne had was conjecture, based on a series of coincidences and his overactive investigative imagination. There was no proof, and having seen Alan mourn his wife, I could not believe he was responsible for her death. But Wayne was right about one thing—I knew on some instinctual level there was a connection between what happened to Maggie Culliver and Bart Jansen.

For once, someone else could be the champion for truth. I did not have the stomach for it anymore.

We were running behind schedule, and in the rush to get moving Josh didn't seem to notice how little I said or how often I got lost in my own thoughts. Much of what I had to do was becoming routine for me, so I managed to cast *Serenity* off without leaving a line tied or forgetting to check the sea cocks. But as soon as I was alone again, standing at the helm, worries crowded in. It took an hour of fresh breeze in my face before my head finally cleared, and I determined to put Maggie Culliver out of my mind.

The wind was light but the direction good, so we motor-sailed most of the way to Morehead, unrolling our jibs to gain a knot or two. We crossed under the bridge between Morehead and Beaufort, rounded the North Carolina Port Terminal, and eased into our slips by four o'clock. Only then did I realize the only thing I'd eaten all day was the donut in Oriental. It's no wonder sailors were skinny.

"Let's do an early dinner," I suggested as Josh, the first at the dock, grabbed my bow line.

"Sounds good. Let me call the rental place first and see if I can pick up the truck tonight," he replied.

We had decided to spend at least a week in Morehead City. We were due in Myrtle Beach for Christmas, having missed Thanksgiving, and that was only a hundred and sixty miles away, an easy three or four days at best. I didn't want to subject Josh to my family any longer than necessary. It's not that I don't love my parents—I do—but one had a doctorate in psychology and the other had a doctorate in mathematics. Talking with them together involved carrying on two completely different conversations simultaneously. They were the perfect example of opposites attracting, which worked for them but could make dinner table dialogue challenging for everyone else involved.

Temperatures were forecast to be in the upper sixties and the water was warmed by the Gulf Stream, so Josh decided we should rent a four-wheel-drive truck and do some off-road beach driving. He lugged a surfboard all the way from Maryland and was eager to use it on the Crystal Coast, some ninety-five miles of shoreline just across the sound. There was also a charter operation out of Beaufort running a shallow wreck dive not far off the coast. Josh had gotten his certification just last summer, and he wanted to try it. It sounded like fun.

And then there was work—the job I had taken on to locate Kathy Dvorak's husband, with a trail leading to this area. I needed a vehicle for that. I hated to admit it, but I missed the thrill of searching out the pieces to puzzles. I felt a sense of anticipation when I thought about looking for Everett Dvorak.

I purposely avoided thinking about Maggie Culliver.

While Josh headed off to check us in with the marina office and call the rental company, I went below and took a long, hot shower. Sea air was invigorating but also sticky, leaving my short hair a mass of tangles and a crust of salt on my lips. By the time I was clean and dressed, the sun was already skimming the tree line along the mainland. I saw Josh had dropped some tourist brochures in the cockpit, so I grabbed a shawl to put over my long-sleeved t-shirt and curled up on a deck cushion to look through them. I discovered several seafood places within walking distance, some fancier restaurants in the historic district of Swansboro, and any number of bar and grill spots out by the beach.

"Take your pick," Josh said, coming down the dock. "We have transportation. Ben, the dockmaster, gave me a lift to the rental office so I could get the truck."

I considered driving over to Atlantic Beach, but I was antsy from the sail and needed to stretch.

"Let's do something local so we can walk. I've done nothing but sit or stand at the wheel all day."

He extended a hand and helped me off the boat, sitting high in the water on an incoming tide.

"Sounds good. I passed a place about two blocks down that looked comfortably disreputable. What do you think?"

"My kind of place."

We strolled down the boardwalk, enjoying the last rays of sun before it slipped behind the buildings. Daylight savings time ended a month ago, but I always found it hard to accept darkness so early in the evening. We commiserated about the shortness of days and Josh half-jokingly proposed we forget Christmas and head south till we reached the Equator, where at least we would be guaranteed twelve hours of sunshine. The way he said it made me wonder if he had the same reservations about meeting my parents that I had felt about meeting his.

We stopped in front of the pub he had picked out, a dark wooden building with a rusty anchor over the door and a blackboard advertising five-dollar-a-dozen steamed shrimp and ten-dollar buckets of cold Coronas.

"Well, we may not have daylight, but at least we have beer," Josh quipped as he held open the door.

Though it was early, the bar was crowded with happy hour customers, all of whom wore the rough, faded clothes and high boots of watermen. I've always taken locals as a good sign—it usually meant the food was better than average and the alcohol cheap and plentiful. The décor inside was nautical, but not the synthesized version you saw in the typical beachy tourist traps. Here the tables were crafted from authentic varnished hogsheads, the walls decorated haphazardly with an assortment of derelict but recognizable boat parts, and the smell of fried fish and Old Bay permeated the dining room. Josh and I exchanged a smile. It was definitely our kind of place.

A broad-faced girl in her twenties, her straight hair pulled back in a tight bun, came out from the back and scooped up menus.

"Welcome to Captain Tom's. Two?" she asked, her voice thick with an Eastern European accent.

We nodded, and she introduced herself as Katya and showed us to a table in a dark corner. It seemed a little chilly for Coronas, but the pub had a surprisingly diverse beer selection, and in the spirit of adventure we both ordered local ales.

"Who were you talking to this morning?" Josh asked, opening his dinner menu as our waitress left.

I started, realizing he had seen me on the phone after all.

"Just Wayne. You know, my friend from D.C.," I said, and even I thought I sounded uncomfortable. "Nothing important."

He caught my reaction. "Sorry—it's none of my business. You don't have to tell me if you don't want to."

I did not, but I also didn't want him to think I was hiding something.

"No, it's just that there's nothing to really tell," I said, pretending to look intently at the menu. "He talked about your aunt. I thought I told you he knew her."

"I don't remember you saying so. How did he know her?" Josh asked.

I had not thought that far ahead.

"Well, your aunt was pretty important, I guess, and, you know, Wayne's a reporter...." I stumbled.

"Oh, right, this is Wayne, your friend who writes for the Post," Josh recalled. "So, he knew Aunt Maggie from working on a story?"

I stifled an urge to clamp a hand over my mouth. Fortunately, Katya came back with our ales before I had a chance to spill out every piece of innuendo Wayne had shared. I smiled at Katya brightly and diverted the direction of the conversation by asking her where she was from. Perhaps because it was a slow night, or perhaps because I feigned such convincing interest, she opened up at once and told us she was in the United States on a guest worker visa.

"I grew up in Serbia," she explained. "There is not so much opportunity there. The American agencies, they look for girls like me. They tell us there are too many jobs here, not enough workers. We don't pay anything—they get us plane tickets and they fill out the papers. When we get here, they give us a job and a place to live."

I said it must have been hard to leave home and move to a new country, but Katya shrugged. The first place she lived was bad, a single room in a dilapidated motel, but now she had a two-room apartment in an old real estate office that was clean and had a small kitchen. She had been here two years, waiting tables during the day, and last semester she started taking night classes at the community college.

"I don't understand American students," she added, gesturing to a stack of books on a nearby table. "The professor, he assigns the reading, and do you know many of them do not even do it? I thought the classes would be hard for me, my English is still not so perfect, but my grades are good. I think now maybe I can study to be a nurse."

Stories like hers reminded me of how much we took for granted, forgetting many of our supposed accomplishments could be credited less to our efforts and more to the lucky circumstances of our birth.

Katya glanced up at the tide clock on the wall and pulled out her notepad.

"I'm sorry. I talk too much, and you are here to eat, not listen," she said.

I assured her we enjoyed hearing her story, which was true. I was also confident Josh had forgotten about my call with Wayne.

I ordered the dinner salad with fried shrimp, which I considered at least half-healthy, but Katya shook her head.

"I am sorry. We cannot serve any salad. It made people sick. Not here," she hastened to add, "but somewhere else, and we get our lettuce from the same...."

She paused as she searched her vocabulary for the right word.

"Supplier?" I filled in.

The girl nodded. "Yes. The same supplier as the places where the sick people ate."

"I heard about that when we were in Norfolk," I said to Josh. "There was a salmonella outbreak. I thought it was in South Carolina."

Katya considered this. "Maybe there too, but my manager told me North Carolina. Bald Head Island, it is a—how do you call it—a country club. It is south of here, but he said it was still in North Carolina."

With anything green under suspicion, I ordered two dozen steamed shrimp and a side of hush puppies instead. Josh did the same. As Katya left, he looked at me worriedly.

"I didn't know anything about a salmonella outbreak. You know I picked up that bag of spring mix for you when I went to Hatteras. It could have been the same brand. Maybe you should throw it away."

"I hate to waste food. Let me look it up," I suggested, pulling out my phone. My search immediately turned up two salmonella outbreaks, both in the past month, covered on every major news website. I opened an article by CNN, paraphrasing for Josh as I read.

Katya was right—the first outbreak had involved Caesar salads served at a fundraising gala in a private country club on North Carolina's Bald Head Island. It had sickened nearly all the five hundred guests, including several congressmen and state officials, sending more than half to the hospital. Sallie Hathaway had also been correct—the second outbreak occurred at a single restaurant in Charleston, South Carolina, a few days before I arrived in Norfolk. This time symptoms affected only a handful of people, but several were still hospitalized. Thus far, officials with the FDA and the CDC had been able to determine the suppliers but were unable to determine the source of the bacteria.

"At least no one was killed," Josh noted.

It was still disconcerting. It wasn't that I worried much about the food I ordered out. After all, I always asked for my meat to be cooked medium rare, despite the dire health warnings on the menu. It was a risk I accepted to eat my burgers the way I liked them. But salad—I wasn't willing to flaunt death for anything under a thousand calories.

"I'll throw the salad mix away. I don't understand, though. I thought we had safety precautions for things like this."

He frowned as he sipped his beer. "Bacteria can come from fertilizers. It could also be in the packaging process, using water that isn't clean, or even from workers not washing their hands. There are a lot of openings along the chain for something to go wrong."

It wasn't a thought I wanted to entertain while we sat in a restaurant waiting for food.

"About tomorrow," I said, changing the subject. "Do you mind if we stop a few places so I can follow up on some leads for Kathy Dvorak?"

He gave me a confused look, and I realized I had never shared my new client's email messagewith him. He listened carefully while I ran over the list of charges, bank account balances, and the ad for a custom boat.

"Sounds like you have a lot to go on. Where do you want to start?"

"I was thinking the restaurant. Waitresses usually remember a regular, especially if he's alone. I couldn't find anything about a biological lab nearby, but maybe he mentioned where he works, or maybe the restaurant gets enough customers from the same company that they'd know what it is."

"If you don't mind a suggestion, I say we try the yacht broker," Josh said, a glint in his eye. "That would be more fun, for one thing. I mean, who doesn't want to look at yachts? Plus, any decent salesman is bound to remember a potential customer looking at a really expensive boat."

I laughed. He made a good argument on both counts.

"Fine, we'll start with the boat," I said. "Just remember, we're there for information. We're not buying anything."

"The boat it is, then!" he declared, raising his beer in a mock toast.

I felt an unfamiliar sense of comradery. So much of what I did I usually did alone. Sometimes I bounced ideas off Wayne, but it was hard to have a frank conversation when you risked ending up as a headline in the Washington Post. Not that he ever used information without my permission, but I didn't always appreciate the consequences of going public until I suffered them. This was the first time I considered how nice it might be to have a partner.

The shrimp came, steaming hot as advertised and liberally doused in seasoning. We took our time, since peeling shells and tails was an interactive and time-consuming dining experience. The talk turned to wave height forecasts and finding the best shore break. Tomorrow we would run down the ad Kathy Dvorak sent me, and in the afternoon, we'd drive out to the beach. The temperature was supposed to top out at seventy-four degrees. I looked forward to finding a wind-sheltered spot on a dune and stretching out in the sun while Josh surfed.

By the time we finished eating and paid the check it was going on eight o'clock. We walked back to the dock slowly, and Josh's arm found its way around my shoulders, welcome heat in the cool night air. As we approached the end of the pier, my phone rang.

"Go ahead. Come on over when you're finished," Josh said, stepping up to his deck. I got out my cell just as the sound died. On the screen was a number I didn't recognize with a North Carolina exchange, and a few seconds later a voicemail notification appeared. It was a short message.

"Sandi, this is Kathy Dvorak. Please call me when you get a chance. Thanks. Bye."

She sounded muffled. I wondered if perhaps her husband had reappeared, or if she had gotten some news of his whereabouts. I pressed redial and she picked up at once, her words coming out in a rush.

"Sandi, I wanted to tell you, you can stop looking for Everett. I'm sorry I wasted your time. If you just send me a bill for what you've done...."

"Kathy, did you hear from Everett?" I broke in.

"No...not exactly. But I know he's all right," she said, but her voice quavered with emotion.

"I don't understand," I said, speaking slowly. "How can you be sure he is okay if you haven't spoken to him?"

"The latest bank statement came today. Everett took the money out of that money market account last month...all of it, and he closed the account. He left me, Sandi!" she wailed.

I had always suspected this was a possibility, but the way he did it surprised me. Not that a late-in-life crisis can't happen, and certainly he would not be the first man to suddenly and impulsively disappear. But everything I had seen suggested Dvorak was a methodical man.

"We don't know that," I said. "He could have been forced to withdraw that money."

"Y-y-you don't really believe that," she stammered between sobs.

She was right, I didn't, but I was trying to be optimistic.

"Did the statement show the branch where he closed the account?" I asked.

I heard her fumbling with some papers, still weeping. "Yes. Beaufort."

"I need you to focus, Kathy. Read me every transaction."

She sniffled loudly, but I could no longer hear crying. "There were only two. Both were withdrawals for cashier's checks. There's no way to see who they went to."

I would bet at least one of them went to Garrett's. It appeared Everett might be a runner after all.

"Send me a copy of the statement and let me look into this. Whatever happened, Kathy, you are owed an explanation," I insisted. "And if he did leave you, you are owed half of whatever he had."

"I don't want his money."

I took a deep breath.

"I understand, Kathy, I do. But you might feel differently in a few months. You moved to Ocracoke for Everett. Now you have a business and a house, and you don't want to lose them. You've earned the right to a secure future and a chance to leave your children an inheritance."

There was a long silence on the other end.

"You're right," she said finally. "You find him, and you tell him that. You tell him I'm calling the children. And I'm contacting our lawyer."

"I will, but I'm asking you to hold off and give me another day. Let me try to get you some answers before you do anything permanent."

Mrs. Dvorak didn't answer.

"Kathy, is there something else you want to tell me?"

She sniffled again. "I don't know if it's important. That's why I didn't say anything before. But now...."

She sounded embarrassed. I knew at once it was about another woman—the missing piece, the only one that would make any sense.

"Go on," I encouraged.

"Everett...he isn't good with his cell phone. He loses it all the time, leaves it lying everywhere. A few months ago, I picked it up and saw he had three missed calls and a new text message. He was out fishing with our neighbor, and I was afraid it might be important, so I checked. They were all from the same number in Maryland. The text said to meet the caller at the airport at two."

"What did your husband say when you told him?"

Kathy hesitated. "I... I didn't tell him. I was afraid he'd be upset I looked on his phone. When he got home, I said I accidentally turned it off when I moved it from the porch. He didn't say anything, just took it back to his study. A few minutes later I heard him talking on the house phone. I picked it up and listened."

"And it was a woman," I finished.

"Yes," she admitted miserably. "I told myself it had to be about work. Everett has never been the type to...I mean, he never has given me a reason...."

"I understand."

"He never told me about the call, and I didn't ask. The next day he said he had some errands to run and left at one-thirty. He was gone for hours, and when he came home, he got out a bottle of scotch and went right to his study. Everett wasn't a drinker, so I could see he was upset, but when I asked what was wrong, he just growled at me and shut the door."

"Did he ever say anything more about what happened?"

"No, and I was afraid he'd get angry if I brought it up. He looked worried for a few days, but then he seemed to feel better. I thought…it just seemed more likely it was something to do with his job."

For every cheating spouse, there were multitudes of friends and relatives who wondered aloud why the faithful partner didn't suspect. They forgot they had the advantage of hindsight. They knew the ending of the story. It was always easier to see the clues when you already had the answer.

"Did this kind of thing ever happen again?"

"No. But in October a friend of mine mentioned she'd seen Everett up in Rodanthe having lunch with a woman. It was on a day he told me he had a dentist appointment in Nags Head. That was just before he left on his last trip."

Her account had all the elements of a textbook affair, but I tried to withhold judgment. "Did you ask him about it?"

"No—I didn't know about it until after he left for work. But Sandi, I remembered the date of the appointment because when he came home, he looked so happy, and he…." She gulped, and the tears started again.

"He what?"

"He brought me flowers!"

A guilty conscience, I thought, or a man who had come to a decision. It would have been nice to have this information earlier, but sometimes denial was the only comfort we had.

"All right. Promise me you'll wait a day or two before you do anything major," I said, by which I meant filing for divorce. "I'm just across the bridge from Beaufort. If he's here, I'll find him."

And I meant it.

I understood gray areas. I was a practitioner of situational ethics. Yet in my heart, there was a puritanical streak, a conviction that right and wrong were absolutes. No amount of explanation or justification could change their reality. If Everett Dvorak truly left his wife for another woman without even bothering to let her know, he was wrong, and he should not be allowed to walk away unscathed.

If he were within a thousand miles, I would track him down.

Chapter 15

"GO OVER IT WITH me again."

Josh rolled his eyes. "We just got a big settlement from a lawsuit, and we've always wanted to move to the Keys and open a charter business. We're looking for a boat to take people fishing on overnight trips. A friend of ours mentioned this boat. We've gone over it a dozen times. Trust me—I've got this."

I knew I was being over-cautious, but I was used to making things up as I went along. That was fine when you worked solo, but I couldn't take a chance we'd open our mouths at the same time and give conflicting answers.

"Oh, yeah, what was the lawsuit about again?" Josh asked. It wasn't a topic we'd discussed, and I could see he was teasing me.

"Slip and fall. In Walmart," I responded immediately. "Legally, we can't talk about the actual amount of the settlement. But between you and me, there are lots of zeros."

His look was a cross between admiration and dismay. "Does it even bother you to lie like this?"

"Occasionally," I admitted. "But I get over it. A necessary evil."

Garrett Bay Boats was a huge operation spanning acres of waterfront, with several large metal buildings where construction was done along with a nicely appointed dockside office. As soon as we walked in, we were greeted by a middle-aged man in Dockers and a polo shirt bearing the company logo.

"Good morning," he said genially, extending his hand. "I'm Tim Davis.

How can I help y'all?"

"We're looking for a boat," Josh said.

"Well, folks, you've come to the right place! What do you have in mind—center console, runabout?"

He had obviously sized us up as belonging in the under-forty-thousand-dollar range. I pulled out a printed copy of the ad Kathy Dvorak sent me.

"We'd like to talk to Greg," I said, pointing to the circled name. "We understand he knows all about this boat."

Tim blinked and took a step backward, reassessing. "You want Greg Garrett. He's out in the shed gettin' a tuna tower refit ready for delivery. If y'all want to come back, I could set you up an appointment."

"Tim, I don't think that's a good idea," said Josh pleasantly. "My wife here's got money burning a hole in her pocket, and this is the boat she's got her heart set on. I don't really care—I saw a Viking I liked just fine, but the settlement's in her name, so it's her choice."

I almost burst out laughing. I couldn't have played it better myself. I could see Tim was weighing the possibility we were pulling his leg against the ire of his boss if he lost a half-million-dollar sale. Money won out, as it always did.

"Let me just give him a holler," Tim said, disappearing through a side door.

"This is more fun than I thought it would be," Josh whispered.

Two minutes later Tim reappeared, following behind a short, stocky man wearing the same company uniform, though in place of blue, his shirt was gold. He grabbed each of our hands and shook them in turn.

"Greg Garrett," he said by way of introduction. "Tim says you asked for me. Have we spoken before?"

There was nothing of southern softness in his voice. If I had to guess, I would say Garrett was a transplanted Baltimorean. There was brisk, no-nonsense directness about him. I surmised he would not be easily manipulated.

"No, sir," I answered truthfully. "We got this ad from a friend, but it's just what we're looking for."

"I'm sorry to disappoint you," Greg said, frowning at the paper I handed him. "That boat was sold in October. We delivered her two weeks ago. We do have something similar under construction now, but it will take at least a month to finish."

I made a face. "I guess Everett was right," I said to Josh. "He said he thought it would go fast."

"You're a friend of Everett Dvorak's?" Greg Garrett asked.

"More like acquaintances," I said. "I know his wife."

This was a shot in the dark. If Everett was parading around with a girlfriend, I might get a reaction. I did, but not the one I expected.

"She didn't tell you?" he said, rubbing his chin. "He bought the boat himself, and I hope she was as happy as he thought she'd be. I've never seen a guy so excited about surprising his wife."

"We haven't talked in a few weeks," I explained hastily, wondering just who the "wife" was Dvorak intended to surprise.

"I guess it must have gone okay, because he hasn't stopped back in. Kind of expected he would, since the window treatments didn't come in until last Thursday. If you see Everett, you might want to mention that. I haven't been able to get hold of him."

I saw the opening and took it.

"We sure will, but he's probably back in Ocracoke, and we won't be heading that way for a while," I said, shaking my head in disappointment. "Do you know if Everett is keeping the boat here in Beaufort? We'd love to stop by and see it." Garrett hesitated, so I added, "It might give us a better idea of whether we'd be willing to wait for the one you're working on to be finished."

Garrett put on a smile. "Sure thing. We delivered it to Mallory's over in Morehead. He told me it was going to stay there through the winter. Unless he's moved it, they had him out on J dock. Ship's name is *Kathy Lee*."

Josh and I exchanged a look. You don't normally name your boat after your wife if you're taking off with another woman. Either Dvorak had a mean streak, or I had misjudged him.

"Thank you. If we run into Everett, we'll tell him to give you a call," I said, turning to go.

"If you think you're interested in this design boat, we can go take a look at the hull right now," Garrett pressed. "Still a lot of the interior to be done, but that'll allow you to customize it just like you want it. We can maybe even cut you a better deal."

"I think we'll take a look at Everett's boat, maybe see what we want, and then we'll get back to you," Josh said, reaching for Garrett's hand.

"We've wasted enough of your time today." Then he took my elbow and guided me swiftly out the door.

"What do you think?" he asked when we were safely out of Greg Garrett's hearing.

"I think we need to visit Mallory's Marina."

Mallory's was across the highway from Dockside. We found *Kathy Lee* at the end of J dock just as Garrett said, and it was stunning. With a sea foam green hull and cream topsides, it stretched the length of the slip. A new welcome mat stood on the dock next to a set of fiberglass boarding steps.

"It looks like someone's home," Josh said.

We knocked on the side of the boat, but no one answered. Without hesitation I climbed aboard, and after a few seconds Josh followed. Deck chairs were out on the stern, and the sliding glass door was unlocked. Inside there were signs everywhere indicating Everett planned to stay aboard—toiletries in the bathroom, sheets on the bed, even food in the fridge, but nothing seemed to have been opened. I checked the date on the milk—it had expired a week ago. On the shelf behind the sofa, there was a framed photo of Kathy and her husband next to a Wall Street Journal dated November eighteenth.

"He wasn't leaving her," Josh said, following my eyes.

"It would appear not," I agreed, looking around with a sinking feeling in my chest. "Don't touch anything."

We made our way carefully back to the deck. As we stepped off the boat, a slim blonde woman in shorts and a long-sleeved white shirt was waiting to greet us.

"If you're looking for Mr. Dvorak, he isn't here," she said.

"Do you know when he'll be back?" I asked.

"Can't say I do. I expected to see him before now. He told us in the office he was going to pick up his wife in Ocracoke and bring her down to the boat. That's two weeks ago now, and he hasn't been back."

I thought a minute. There were times when you had to give a little information to get some, and it was clear the woman in front of me was already curious.

"My name is Sandi Beck, and this is Josh Culliver," I said. "I'm a friend of Everett's wife, Kathy. To be honest, she asked us to come down and find out what's going on. She hasn't been able to get in touch with him, and she's afraid something happened."

The woman's eyes grew round. "My goodness. I had no idea. I hope he's all right."

"We do, too. Can you tell me the last time you saw Mr. Dvorak?"

She frowned. "Let me think…the boat was delivered on a Thursday evening, I guess that would've been the nineteenth of November, and I talked to him Friday morning. That's when he told me he was going home to pick up his wife and bring her back for the weekend. He had a friend come down just as I was going to pick up parts in Jacksonville, but his car was gone when I got back, so I figured he left Friday afternoon."

"Do you remember the name of his friend?"

She shook her head. "He didn't introduce us. I was busy writing down readings on the electric meters, and I was halfway down the dock. But I noticed Mr. Dvorak looked kind of unhappy, and I heard him mention the lab. I knew Mr. Dvorak was a scientist, so I just assumed it was someone he worked with."

"Can you describe his visitor?"

The woman hesitated. "I don't know. I didn't really pay much attention."

"Anything you remember might be helpful."

She thought. "He was tall, that's for sure, really big build but not fat, if you know what I mean. Short hair. He looked familiar."

No wonder. With two bases nearby, it was a description that could fit any of a thousand men in this area.

"Maybe you should talk to Mr. Mallory, the owner," she said. "He'll be in tomorrow."

I doubted that would help. "Thank you. Maybe we'll stop by tomorrow."

She followed us down the dock and watched as we got in the truck. I saw her read over our license plate as we pulled away.

"You think he's dead, don't you?"

Josh's voice was surprisingly matter-of-fact given the subject.

"I think it's a possibility, yes. Even after he paid for the boat, he should have had over three hundred thousand dollars. He could have been robbed or even kidnapped. But if he was doing something illegal…."

He nodded. "None of those are great scenarios, given he's a biological weapons scientist. Do you want me to call my father?"

"No," I said, then seeing his expression, "at least, not yet. I need to talk to Kathy Dvorak first."

He turned into our marina parking lot and shut off the engine. His voice was soft when he spoke.

"We're talking about a potential threat to national security, Sandi."

"I know, Josh. But we're also talking about a woman who has been married to this man for more than thirty years."

He pressed his lips together. "Do what you need to do. I'll be down on my boat."

I waited till he was out of sight, then dialed Kathy's number. In as calm and professional a manner as possible, I spelled out everything we had learned at Garrett Bay and described what we had seen on the boat. When I finished, I heard her take a shaky breath.

"You say he named the boat for me?" she asked.

"Yes. *Kathy Lee.*"

"And he wasn't going to leave me," she said, more to herself than to me.

"It doesn't look like it, no."

"Then where is he?" Kathy asked, and for the first time I heard real terror in her voice.

"I don't know. I wish I did. Given what we've learned, and with the money Everett was being paid…." I tried to think of a way to word it gently, but none came to mind.

"You think he was doing something wrong?"

I heard the defensiveness in her tone. "I think he might have been unaware of exactly what he was doing. If he had an accident, by now you would have gotten a call from someone—police, a hospital, something. I think we have to consider the possibility Everett is in trouble, and we may need to go to someone for help."

"What should I do?" Kathy asked. "If we call the police, wouldn't that put him in greater danger?"

"I know someone in law enforcement, the father of a close friend," I said carefully. "I'm sure he has worked on cases like this before. He may even know Everett. I'd like to ask him what he thinks."

"All right," she said, sounding close to tears. "How soon can you call him?"

"I'll try as soon as I get off the phone with you, but I might not get anyone right away. I promise I'll call you back as soon as I hear anything. And if you decide then you want to go to the police, or whatever else you want to do, that will be up to you."

"All right," she said weakly. "Thank you."
And she hung up the phone.

Chapter 16

ANDREW CULLIVER DID NOT SOUND particularly happy to hear from me.

I tried not to take it personally. I understood his wife did not view me as daughter-in-law material, but I thought Josh's father was more open-minded. In this case, maybe it was the message rather than the messenger that concerned him. No one in the FBI wanted to be told a scientist with explicit knowledge of biological weapons had gone missing. I don't think his reaction was necessarily a reflection of his feelings for me.

At least, I hoped not.

"To the best of my knowledge, there are no legitimate military contractors working on counteracting biological agents outside of secured military facilities. It is possible his wife misunderstood, and he was working on a new drug or vaccine for a pharmaceutical company. However, Dr. Dvorak's level of compensation suggests whatever research he was completing was outside of existing regulations," Mr. Culliver said.

In other words, no one got paid that much for doing something legal.

"So, what do we do now?" I asked.

"I need you to email me the documents you received from Mrs. Dvorak along with a statement detailing what you just told me. No conjecture, just facts. I will share this with officials in the Justice Department and Homeland Security and we'll launch an investigation. Your involvement ends here. This is now a national security matter," Josh's father said bluntly. "Do you understand?"

I knew he was right, but at the same time, I could not simply walk away from Kathy Dvorak. She had come to me, had trusted me.

"I'd like to keep in touch with my client," I said.

Andrew Culliver sighed. "Sandi, if you want to speak to Mrs. Dvorak in a private capacity, I can't stop you. However, I'd like you to ask yourself how you are helping by remaining involved. You were correct in calling me—you don't have the resources or clearance for this type of investigation. You need to let me do my job."

I suppressed my urge to argue back.

"Fine," I muttered.

"I really do appreciate the work you've done here," Josh's father said, his voice softening to something close to human. "This could be a serious situation, and I'm grateful you brought it to our attention."

I murmured something about being glad I could help, though I felt like a child who had been summarily dismissed. I handed the phone back to Josh and went to sit in his cockpit. A few minutes later he came out to join me.

"I'm sorry if he came off a little gruff," he apologized.

"I understand."

"He told me I needed to keep you out of it, for your own safety," Josh said with a faint smile. "I told him I didn't think I had much power to make you do anything."

I studied his face carefully. "Does that bother you?"

"Not at all," he said, and the smile widened. "I like independent women. Just try not to get yourself killed."

I noted I'd been moderately successful so far, which wasn't exactly true. It had been barely a month since Patricia Grady threatened to shoot me over the small matter of her son's inheritance after her husband's murder. But Josh didn't know that whole story, and this was not an opportune time to share it.

Josh glanced at his watch. "Why don't you call Kathy Dvorak back and let her know what's going on. I'll pack up some sandwiches and drinks, and then we're going to take the rest of the day and go to the beach. I think you need to have some fun."

While he got the cooler together, I went back to *Serenity* and put together a statement to send to Josh's father. Then I changed into shorts and grabbed a beach bag, dialing Kathy as I went. She answered on the third ring. I told her about my conversation with Andrew Culliver, and she sounded relieved. It was clear she no longer feared her husband's displeasure; she feared for his life. While we were talking, she got a second call, this one from a D.C. number. She read it aloud, and I recognized it at once as the number of Josh's father.

"Take it," I said. "Call me later."

"Thank you," she said breathlessly, and she was gone.

Everett Dvorak's fate was out of my hands.

Josh and I drove the truck across to the coast, parking on a stretch of sand where the waves were breaking in slow, systematic lines of foam. The oceanside vacation homes behind us were empty, their windows covered by hurricane shutters, and the beach was deserted but for sea birds and ghost crabs. Josh unloaded his board and pulled on a wetsuit, while I chose a spot for my blanket and laid out in the sun. I propped myself up on both elbows and watched him as he paddled out and floated on the swells, waiting for the right wave. When he finally stood, he rode the curl of white with power and grace, his body in tune with the movement of the board and the water.

He came in after a dozen good rides, his board under his arm, his face alight. He stripped off his wetsuit and toweled off, the first time I had really seen him without a shirt. His body was lean and muscled, skin crazed by thin white scars made more visible by the last remnants of a faded summer tan. He reached in the cooler and grabbed two bottles, handing me one as he flopped beside me on the blanket, still breathing heavily from the exertion.

"You really can surf," I said.

He grinned. "Don't sound so surprised. I am a man of many talents."

"Oh? What are they?" I teased.

He leaned over, his face close to mine.

"Let me show you," he said softly, and he pressed his lips against mine. I breathed in his breath, and then his hand was behind my head, lifting me to him as the kiss deepened. I closed my eyes, and time slowed to nothingness.

This…this was what I had been waiting for. I knew it, could feel it in every nerve ending. It was the free fall, the lightning strike. It was breaking the surface and being blinded by the sun. As he drew back, I opened my eyes.

"I'm glad we got that over with," he said lightly. "The suspense was killing me. How about a sandwich?"

He pulled out a roll of paper towels, bags of chips, and several sandwiches while I stared at him blankly, still trying to clear my head. He handed me one, then sat beside me on the blanket to eat.

"Ham and provolone, spicy mustard," Josh explained, then unwrapped his own sandwich and began to eat.

Perhaps it was the impact of the kiss, but I found the sharing of a packed lunch endearingly romantic.

After we finished eating, we took a long walk along the water's edge, stopping to pick up shells and laughing when a larger wave would swirl around our legs, nearly knocking us to our knees. Josh would put his arm around me then, and I leaned against him, so we steadied each other. When we had gone so far that the truck was just a dot on the horizon, we turned back, and when we reached the car, he kissed me again.

"Thanks for coming along," he said. "I had a good time."

"Me too."

Sticky and damp, we packed everything in the truck and drove back to the marina to shower. Afterward we met on Josh's boat, where he had already poured two glasses of wine.

"To us," he said.

"To us."

We both took a sip of wine. Josh looked at me seriously.

"There's something I want to talk to you about," he said.

I felt my face stiffen. Those words seldom prefaced anything good.

"I've been thinking about our trip from here, and it would make more sense to take just one boat," he began.

It was something I had thought myself, especially on that miserable sail to Oriental. But as soon as he said it, my mind rebelled. The rosy glow of the afternoon was gone, replaced by concern bordering on panic. Did he really expect me to give up *Serenity*?

"I'm not saying which boat," he said quickly. "We'd need to look at equipment and what would make each of us most comfortable. I just wanted to throw the idea out there and let you think about it. Single-handing is difficult. In terms of safety, especially offshore, we would both need to take on crew. Dockage as we go south is going to get more expensive. It makes financial and logistical sense to sail together."

He was right, of course, but I had lived alone for three years, and I had not once considered giving up my independence. Whether we took *Serenity* or *Andromeda*, every move, every decision would be a collaboration. I wasn't sure I was ready for that.

"You don't have to come up with an answer right now," he said. "Just think about it."

I opened my mouth, but I was cut off by Josh's phone. He glanced at the screen, then looked at me apologetically. "It's Uncle Alan."

"Go ahead," I said, relieved I would have more time to work out what I was going to say.

As soon as Josh took the call, I could see something was wrong. His brow furrowed, and his fingers tightened their grip on the phone.

"When?" he asked, and after a brief pause, "Have you talked to your lawyer?"

I froze when I heard the words. Somehow, between the search for Dvorak and the distraction of the kiss, I had managed to put the conversation with Wayne Kremm totally out of my mind. I watched as Josh got up abruptly and went to his nav station, a small desk built in the corner by the pantry. Grabbing a pencil and paper, he scribbled down a name and phone number.

"I'll be there in four hours," he said. He ended the call and stood staring at the cell phone in his hand.

"What's wrong?" I asked, a catch in my voice.

He looked up at me, his face a mixture of anger and confusion. "Uncle Alan has been taken in for questioning. The police are planning to charge him in Aunt Maggie's death."

"Oh, Josh...."

He turned away and opened a closet door. He pulled out a duffel bag and began shoving clothes inside.

"I'm sorry, Sandi, but I've got to get up there," he said over his back. "Uncle Alan hasn't been able to reach his lawyer and he won't call my father. He's afraid it will jeopardize Dad's career to get involved. He sounds—God, he sounds awful. He needs me."

He turned to face me, his expression pleading. "Do you understand? I've got to go."

I rose and went to him, giving him a hug. "Of course, I understand. Call me when you get there. I'll shut everything up on *Andromeda*."

"Thanks," he said, hugging me back. Then he slipped free and went to the head, returning with a shaving kit and toothbrush, and dumped them in his bag. Josh looked around distractedly, then stopped when his eyes met mine.

"I'm really sorry. I'll have to take the truck. Will you be all right?"

"I'll be fine. Don't worry about me."

I followed him out to the deck, where he gave me a quick kiss goodbye. I watched as he left, waiting until the truck's tail lights disappeared before I dialed my phone.

Wayne picked up on the first ring.

"If you're calling about Alan Culliver, it wasn't me," he said at once.

"Why didn't you tell me this was going on?" I snapped.

"Because I just found out about ten minutes ago. Look, San, I got sidetracked by another story and I never even started digging. But when I asked Elsa whether there was anything more on Maggie's death, she started putting things together. Before long, she heard the same rumor you did, about the Cullivers' marriage having problems. She's the one who went to the police. I didn't know anything about it until her piece came across my newsfeed."

His voice was earnest. Wayne is many things, but he is not a liar. I sighed.

"Do they have enough to arrest him?"

"Maybe. If what Elsa wrote is everything, it's all circumstantial," he said. "She found out Alan Culliver was a diver, and she got two people in his neighborhood to say they saw him in a wetsuit on the day Maggie died. She showed his picture to the guy from the Navy story she was working on, and he said Alan looked like the diver who walked through his yard. Then she went back to the waterman and showed him some photos of hooded divers surfacing by a boat. He said yeah, that could have been what he saw."

"That's not enough to bring him in on," I protested.

"No, it isn't. Then she went to Alan Culliver. I don't know what story she used to get an interview, but she got him to admit he thought Maggie was having an affair."

"That doesn't mean he killed her!"

There was a pause.

"What aren't you telling me, Wayne?"

"Remember I thought there was a link between Maggie's and Jansen's deaths," he said. "You never mentioned Alan Culliver drives a red Corvette."

"He doesn't own the only red Corvette on the East Coast. That could have been anybody and you know it," I argued.

"The police don't think so. They're reopening the investigation into Jansen's death. Elsa has a source who claims Culliver thought Jansen was his wife's lover. His name isn't in the report, but he was her diving instructor, so it must be the same guy you overheard at the memorial service. According to this witness, Maggie told him last September that she was afraid of her husband. She said Alan accused her of running around with her old boss."

I thought back to the conversation between Holtz and Gardner. It was possible the I.U.S. CEO thought Holtz was going to confront Alan about Maggie's death, but he hadn't, he had merely offered condolences. Nothing in the way he spoke to Maggie's husband suggested he thought Alan was responsible for her murder. I pointed this out to Wayne, adding, "It doesn't make sense. Why wait till now? And besides, there's no way to prove Holtz is telling the truth. The only person who can confirm what he's saying is dead."

"Like I said, it's all circumstantial. But Alan Culliver has no alibi for the morning of Maggie's death, and he didn't report her missing until after nine a.m. There's another thing—both he and Maggie had life insurance policies for five hundred thousand dollars. Alan took them out last spring."

My frustration bubbled over. "None of this proves anything, Wayne! Who has an alibi at six o'clock in the morning?"

"San, be honest. It's at least enough to be suspicious. You can't blame Elsa for writing the story."

"Do you remember Bernie Wathen?" I asked sharply. He was a man both of us had believed to be guilty of murder. I gave Wayne the tip, he printed the story, Wathen was arrested and then hanged himself. It was only after the fact I discovered he was innocent. "We put the noose around his neck, Wayne, you and I. Do you want this reporter to do the same thing to Alan Culliver?"

I knew I had struck a nerve when he didn't answer.

Yet Wayne had a point. If I were in Elsa's position, I might have printed it. The difference was that I had seen the naked grief Alan felt at Maggie's death. I might have believed he pushed or struck Jansen in a moment of anger, but he would never have planned and executed the cold-blooded murder of his wife.

But gossip was an insidious adversary. I heard about Maggie's alleged infidelity from Sallie Hathaway and from Josh's own mother. If they knew, how many others had some inkling the Cullivers' marriage was in trouble? How long before they were drawn to tell their stories to police or reporters, whether out of guilt, a sense of responsibility, or the thrill of temporary notoriety? Even circumstantial evidence, when it flooded in from all sides, could be compelling. A few more voices raised against him, an anecdote or two about the discord in his home, and there might be enough to hold Alan…maybe even enough to sway a jury.

Poor Josh. This was going to crush him.

"I'm sorry, Wayne. I just think you're wrong," I said tiredly. "Please, if you hear anything else, let me know."

"What are you going to do?" Wayne asked.

"Nothing," I said. "There's nothing I can do."

It was a hopeless feeling, and for once, it was the truth.

Chapter 17

JOSH CALLED ME THAT night from Virginia Beach. His uncle's lawyer had finally gotten to the police station just as Alan was charged with murder in the first degree for the death of Maggie Culliver. As Wayne had suggested he might be, Alan was also wanted for questioning in Maryland regarding Bart Jansen's death. Jansen's house was still on the market, and the police told Alan's lawyer an investigative team was combing the house for fingerprints or DNA evidence placing Culliver there. They needn't have bothered—as soon as they asked, Alan admitted he had gone to see Bart Jansen on the day the former intelligence official died.

"It wasn't because he thought Aunt Maggie was having an affair with him," Josh insisted. "He wanted to ask Jansen to stop calling her. She was supposed to be retired. He said she wasn't sleeping, she was upset, and he was trying to protect her."

I couldn't tell if he was trying to persuade me or himself.

"I'm sorry, Josh," I said. I didn't know what else to say. And I was sorry, sorry I had ever talked to Wayne about Alan and Maggie Culliver, sorry Josh was caught in this situation, sorry people were fallible and prone to the most terrible of mistakes.

"This is just a…a big mess, Sandi. Alan told us he and Aunt Maggie were having problems, and he did think she was seeing someone. She lied about being someplace and he found out. But he never confronted her, never told her what he suspected. He said about a month ago it all stopped, things went back to normal, so he let it go. He was just glad everything was better."

There was a pause. Despite his love for his uncle, Josh was not the kind of man to lie to himself.

"I know it looks bad but—damn it, Sandi, he would never hurt Aunt Maggie."

I heard what he did not say. Like me, he wasn't as certain about Bart Jansen. Just below the surface, Josh was afraid he didn't really know his uncle. He was looking back even now, remembering forgotten conversations—a word here, a look there—and wondering if he had been blinded all along to the man Alan was.

This was what the search for truth could yield: a loss of trust, a breakdown of family. It was why so many of us chose to ignore faults, overlook behaviors, pretend everything was fine. Lies were easier to bear.

"The bail hearing is set for tomorrow, but the prosecutor isn't pressing for a quick trial date. I think they're hoping to have something more from the Maryland investigation, so this whole mess could drag on for months."

"Oh," I said, as our plans for Christmas and the cruise south crumbled.

"I'm only staying in Norfolk till the end of the week," Josh added quickly. "Once Alan's out on bail, there's not much more for me to do."

I knew I should tell him it was no big deal, not to worry, but I wanted him with me.

"Good. I've kind of gotten used to you," I said, and I could hear his smile.

"I've kind of gotten used to you, too. I've got to go now. I'll call you tomorrow."

I slept fitfully that night. I had spent less than a month with Josh, but I could sense his empty bunk on *Andromeda* even in my sleep. I hadn't just gotten used to him—I had become dependent on the comfort of having him there. He was the first thing I thought about when my eyes opened and the last thing on my mind when I crawled into bed. The realization came with a rush of what was either giddy anticipation or paralyzing terror.

The poets called it love.

I got up and dressed at six a.m. It was still dark, but I made a cup of coffee and set out to create a list of jobs for myself for the rest of the week. Sitting around missing Josh and worrying about Alan was not a productive use of my time. I'd found that keeping busy was, if not a cure, at least a treatment for what bothered me.

I needed to do some grocery shopping, though I'd have to beg a ride from the marina staff. The teak could use a fresh coat of oil. I hadn't been under the boat for more than a month, so I could do a dive and clean the propeller, weather permitting. I finished out my list with a few other odd jobs, and by then the sun was up. It was a cool morning, clear and bright, and I felt a rush of caffeine-induced optimism. I toasted a bagel and slathered it in cream cheese, poured a second cup of coffee, and went out on the deck to welcome the day.

The docks in Morehead stayed full year-round, the temperatures moderate enough that most boats were seldom winterized. It was both a tourist town and a working town, and on warm weeks like this one, the inlet was busy with recreational fishermen and commercial watermen coming and going. This morning Ben, the marina manager, was supervising as a group of men loaded coolers and poles aboard a large sportfisher at the end the pier. When he saw me, he walked over to say hello.

"You're here early," I noted.

He adopted a doleful expression.

"Tell me about it."

Ben Lancome was perhaps thirty, wiry and thin with thick glasses. He looked like an engineer or an accountant, and he would have been one or the other except his family moved to Morehead from Jersey and bought a marina when Ben was in high school. Four years later his father developed Parkinson's and Ben dropped out of Duke in his junior year. He took over the day-to-day job of running the business, which he did in a far more organized and efficient manner than I was accustomed to. He was also likable, with a slightly edgy sense of humor and a knack for saying outrageous things with such a straight face you were never sure if he was joking.

"It's purely self-serving. Dennis over there can't get his boat out of the slip to save his life," he added, holding up a handheld VHF. "If I don't talk him out, it'll cost me two posts."

Dennis Walters was the owner of *White Caps*, the custom forty-eight-foot yacht loading at the end of the dock. As the name suggested, he was also a practicing dentist, though only part-time. He had recently retired to the Crystal Coast from Alexandria, Virginia. A big man with a florid complexion, he had copious amounts of money and very little boating experience. I had personally seen him come in on the wrong side of the channel markers twice, and we had only been in town two days.

"Any chance you can give me a lift to Food Lion? Josh had to go to Virginia Beach with the truck, and I'm not sure how long he'll be gone."

"Everything okay?" Ben asked, looking at me curiously. I'm sure he was wondering if we'd had a fight. The couple with two sailboats was already the talk of the Morehead City waterfront.

"Family emergency," I said.

"Too bad. Hope everything works out. If you can wait till after one, I can give you a ride. Otherwise, you can borrow the van. I've got a delivery coming in this morning."

I assured him waiting was no problem as I planned to dive my boat this morning anyway. Ben looked at me with renewed interest.

"I didn't know you dove," he said. "Brenda Pullen over at Mallory's called me yesterday to ask if I knew of an available diver. Chuck Donaldson usually takes care of anything we need, but he sliced his hand down to the bone a week ago, and the doctor won't let him back in the water till it heals. You wouldn't be interested in making a few dollars, would you? Brenda said some woman dropped a diamond tennis bracelet off her boat, and she was hysterical about finding it."

"I don't mind taking a look," I said. "Is Brenda the blonde dockmaster? I think I met her yesterday."

"That's her. If you don't mind, I'll give her a call as soon as I get Dennis as far away from my docks as possible. If she still needs you, take the van. You don't want to have to drag a tank across the highway. Nine o'clock sound okay, or do you want to go later?"

I glanced at my watch. "Nine will work. That gives me plenty of time to finish my breakfast and get suited up."

Ben nodded, his attention back on *White Caps*. Dennis Walters was gunning the engines, and his guests were frantically throwing off lines in every direction as the boat bounced against pilings like a pinball. Ben shouted and began running down the dock.

I was watching the local weather channel when Ben stopped by fifteen minutes later to say they still needed a diver at Mallory's. I hauled my gear up to the van and found it unlocked. Ben had already placed the keys in the console. I went back to *Serenity*, donned a bathing suit followed by a full wetsuit, then sweated as I drove across the street. Brenda was waiting for the van in the parking lot, and she recognized me at once.

"Aren't you the friend of Everett Dvorak's?"

"His wife's," I clarified, opening the rear doors. "Do you have a dock cart?"

She went to fetch one, but she was still frowning when she returned.

"You know, I got a call this morning from the FBI," Brenda said, and there was no missing the accusing tone.

I stopped unloading my equipment and faced her. "I'm sorry, Brenda. But Everett Dvorak's wife really believes he may be in danger. Since Dr. Dvorak used to work in a classified position for the government, the FBI is investigating his disappearance."

Her eyes widened.

"I understand someone lost a tennis bracelet?" I prompted.

The question refocused the dockmaster on the present situation. "Yes. Angela DeGrasse. Her boyfriend owns *Realty Rewards*," she said, pointing to a sizeable yacht about halfway down the dock, just across from *Kathy Lee*. "They were coming into their slip yesterday, and when she threw me a line the bracelet popped right off. I watched it sink down by the post."

I couldn't help but wince at the boat name. *White Caps, Realty Rewards*. When did it become fashionable to name your vessel after your place of employment?

"Can you point out exactly where you saw it go in?" I asked, shutting the van doors and maneuvering the cart toward the dock. Brenda fell in step beside me.

"Sure."

We reached the post at the boat's starboard bow. The dockmaster pointed in the water, about a foot from the post.

"How deep?" I asked, peering into the darkness.

"When the tide's in like this, eighteen feet, give or take."

The water was relatively clear for the ICW, perhaps eight feet of visibility, but I certainly couldn't make out the bottom, much less a tennis bracelet. I hooked up my equipment while Brenda continued talking.

"That man who called from the FBI? I couldn't tell him much. Everett paid in cash, never wrote down any information about where he worked, and whenever you asked a question about his job, he found something else to talk about," she said. "Come to think about it, that's strange. Most of the boat owners here try to peddle whatever it is they're selling, if you know what I mean. Like Steve Edsen, who owns this boat. He specializes in high-end vacation homes, and he tries to sell property to everybody in the marina. But all we knew about Everett was that he was a scientist. We don't get a lot of those."

No doubt. Research science was not a field usually associated with sumptuous salaries.

I turned on my air and sat on the dock, working my arms and shoulders into the BC, balancing the full tank against my back. Just as I was ready to go in, the glass doors on *Realty Rewards* slid open, and a slender woman in lacy underwear stepped out on the deck. She was petite, about my age, with a mane of vivid blue-black hair that hug to her waist. It was so uniquely magnificent that for a moment I did not register how little she was wearing.

"Finally! I didn't think you'd ever get someone!" she complained to Brenda in a sharp, strident tone.

I assumed this was Angela. She folded her arms across the skimpy camisole that barely contained her chest, suddenly aware of the cool air.

"How long will this take?" she demanded. This was directed at me.

It's not that I didn't like rich people—I was sure some of them were fine individuals. I just hadn't met many.

"Ten minutes," I said.

Angela raised her perfectly manicured jet-black eyebrows dramatically. "How can you be sure you can find my bracelet in ten minutes?"

"I can't. That's how long I'm going to look," I said. I put my regulator in my mouth and lowered myself into the water.

Even below the surface, I could hear Angela's protests. I bled the air from my BC, sinking slowly to float about two feet off the bottom, being careful not to disturb the sand with my fins. I pulled a small waterproof flashlight from my pocket and focused on the soft silt beneath me. No glint of metal or stone. I moved delicately around the post first, then swam underneath the hull, covering the front quarter to the bow of the boat in a gradually widening semicircle. Still nothing. Above me the sun disappeared behind a cloud, and the water around me grew darker.

It was possible the bracelet had been carried beneath the pier as it sunk.

I backed around the post and began the same search pattern under the dock. I moved inch by inch, my mask just above the bottom, my breath slow and even. One foot back…two feet back…a fish flashed beside my face, startling me, and my sudden movement sent a cloud of silt swirling around me. My visibility closed to nothing, and I felt the claustrophobic panic claw at my throat.

I did the Devil's Den once in Florida, and I felt now as I had then, as if cave walls were closing in around me. I concentrated on keeping my body still and breathing slowly, in and out, letting the tide pull me under the pier. The water around me swelled and undulated, pushed by the wake of a passing boat, carrying me. Looking down, I caught a quick reflection of an object sticking up on the bottom. I reached down, pulled it from the sand, and brought it to my mask. A cell phone. I slipped it into my pocket and continued my search.

Even the small movement of retrieving the phone sent another haze of silt into the water around me, again reducing visibility to less than a foot. I felt something flutter against my side, softly skittering along my wetsuit once, twice. So close to the inlet, I had no doubt there were sharks in this water, and my heart began to race. Stop. Relax. It's just a fish. I turned my head to the left where a light-colored shape floated beside me, just on the edge of my field of vision, surrounded by tiny silver flashes. I rolled to my side and kicked my fins gently, pushing my face closer. A school of fish, scales gleaming, churned around my head, then darted away. The pale shape drifted toward me, swaying to and fro in the current, just as the silt cleared.

I opened my mouth to scream.

A hand, the flesh pallid and torn, raised its curled fingers and brushed against my mask.

Chapter 18

I KNOCKED THE HAND away and began to flail and kick, struggling to get free of whatever else might be there. For a wild moment I was sure I was seeing the remains of a shark attack, and I half-expected teeth to clamp down on my leg. I swam frantically to the back of *Realty Rewards*, as far from the hand as possible, and hoisted my body onto the swim platform. The splashing drew the attention of Angela, who shouted at me from the bow.

"Did you find my bracelet?"

I spit out my regulator, pulled off my mask, and vomited on the deck.

"What the hell are you doing?" she shrieked.

Brenda, who had heard the commotion from the dock, boarded the boat and rushed to the stern. I splashed water on my face, trying to control the shaking of my hands.

"Call 911," I choked out, and then I was doubled over, coughing up what was left of my breakfast.

Brenda was pulling out her phone as she spoke. "Are you hurt? What happened?"

"It's not me," I managed, trying to clear my throat.

"Then what is it?"

"There's a body on the bottom by *Kathy Lee*," I said. "It might be Everett Dvorak."

The police arrived ten minutes later, followed by an ambulance and a two-man underwater search and recovery team. By then I was sitting on the dock sipping a bottle of water, my back against a post, shivering in my wetsuit despite the sun. I had stripped off the rest of my gear, and Brenda carted it up to the van while the deputy in charge spent his first fifteen minutes on scene calming a near-hysterical Angela DeGrasse. He finally gave up and ordered her back to her boat, which precipitated a brief screaming match before a second officer escorted her off the dock. None of that had done much to improve the mood of the deputy, who was now interviewing me. He asked for my name and contact information and wanted to know why I was in Morehead City, all the while making a face suggesting not one of my answers was satisfactory. When we finally got around to talking about what I'd found, he didn't bother to hide his skepticism.

"You only saw the hand?" the officer asked.

I nodded.

"And you're sure it was a hand? Not, say, a plastic bag or a fish head?"

"It bumped right into my mask. I know what a hand looks like," I snapped.

"So, you saw a hand," he repeated dubiously. "What makes you so sure there is a whole body there?"

I reflected a moment. It was a good question.

"The way it floated," I said finally. "It was tethered, it wasn't moving freely. The visibility was pretty poor, but I got the impression of a large shape just behind it, up against the piling."

He snorted softly at the word impression. "You told Mrs. Pullen you thought it was Everett Dvorak, the owner of that boat over there. Why did you say that?"

"Because he's missing," I said. "I reported it to the FBI yesterday."

This was apparently news to the Carteret County Sheriff's Office. The deputy frowned.

"Can you explain what you mean by missing?"

I gave him an incredulous look. "Missing. As in, whereabouts unknown. No one has seen him in several weeks."

He made a note on his report. "Are you related to Everett Dvorak?"

"No."

"Friend?"

"No."

The deputy exhaled in frustration. "So, you don't really know Everett

Dvorak, but you know he's missing. And rather than contact the local police department, you took it upon yourself to call the FBI?"

I wasn't quite sure how to explain my actions without including information about Dvorak's unique credentials, and I doubted Andrew Culliver wanted the rest of the world to know a bioweapons expert had disappeared.

"I'm afraid I am not at liberty to say. You'll need to contact Senior Analyst Andrew Culliver of the FBI's Counterterrorism Division," I said.

The officer's eyes widened. He jotted down the name, which he asked me to repeat, along with the title. As he did so, there was excited noise from across the dock.

"Joe, they've got him," someone called, and the deputy and I both turned.

The men on the pier began hauling up ropes, slowly raising a bulky shape wrapped in heavy black plastic.

"Miss Beck, can you at least identify Everett Dvorak?" the deputy asked.

"I don't think so. I've never met him."

The officer looked like he wanted to say something, but instead he made a disgusted noise under his breath and stalked over to where the men were draining the body. It was true I had never met Kathy's husband, though I did know what he looked like from photographs. Perhaps I would have recognized his body, but based on the condition of the piece I saw, I didn't think there would be much of a face left. It wasn't an image I wanted to carry with me the rest of my life.

I heard a chorus of gasps and groans as the remains were exposed, and I turned my head away.

One of the rescue divers came to sit beside me while the corpse was carried to the waiting ambulance. He offered me a fresh bottle of Gatorade, which I declined.

"Still feeling pretty sick?" he asked sympathetically. He was about my father's age, with gray in his beard and kind eyes.

"I've felt better," I admitted, embarrassed at how I had come apart.

"I tossed my lunch every time I pulled out a body for at least the first year," the man said. "Don't beat yourself up."

I managed a wan smile. "Thanks. I hope this is my last."

"Me, too. By the way, in case you are wondering, this definitely looks like an accident. Guy's fly was unzipped."

I looked at him curiously. "How does that make it an accident?"

"Most male drowning victims are found that way, especially the ones who go over at night. They unzip, lean out a little too far, fall, hit their head, end of story."

I shook my head. "I guess there are advantages to being female."

He laughed. "See? I told you you'd be fine. By the way, the victim had a wallet in his pocket. It looks like you were right. All the identification belongs to Everett Dvorak. The deputy called your friend at the FBI and reported it. They're sending their own medical examiner down tomorrow."

The diver rose to go. He held out a hand and I took it, letting him pull me up from the dock. We walked back toward the parking lot.

"Everett Dvorak's been missing for a couple of weeks," I said thoughtfully. "Doesn't a body usually float to the surface by then?"

The man shrugged. "Sometimes. Not always. It depends on the water temperature, salinity, everything that affects the rate of decomposition. But it wouldn't have mattered this time. There was an old wreck on the bottom, the remains of a sunken sailboat. I'm surprised you didn't see it. The upper body got wedged between the keel and the post."

"How would that happen?"

He shrugged. "Could have been pushed by a wake caused by a boat coming in or out of its slip. Could have just settled near there and worked itself in over a couple of days."

An EMT in the parking lot called the diver away just as another man walked up, this one with slightly longish chestnut hair. He was hugging a vinyl folder. I was struck by his clothing: a sweater vest, plaid button-down shirt, and a bow tie. He looked like a character in a 1970s sitcom, the impression made worse by the fact he was probably only a few years older than I was.

"Morning, ma'am," he said, extending a hand. "Dave Burliss, Burliss Insurance."

He had a deep southern twang, something I had heard very little in this town of transplants. I shook Burliss's hand briefly. It was soft, pink, and without callouses.

"I manage the policy for Mallory Yacht Basin," he explained. "I understand you were divin' down off the dock and discovered the body.

Now, are you a licensed commercial divah, Miz Beck?"

"No," I said, wondering where this was headed.

"Do you carry liability insurance for this here divin' business you're doin'?"

"Dave—Burliss, was it? Well, Dave, I am not a professional diver. I don't have a diving business, and I don't make a living diving. My boat is over at Dockside Marina, and Ben Lancome, the manager, told me Brenda needed someone to look for a lost bracelet. He asked if I could help. That's it."

My attitude was bordering on hostile. In my defense, bumping into a corpse underwater was an emotionally taxing experience. Dave had the grace to look embarrassed.

"I don't mean to cause offense, Miz Beck. I just—after the fact, people do look for someone to blame—"

I turned on him. "Are you suggesting it was my fault someone drowned because I happened to find him?"

He stammered. "No ma'am, no, I, um, heah now, I was trying to determine if you felt, uh, you had sustained damages."

"Dave, have you ever had a dead man's hand hit you in the face?"

The insurance salesman swallowed. "No, ma'am, can't say as I have."

"Well, it's not that easy to get over. So yes, I have sustained damages. But if you are asking whether I blame Brenda, or Ben, or Mallory's—of course not!"

I stomped off in the direction of the van. He let me go a few steps, then caught up with me.

"I sure am sorry, Miz Beck. Tell you the truth, this sort of thing hasn't happened to me before. It's put me right outta' kilter, if you get my meanin'. I mostly do homeowners policies and car insurance. Mallory's right here is my only marina."

The dock cart with my gear was by the back of the van. Ignoring Mr. Burliss, I opened the cargo door and began to load my equipment.

"My office is over in Swansboro, right on Front Street," he continued. "I do believe it's Miz Sandi, am I right? Miz Sandi, here's my card. I sure am sorry we had to meet under these circumstances, and I hope you'll let me make it up to you. If you need anything a'tall, or if you'd just like to get together and shoot the breeze sometime, you give me a call."

I took the card, biting my lip at the absurdity of the offer. Whether this was damage control, salesmanship, or flirting, Dave Burliss needed major work on his sense of timing.

He insisted on helping me load my gear, getting saltwater on his sweater vest and khakis and tripping over the vinyl folder he laid on the ground. When we finished, it was all I could do to skirt around him and into the driver's seat. He leaned into the open window.

"So maybe I'll see you around?" Dave asked.

I started the engine.

"Maybe," I said and gave it gas. He stepped back hurriedly as I put the van in reverse and backed out in a spray of gravel. Undeterred, he followed me, waving goodbye.

Everyone from the office and shed came out as soon as I pulled into the Dockside parking lot. Mallory's was only a few hundred yards away, close enough to have watched the whole show. Ben helped me unload my equipment, all the while apologizing for ever getting me in "such a frickin' sick situation." I assured him it wasn't his fault, though as far as the description went, I couldn't have agreed more.

I knew I needed to call Kathy Dvorak, regardless of what Andrew Culliver had said. I should have done it as soon as I got back to the van, but the insurance salesman distracted me. The authorities would likely send a local Ocracoke officer to her shop to tell her Everett's body had been found, but if they chose to call instead, I wanted to spare her the cold, impersonal words of a stranger. Still shivering in my damp wetsuit, I stood on my deck and dialed her number.

Reporting a death is never easy, and in Everett Dvorak's case it felt like a personal failure. Granted, he had probably been dead long before Kathy asked me to investigate his disappearance. But I prided myself on arranging happy endings, and I was sorry I could not provide one for Kathy Dvorak.

I was both relieved and sorry when she did not pick up the phone.

In my voicemail, I asked her to call me as soon as possible. Then I went below and peeled off the clammy neoprene in the shower, letting the hot water wash over me and penetrate my cold skin. I covered myself with liquid soap and vigorously scrubbed the saltwater from my hair, trying to forget it contained the detritus of Everett Dvorak's body. When I was done, I dressed in jeans and a turtleneck despite the sun and went out on the dock to rinse off my equipment. It was only then, when I got to the

BC, that I remembered the cell phone in the pocket.

It was an iPhone, enclosed in a protective plastic case. I didn't see any water inside, but when I tried to power it on, nothing happened. Reasoning the battery could be dead, I took it to my cabin and plugged it into my charger. Immediately the screen lit up and opened to a photo of a young Kathy and Everett on their wedding day, the background for the phone's lock screen. It was Dvorak's, then. Kathy had said her husband didn't bother with passwords, so I touched the home button, and sure enough, the main screen opened.

At this point, the right thing to do as Kathy Dvorak's personal advocate was to turn off the phone and wait until I heard from my client. It was her husband's phone, and it might contain private information she wouldn't want others to see. From a legal perspective, I should immediately call the police and tell them what I had, since the phone was a part of the accident scene. By failing to do so, I could be obstructing an investigation. And let's not forget Andrew Culliver and the FBI. I was pretty sure he wouldn't be happy with what I did next.

I looked through the notifications on Everett Dvorak's phone.

Under the "recent" folder there were twenty-one missed calls, two from Garrett's, and all the rest but one labelled as Kat. I assumed this was Dvorak's iPhone nickname for his wife. These calls began on the twenty-first of November and ended just yesterday. There were also ten voicemails, nine of which were also Kathy's. I didn't listen to them. It made me sad to think of the phone ringing underwater all the time she was leaving those messages, believing he was still alive.

I looked back at the one missed call and voicemail not attributed to Kat. It had come in on the nineteenth at ten p.m. The number was on Everett's contact list, identified only as G. I played it.

"Everett, I just got your resignation letter, and I am very concerned. I thought I was clear about the duration of our agreement. You work for me as long as I say you do. You cannot unilaterally decide to walk away. I don't think you understand just how serious this can become. Call me before it is too late."

The man's voice was clipped and angry, and the way he emphasized the words serious and too late sounded like a threat. This call, coupled with the amount the scientist was being paid, implied involvement in a shady enterprise.

I re-played the message. No background noise, nothing to point to where it originated. There was something familiar about the pronunciation of the words, but I couldn't place the voice. I checked for any calls prior to the nineteenth, but they had all been deleted. So had all his text messages.

I debated what to do. The rescue diver had been certain Dvorak's drowning was accidental, but if the FBI believed the scientist was involved in something illicit, they would launch a full-scale investigation. If they found Everett's money came from illegal activity, they could potentially seize the scientist's property. Kathy's inheritance would be gone, as would her reputation and that of her late husband. Wouldn't it be better to know a little more, perhaps find some evidence in Everett's favor or at least determine the extent of his wrongdoing, before exposing Kathy to that kind of circus?

I looked at my watch. It was after one, and I was supposed to meet Ben to go grocery shopping. I left the phone on charge, hidden behind a stack of books, while I considered my options.

For me, traumatic events triggered one of two responses: either I didn't eat for days, or I had desperate food cravings. You might think finding a dead body would fall into the first category, but instead I was feeling an intense desire for meatloaf and mashed potatoes. When Ben dropped me off at Food Lion with my basic provisioning list, I picked up all the necessary ingredients for a home-cooked meal, along with a bottle of cabernet and a Hershey bar. There wasn't much that wine and chocolate couldn't fix.

I was just leaving the checkout line when Josh called, so I wheeled my shopping cart to a corner by the front window where I could watch for Ben as we talked. Josh was more cheerful than yesterday, and with good reason. The bail hearing had been postponed until tomorrow, but a witness had come forward claiming she saw Alan at his home during the time Maggie had been killed. An exchange student from Norway, she was walking her host family's border collie along the beach that morning. Just before sunrise she recalled stopping because a man was in his yard wearing a wetsuit and hood. The location of the house matched the Cullivers'. Since the dog was known to be skittish about masks and hats, she played fetch for fifteen or twenty minutes while the man pulled up and cleaned an oyster cage that was submerged off his beach. When he finished and went back in the house, she walked across his yard.

She remembered checking her watch when she went past his deck. It was seven o'clock. "This proves there was no way Alan could have been anywhere near Maggie's kayak at dawn," he asserted.

"That's wonderful, Josh," I said, relieved for both him and his uncle.

"Uncle Alan's lawyer thinks the DA is going to drop the charges. Their only witness is the guy who picked Alan out of the line-up, and it turns out a reporter had already shown him a picture of Alan, so the identification won't hold up in court," Josh continued. "This should all be over by tomorrow."

"What about the other investigation, the one into Bart Jansen's death?" I asked.

"They've already dropped it. Jansen's time of death was four p.m. There's a record of Uncle Alan's EZ Pass on his Corvette going southbound across the Bay Bridge Tunnel at three-thirty. He wasn't even in the same state." He paused, and I felt momentary guilt for ever believing Wayne's version of events.

"Where are you?" I asked.

"I'm at the city jail. I have a meeting in five minutes—the prosecutor wants to meet with Alan and his lawyer and Alan wants me there."

I heard voices in the background. Josh spoke softly, pitched for my ears only. "Sandi, as soon as we get this settled, I'd like to bring Alan back to Morehead with me. His face has been on the evening news for the past couple of days, and I think it would be good for him to get away and let it blow over."

His voice was tentative, and I understood that he was asking for my approval. Having Alan here would change the dynamic between us.

"I think that's a great idea," I said with forced enthusiasm. At the far end of the parking lot, I saw the marina van turning into the shopping center.

"I told him you'd feel that way. I'll call you tomorrow. If we find out something by then, we'll drive back on Thursday. Do me a favor and take a look at *Andromeda*? I left in such a hurry, I don't remember what kind of a mess it was in. Uncle Alan's never seen her, and—"

I cut him off. "I'll clean her up. Don't worry. Something happened while you were—"

"They're calling for me. I've got to go." Josh interrupted. "I'll talk to you tomorrow."

He hung up without letting me finish, without hearing about Everett Dvorak's death. I dropped the phone in my purse and pushed my cart through the automatic door, trying to ignore my bruised feelings. Ben pulled to the curb, heavy metal blaring from the front seat. I loaded my bags in the back, then slid in beside him. He turned down the volume slightly.

"Need anything else?" he asked loudly.

I shook my head, and he turned up the stereo.

Josh hadn't asked where I was, what I was doing, or even how I was feeling. I felt the seed of anger swelling in my chest. Since I left Irvington, my life had been dictated by Josh's circumstances. I had been understanding and sympathetic about his aunt, had put up with his mother's barely veiled disapproval, given up Thanksgiving with my parents, and now I was going to have to entertain Josh's uncle—and what did I have to show for it? A solo meal of meatloaf and mashed potatoes.

By the time we got back to the marina I was inwardly seething. This was supposed to be my time, I told myself bitterly, and once again my life revolved around the needs of someone else.

I put my groceries away and changed into a pair of black jeans and a tight white sweater. I was not going to huddle in my cabin and eat my dinner alone.

Chapter 19

BY THE TIME I walked down to Captain Tom's, some of my righteous indignation had faded. The warm weather had brought out a crowd, and I could see through the windows every stool was taken. Suddenly the press of people and the necessity of conversation were not as appealing as they had seemed a few minutes before.

I took a step backward, running right into someone behind me.

"I'm sorry," I said, turning to find my face inches from Dave Burliss's sweater vest.

"Oh, Miz Sandi! Hey!" he said happily. "Are you meetin' someone?"

I was too tired to lie.

"No, I was just getting some dinner, but now I'm not sure. They look pretty busy...."

"That's jest the bar. Look, there's plenty of room at the tables. Why don't you let me buy you suppah? I feel terrible about earlier," he said. "If I had a dollah for every time I put my foot in my mouth—well, I'd be makin' a lot more than I do sellin' insurance."

His earnest brown eyes were pleading. I weighed the awkwardness of dinner with a stranger against going back to the boat alone.

"You don't have to do that, but you're welcome to sit with me and eat," I answered.

"Oh, no. Suppah is on me. I insist." Dave beamed as he slipped by me and opened the door.

Katya was at the dining room entrance. She raised her eyebrows when she saw who was with me, and she maintained a critical expression throughout our drink order, though Burliss did not seem to notice.

"So, how are you feelin'?" he asked, leaning closer as Katya walked away.

Not an overtly emotional person, I could count on one hand the times I had teared up in public places. But the events of the day—finding Dr. Dvorak's body, the conversation with Josh—overwhelmed me with an unexpected suddenness. Too late, I tried to blink back the burning behind my eyes.

"Lord, I'm so sorry. I should've known better," he said contritely, offering me a napkin. "How would you be feelin' after the day you've had? Don't pay me no mind. Why don't we talk about somethin' else? How do you like it down heah in Morehead City? What all have you seen in town so far?"

An image of the ghostly hand appeared in my mind, and I grimaced. Dave, realizing his mistake, slapped his hand against his forehead.

"Danged if I didn't do it again. I don't guess you're thinkin' about seein' anything but that poor fella in the water," he groaned. "Now you understand why I'm not exactly tearin' up the spreadsheets."

Katya came back with our drinks and her discerning eyes registered the wet spots on my cheeks. She must have reassessed my situation and determined I was a jilted lover, because she was considerably warmer while she took our food order.

As she left, the insurance salesman looked at me ruefully.

"Believe me, this is the story of my life. If there's a wrong thing to say, I say it. My ex-wife says I'm like a dog in a pig pen—always steppin' in the sh—well, you kin fill in the rest."

I couldn't help but smile at his reluctance to use a curse word, however mild. He took this as encouragement and continued.

"To be honest, the only reason Burliss Insurance is successful a'tall is my daddy. It was his company till three years ago, when he jest up and retired and gave it to me. Most of our customers stayed on for the first year, but since then I've lost a few every renewal. If it hadn't of been for I.U.S., I'd of thrown in the towel and gotten a job at the Walmart."

His last sentence caught my waning attention. "I.U.S.? The defense contractor? I didn't realize they had a plant here."

He sat up straighter. "Yes indeed, but that's not all they do. They opened a big U.A.V. facility west of Hubert, more than eight hundred employees, and they signed on with me for everything: employee health and life insurance, property insurance, and commercial coverage for the plant. I tell you, it didn't just make my day, it made my whole dern decade."

"It sounds like you must have done something right to land an account that big."

Dave shook his head. "Wish I could say I had, but not really. Mr. Gardner came to me. He just showed up in my office one day, said he heard I was an honest guy, and told me what he wanted."

"See? He came to you because of your reputation," I said.

"I don't know. I think he just wanted somebody who wouldn't waste time askin' a lot of questions and was willin' to give him exactly what he wanted. Some of the facility wasn't done, so I couldn't get an accurate valuation, but he gave me an estimate and that was good enough. I guess some folks woulda' been a stickler on details, but good gravy, the company works for the U.S. of A. If Uncle Sam trusts them, I sure as heck can."

I had my doubts about that. From what I had seen of Jack Gardner's greed on display at Maggie's memorial service, I wouldn't put it past him to burn down his own building to make a profit.

"So, Sandi, what do you do?" Dave asked, changing the subject.

I gave him the abbreviated version of my career choice, and Dave was fascinated with the lack of rules and structure my business entailed.

"You see a problem and—bang—you kin just fix it," he said admiringly. "I have to submit six different forms and wait for approval before I kin tell my customer we'll cover him. You have a roof blown off, you're not in the mind to wait on red tape. I mean, I don't have to be a plumber to know what a busted pipe looks like. But you, you jest make up your mind and get after it."

I had never thought of it that way. It made me feel sorry for insurance agents.

Our food came then, and the conversation turned to why I was in Morehead City. Dave's genial expression deflated when I mentioned Josh.

"Sailin' off to the islands. Sure sounds romantic," he said, but his voice lacked enthusiasm.

My mouth was full, but I managed a small sound of agreement. I did not mention the romance thus far consisted of a single afternoon. Dave concentrated on his fish for a few minutes, then looked up suddenly as if he just had a revelation.

"You and Jason are datin', but y'all are not livin' on the same boat?" he asked.

"It's Josh. Yes, for now. We're…negotiating," I said, adding, "It's complicated."

Dave digested this for a moment. "So where is Josh off to tonight?"

"He had a family emergency," I answered. I couldn't imagine Dave's reaction if I said he was visiting his uncle in jail.

"So, he's out of town?"

"Just for a day or two."

This seemed to give Dave renewed life. His face lit up, and his voice became animated. "I'd be glad to show you around town while he's gone. Wednesdays are always slow. I could pick you up tomorrow and we could have lunch in Swansboro, maybe take a little drive up through Beaufort."

"I'm not sure what my plans are," I stalled, scouring my mind for some polite excuse.

"Or we could do breakfast. Or supper. Whatever you'd like."

Katya saved me from responding by showing up and asking how we liked our meal. When she left, I deftly turned the conversation back to Dave's business.

"I've always wondered how insurance companies determine risk. It must be very involved."

"Oh, it is. It's fascinatin', really," he replied, warming to the topic immediately. "There are actuary tables for everything. They assess risk based on elements like family history, employment type, individual behaviors, geography—"

"Geography?" I interrupted, curious.

"Mm hmm. You'd be surprised what a difference that makes. People livin' in poorly serviced rural areas, for example, have much higher mortality rates."

I thought about this. "What about living on the water? Does that increase risk?"

"Sure enough, dependin' on where you are. Mind you, that's partially related to behaviors. People who live on the water boat, and boaters have an increased risk of drownin'. Or take divin'—that's a very high- risk activity," he continued.

"I guess I'm not a good candidate for life insurance."

Dave's face reddened. "I, uh, didn't mean you, of course. I'm jest… those are jest the statistics."

"Then a drowning death for an elderly man like Everett Dvorak isn't going to raise any red flags? It's expected?"

"Oh, I wouldn't say expected," Dave responded hastily. "It jest falls within an anticipated range."

"If I told you two people who knew each other, both boaters, both over sixty-five, drowned in the same year," I persisted, thinking about something Wayne had said, "would you consider that unusual?"

"Did they happen in the same location?"

"No. Two different states."

Dave looked at me with mild concern. "Why are you askin'? Did this actually happen to some folks you know?"

"No. Hypothetically," I lied.

"Well, then," he said more easily, "statistically I'd say each one had the same chance of accidental death based on age and behaviors. The only other factor might be where they lived, whether it was a lake or tidal water. Knowin' each other was coincidental."

I must have looked puzzled, because he tried again.

"Let me explain it another way. Say you have two men who were college fraternity brothers. They went rock-climbin' all the time together. After college, they move to different states. They each still spend their recreational time rock-climbin', but they climb out in the woods, miles apart."

I nodded to show I was following him.

"Okay, let's say one in five wilderness recreation accidents involves rock-climbin'. That's a high-risk percentage. So, each one of these men has a one in five chance of bein' injured."

"Okay, but still, the fact that they know each other…."

"Let me put it another way. Let's also say one in five people who eat at McDonald's will order a Big Mac. If both these men ate at McDonald's, would you consider it unusual if in the course of a year they both ordered a Big Mac?"

"No," I said, smiling.

"Statistically, it is no more unusual than if both of them received an injury rock-climbin'. Do you see? People like to believe in unseen forces, but all it really is, is jest data patterns."

I had to admit it was a convincing argument. Yet the deaths of Maggie Culliver and Bart Jansen, and now Everett Dvorak, were starting to bother me for reasons I couldn't explain. With Alan no longer under suspicion, there was nothing the first two shared besides a work history, and there was no known relationship between them and the scientist. All three worked with classified information, but so did hundreds of thousands of government employees. The only thing the accidents had in common was I knew about them.

We finished our dinner pleasantly enough, and Dave was adamant about paying the bill. He also insisted on walking me back to my boat.

"I have to go right by there anyhow. I'm still parked over at Mallory's. I was there all afternoon," he said.

The night air was cool, a brisk wind blowing straight down the channel. The buildings offered little protection, making me wish I had brought a jacket. We kept our heads bent and increased our pace. When we reached the marina docks, I headed for the restrooms rather than *Serenity*. I had lived alone a long time now, and while Dave seemed harmless enough, I didn't want to be pressed into inviting him aboard. He followed me to the door.

"Thanks again for dinner," I said. "Goodnight."

"What about tomorrow? Do you want me to pick you up?"

I shook my head. "No, I have some things I promised Josh I'd do over on his boat. Thanks anyway."

He stood by uncertainly while I opened the bathroom door. I stepped inside, and as it shut, I called out another goodnight. Then I waited ten minutes, just to be on the safe side, before I stuck my head out. The insurance salesman was gone.

As I walked down the dock to *Serenity*, I felt mildly guilty. Dave wasn't a bad guy, not really, but I certainly didn't find him attractive. Still, it had been an interesting night. If I.U.S. owned a facility nearby, perhaps Alan or his partner would know something about the lab where Dvorak worked. Even if Dvorak had been doing questionable research, his employer might be masquerading as a legitimate military contractor. Perhaps Everett didn't even understand what he was doing at first, and he quit when he realized how his work was being used. That theory fit with the voicemail I heard. I didn't need to know all the details, just enough to decide how to best protect Kathy Dvorak.

I opened the companionway hatch and descended the steep stairs. I left a light burning and a heater on low, so the cabin was warmly inviting. I put on a pot of herbal tea, washed my face, and changed into pajamas pants and a plush sweatshirt. I had not taken my phone with me to Captain Tom's, and I was half-afraid to look at it now. One missed call from Josh, no message.

There was no point in calling back at this hour. It was late, I was tired, and as long as I was being honest with myself, I was still feeling a little hurt. Better to wait until morning.

I curled in my berth with a cup of tea and my laptop and watched the first few minutes of a Netflix movie, but my eyelids were heavy. I put everything away and turned off the light, snuggling beneath the covers, but though I was exhausted, sleep would not come. I had the ominous feeling I was missing something important. I lay there for an hour or more, bone-tired but unable to close my eyes, when I had a sudden vision of standing on Mallory's dock with Josh and Brenda. I heard her voice.

"He had a friend come down just as I was going to pick up parts in Jacksonville, but his car was gone when I got back. I figured he left Friday afternoon," she had said.

If Everett Dvorak drowned in the marina basin two weeks ago, who had his car?

Chapter 20

I SET OUT FOR Mallory's as soon as I finished my morning coffee.

We had six days to go until the official start of winter, but in North Carolina the weatherman seemed blissfully unaware of the calendar. It was mild out with a cloudless sky, the wind coming from the southeast. I breathed in the salty tang of ocean air as I walked through Dockside's yard.

My goal for today was to discover what happened to Everett Dvorak's car. If he had fallen overboard, surely it would still be in the yard. Maybe it was parked behind a truck or van and Brenda had just missed it. Or perhaps the scientist had engine trouble when he went to leave Friday and instead had the vehicle towed for repairs. That would explain the missing car and why he didn't go home as promised. If that was the case, I should be able to find it by canvassing local repair shops. If not, then the only other plausible explanation was the car had been taken by the visitor Brenda saw. Since she heard Dvorak and the man mention a lab, he had to be someone from the scientist's place of employment. Either way, the car's whereabouts might provide some answers.

I crossed the highway and passed the squat concrete building in front of Mallory's parking lot. I had driven past it several times, but this was the first time I had really noticed it. The cinderblock was painted in peeling yellow, and a defunct and rusted real estate office sign hung on a wooden post out front, but it was clear the building had been converted into a duplex some time ago. Frilly curtains hung in all the windows, and there were two separate entrance doorways, one with a child's bike leaning beside it, the other with a homemade seashell wreath. I took a shortcut around the side, along the tiny square of grass that constituted the back yard, and nearly tripped over a woman in shorts, perched on a lawn chair.

"Katya?" I said, surprised.

The waitress from Captain Tom's looked up from her book.

"Sandi!" She started to get up, but her lap was weighted down by an economics textbook and a notebook. A notebook computer was open on an upside-down plastic milk crate beside her.

"That doesn't look like much fun," I remarked.

Katya snorted. "Fun. That is a joke. Is work, not fun, but that's okay. I have a final Thursday."

"I didn't know you lived here. You should come visit. I'm right across the street."

"I know. I saw you yesterday morning with the ambulance and all the police. I wanted to tell you last night I am sorry for what happened, but it was so busy, and I did not know your new friend."

I smiled at the censure in her tone. I don't know what it is about Josh that inspires such loyalty in people he barely knows, but it was apparent Katya was still trying to decide if my dinner with Dave constituted betrayal.

"He's not a friend. I met him yesterday at Mallory's. He handles their insurance. I just bumped into him last night outside of Captain Tom's."

She looked only slightly mollified. "It is not safe to sit down with strangers. I think your boyfriend would tell you the same thing."

"Probably," I agreed, "but he's in Virginia Beach visiting family." I looked across the patch of brown grass to the docks. "You have a good view of the water here."

"It is nice, yes," she agreed.

"You saw the whole thing yesterday?"

"Not all of it. I saw you talk to the loud woman and then go into the water across from the green boat. You were doing the scuba diving. Then all the police came, but I could not watch any longer," Katya explained. "I worked the lunch shift, so I did not see them pull out the body, but I heard from Marvin next door you found a dead man." She added, shivering, "I do not know how you could go out for dinner after seeing such a thing! My heart would have stopped."

"Believe me, it did," I said, but my mind was skipping backward. "Katya, do you sit out here every day?"

"Always if the weather is good, yes," the young woman answered. "I spend so much time inside at work, I miss the sun. I do all my homework here."

"Do you remember if you sat out here about two-and-a-half weeks ago on a Friday? It would have been the twentieth of November—the Friday before Thanksgiving."

She answered without a pause. "Yes. I was right here until two o'clock. I was finishing a paper for English class, very long, and it had to be in by midnight. I worked from three until closing and I needed to finish before I left."

"The green boat, the *Kathy Lee*. Did you see anyone on it?"

"The little man with the glasses. I think he is the one they say is dead. He was there on the dock when the boat came in the day before. Mr. Garrett was driving, and he and the little man shook hands. Mr. Garrett is one of our regular customers."

"Did the little man take the boat out himself?"

"No. He left in the car and came back with shopping bags. Maybe he went out while I was at work, but he was there when I got back. He slept on his boat."

"How do you know?"

"There were still lights on when I went to bed," she answered. "I notice this because no one stays during the week since maybe October except sometimes the boat across from him, with the loud black-haired woman."

"What about Friday? Did you see anyone else visit him?"

Katya nodded at once. "Yes, two."

I looked at her in confusion. "What do you mean, two?"

"Two men visited him. One was early. I was at the sink doing dishes when I saw him walk down the dock. The little man was putting out the…balloons—no—what do they call them?"

"Bumpers?"

Katya snapped her fingers, pleased I understood. "Yes! Bumpers. The visiting man, he went on the boat. He did not stay long, because when I took my computer outside, he was leaving."

I asked if she could describe him, and her remembrance matched that of Brenda, the manager.

"What about the second man? When did you see him?"

She thought for a moment. "It was maybe one o'clock. I went in to get my lunch, and when I came out, I saw his back when he got on the boat."

I sighed. "You didn't see his face?"

"No, but…." she began, then stopped abruptly. "The little man with glasses—he is the one who died?"

I nodded.

"You are thinking this other man killed him?"

"No," I said quickly. "The police think it was an accident. I'm just curious."

Katya looked at me with shrewd eyes.

"I do not want to get involved. Is not good for someone in my position."

"I'm not asking you to get involved. I'm asking you to tell me. I promise, I will not repeat what you say to anyone."

She pulled at her ear, thinking.

"All right," Katya said finally. "But I am telling only you."

"I understand."

"He was tall, like the first man, and wide here," she said, gesturing to her shoulders, "and he had red hair, very bright. The first man, in the morning, I am sure I have seen him before. This man, no. He was someone you would remember."

I considered her words. The second man could have been from Garrett's, checking on how Everett was making out with his new boat. He could've been a friend, though the scientist did not strike me as a social being. He could also have been another co-worker, sent to pressure Dvorak into returning to his job. If I called the yacht brokerage to check on the first possibility, they might want to know why, and I couldn't think of a plausible explanation. In a community this size, I was sure they heard about Everett's death.

I thanked Katya for the information, though I wasn't sure what use it would be. She looked at me astutely.

"My grandmother had a saying: 'Do not borrow trouble because you cannot give it back.' I think you don't need to borrow trouble, Sandi."

Her words were spoken darkly, and they sounded like an omen. I tried to smile.

"I'm not. Really."

I thought she might argue with me, but she just shook her head.

"Maybe I'll see you tonight," I said.

Katya mumbled an assent, her head already bowed over the pages of her book.

I headed across the parking lot to the yacht basin's office, but Brenda wasn't in. The assistant dockmaster's name was Kristopher, and he answered every question I asked with "I couldn't say." I gave up and started to leave when a uniformed officer and a man in a dark suit came through the door. I recognized the policeman as the sheriff's deputy I talked to yesterday. Unfortunately, he recognized me as well.

"Miss Beck, I'm glad we ran into you. This is Special Agent Neeman from the FBI. He's looking into Everett Dvorak's death."

The suited man did not extend his hand. He was of average height and weight, with nondescript brown hair and plain, generic features. Like background music, he would only be noticeable in the total absence of other noise. Now the space around us grew silent, and I found myself hypnotized by his eyes, hard-edged and black as coal.

"Agent Neeman, Miss Beck is the diver who found the body," the deputy said, after a long pause in which the suited man only stared at me. "She's also the person who gave me your boss's number."

The agent's forehead creased. "How do you know Senior Analyst Culliver?"

I shook the paralysis of his gaze and said the first thought in my mind. "I'm dating his son."

Agent Neeman digested this with the expression of someone who had eaten food that did not agree with him.

"And what made you believe your boyfriend's father would be interested in a body you found in North Carolina?" he asked, his frown and voice deepening simultaneously.

I wanted to tell him. The black eyes bore into me, and I wanted to share every secret I had ever kept, from the plastic yoyo I stole at the county fair when I was seven to how I always forgot to save expense receipts for my taxes. Still, I hesitated. "I'm not sure it's something we can discuss here," I ventured, trying to keep my voice from shaking.

The sheriff's deputy made a disgusted noise. "Miss Beck seems to think we have a top-secret case here, Agent Neeman. Where do you think we can discuss this safely, Miss Beck?"

I bristled at his tone, a reaction which fortunately took my attention off Agent Neeman's incapacitating stare. "You misunderstand the situation, Officer," I said, turning to him. "It doesn't matter to me. I just thought before we started talking about biological weapons, Agent Neeman might want to go someplace more secure."

The officer began to laugh derisively, but he stopped when he saw the FBI agent's face.

"Miss Beck, let's take a walk down the dock," Neeman said in a steely voice. "Officer Prentice, you can stay here and get the extra key to Dvorak's boat."

Officer Prentice opened his mouth to protest, but he got the full power of the eyes and nodded his agreement. He slunk toward the dockmaster's desk as Neeman put a firm hand on my arm and steered me out the door. We were halfway down the pier with no one in earshot when the agent stopped and turned on me, the quick movement exposing the gun beneath his coat.

"How do you know about Dr. Dvorak's work?"

There was barely concealed violence in his question. I don't normally frighten easily, but the combination of his eyes and the weapon were too much. I gave up any pretense of non-cooperation and spilled everything I had. I described my meeting with Kathy in Ocracoke and how I agreed to help locate her husband. I took him through my visit to Garrett's and then our boarding of *Kathy Lee*.

"The boat was open?" he asked tersely.

"The doors were closed, but they were unlocked."

This was a clear admission of illegal trespass, and I fully expected him to slap on the cuffs. To my surprise, Neeman showed no reaction at all. He seemed lost in thought. Perhaps Andrew Culliver had given instructions not to incarcerate me. If so, I bet he didn't discuss that decision with Josh's mother.

Neeman rubbed both sides of his nose as he mentally reviewed my statement. I stayed as still as I could, but the waiting made my throat tickle, and eventually I could not hold back a tiny cough. He looked at me as if wondering why I was still there.

"Miss Beck, the details of your investigation will remain confidential," he said, dripping disdain. "At this stage there is zero evidence Everett Dvorak's previous career is in any way connected to his death. However, as a result of your phone call, the FBI has launched an investigation. If you are in possession of any additional facts having a bearing on that investigation, you need to share them at this time. If you do not, you intentionally hamper a federal investigation, and you will face charges. Is that clear?"

I swallowed. Across the highway, I could swear I heard Dvorak's phone ringing out an accusation.

"Yes, sir."

My terrified expression was like a beacon, and Neeman homed in on it at once. "Miss Beck, I am going to repeat this one more time. If you have any other information, this is your last opportunity to share it without consequences."

There was the missing car, which I had no reason not to share. I also had what Katya told me, but if I mentioned her name she would be questioned, and I had given my word. As for the phone, while I hated to part with it, the possibility of accommodations in a federal prison loomed large in my imagination.

"There are, um, two things," I began in a small voice. "Dvorak drove a Subaru. Brenda in the office said it was here when she went out to pick up parts on the twentieth, but it was gone that evening when she got back. She assumed Dr. Dvorak had gone to pick up his wife. The car never came back."

Agent Neeman nodded curtly. "I'll check into it. What else?"

I paused. I wondered what it would take to drive someone as straight-laced as Neeman to explode.

"Miss Beck, you said there were two things. What else do you have?" he barked.

It was now or never.

"His phone."

"Are you saying you took Everett Dvorak's phone?" he asked, granite-faced.

"Not intentionally," I amended hastily. "I found it under the pier when I was diving. That was before I saw the body. I forgot all about it until I got back to my boat. I wasn't even sure it was his until I charged it up. Um, would you like me to go get it?"

"We'll go get it together, Miss Beck. My car is right over there."

I started to say I was just across the highway, but Agent Neeman did not look like someone who took leisurely strolls. We got inside his navy sedan, where he listened to my stammered directions, then drove in uncomfortable silence to the Dockside parking lot. When we reached *Serenity* he hesitated, processing the distance between the dock and my deck. It was nearly high tide and getting up required some finesse.

"I'll wait here. You go get the phone," he commanded.

I climbed on my boat with an ease borne of practice, hoping he noticed. I retrieved the phone, unplugged it and shut it down. When I handed it to Neeman, he slipped it into a plastic bag he took from his jacket pocket. He then reached in his lapel and took out a card.

"I expect you to call me if you hear any new information regarding Everett Dvorak."

I promised I would, a vow he met with the slightest curl of his lip.

"Good afternoon, Miss Beck," the agent said, though I believe the words he wanted were "You're under arrest."

I watched as he stamped to his car and didn't let out my breath until I saw him drive away. I had lost the phone, but I still had another clue Neeman did not.

I needed to find the red-haired man.

Chapter 21

I TRIED TO CALL Josh twice that morning, both times getting his voicemail. I left a brief message asking his plans, then went to *Andromeda* to do some straightening up.

It felt odd to be in the cabin without Josh. Like *Serenity*, it was an older boat, but while Ryan and I had refurbished our interior with lighter finishes, tile, and bright colors, Josh's was dark and sparsely decorated. His boat was three feet shorter and had a narrower beam than mine, with a head the size of a 1950s telephone booth and a curtainless shower guaranteed to wet down the entire room. The V-berth didn't even have its own stateroom—it was separated from the cabin by heavy cabinet doors, so it was like sliding into a coffin to sleep. Worse, without Josh's presence, I saw the cabin for what it was: stark and impersonal, every space functional. A soldier's barracks. A way to get from one port to another.

But not a home.

The phone in my pocket began to ring. It was Josh, bursting with the news that the charges had been dropped this morning and Alan was free. I was glad for him and said so, but my cheerfulness was discernibly forced.

"Is everything okay, Sandi?" he asked. "You sound like you're upset."

"Everett Dvorak is dead."

There was stunned silence on the other end of the line.

I filled him in on the events of the past thirty-two hours, starting with finding Everett Dvorak's body and ending with my discomfiting encounter with Agent Neeman. It was possible my words carried a faint whiff of recrimination for being left alone.

"Why didn't you tell me any of this last night?"

"You didn't give me a chance."

There was a brief pause while Josh considered this.

"You're right. I'm sorry, San," he said finally. "I knew I cut you off, but there was no way I could...I had no idea what you'd been through. I did try to call you back later. You didn't pick up."

"I didn't take my phone with me when I went out to get dinner, and then it was so late when I got back, I didn't want to bother you." Now that I heard his voice, my reaction seemed out of proportion and a little foolish.

"Sandi, I really am sorry," he repeated. "For future reference, bother me. Anytime, day or night. That's what I'm here for. All right?"

Warmth spread in my chest.

"All right."

"So besides bumping into a body and tangling with federal investigators, did anything else happen while I've been gone?"

I smiled despite myself. "No. I think that about covers it."

"Then I should be there in about six hours. Send me a text if you want me to pick up anything on the way."

"What about Alan?"

"He's coming down Friday. He said he needs a little rest. This whole thing has taken a toll on him, San. I'm coming up on the tunnel now. I'll let you know when I'm a half-hour away."

I said goodbye with a lighter heart. As sympathetic as I felt toward his uncle, I was glad we would have the time alone.

I finished straightening *Andromeda* and looked at my watch. It was a half-past noon, with no return call from Kathy Dvorak. I was certain the police had contacted her by now as next of kin. If she needed to grieve alone, I understood.

I decided to walk to a deli along the boardwalk, two doors up from Captain Tom's, to pick up lunch. The boats along these docks included private powerboats, an occasional sailboat, and a range of fishing and diving charters. The last of the morning trips were unloading and spraying down their decks, while a few afternoon groups were loading customers and coolers and preparing to go out. A half-dozen tanks were lying on the dock in front of World Dive's catamaran as a crewman finished hanging wet dive gear on a rack.

I stopped to watch Fintastic, a big charter, depart from the next slip down with a cockpit full of hopeful anglers. Just in time, I saw their stern line was still attached to the cleat, running around and under the tanks. I shouted and waved as I saw it tighten. The man on the dive boat heard me and rushed forward just as Fintastic's captain realized his crew's mistake and dropped out of gear. I ran to free the line from the cleat as the man pulled his tanks clear. Shouting apologies, the red-faced charter crew took off, but I barely noticed. I was focused instead on the man from World Dive.

It was Chris Holtz.

"Oh, hey. I know you," he said, giving me a friendly smile and reaching to shake my hand. "You're Alan Culliver's nephew's girlfriend, right? You were at the memorial service. I owe you one. That could have been a helluva mess."

He said Alan's name without rancor. Nothing in Holtz's face or voice suggested he blamed Maggie's husband for her death.

"You're welcome," I said. "Chris, right? I remember seeing you with Alan."

"Yeah, damned shame," he said, shaking his head. "Maggie was a great woman. What are you doing down here in Morehead?"

"Josh and I are on our way south for the winter. We're sailing to Florida, then maybe the Bahamas."

"Very cool!" he enthused, bending over to pick up a tank. "You see Alan, tell him Chris said hi."

A hello from the man whose information helped to land Josh's uncle in jail?

"I will. He should be down here on Friday," I added. "Josh called this morning to tell me all the charges had been dropped."

Chris had shouldered two tanks, but now he put them down and stared at me. "I'm sorry. Did you say 'charges'?"

His surprise seemed genuine. "Yes. I thought you knew. Alan was being held for Maggie's murder."

The man stumbled backward slightly as if pushed. "What the hell? You've got to be kidding me. That was an accident."

"The police weren't so sure. A few witnesses came forward and claimed

Alan thought Maggie was having an affair."

"That's ridiculous. What idiot would say something like that?" Chris spit out.

I looked directly into his eyes.

"From what I heard, you did."

He took a step toward me, and I was suddenly aware of how big Chris was. "What do you mean?" he rasped.

I edged backward, keeping my voice matter-of-fact. "The police said Maggie's former dive instructor told them Maggie was afraid of her husband. According to him, she said Alan was jealous and accused her of having an affair. Since you taught Maggie, everyone assumed it was you."

Chris's face grew red. "I don't know who would say shit like that, but it wasn't me. Maggie Culliver was never afraid of anybody or anything, I can tell you that. This whole thing sounds messed up." He paused. "You say Alan's okay, though?"

"Yes, he's fine. He's back home, but he's coming here to stay with us for a few days."

He nodded, though he sounded troubled. "I'm glad. Alan's good people. You tell him it wasn't me, okay?"

"Okay."

Chris picked up the tanks again and started up the walk toward the dive center. I tagged along beside him. A German shepherd tied to a bench on the building's porch began barking as I got closer.

"It's okay, girl," he said, and the bark was replaced by a wagging tail. "That's Ripley. She's a retired service dog. I adopted her last year."

"Is she friendly?" I asked, hanging back.

"As long as you are. She's sensitive to noise and sudden movement, but otherwise, she's a great dog."

I moved forward, hand outstretched. Ripley sniffed it, then positioned herself so I could scratch behind her ears. I crooned to her in the same voice I used for small children, and she muzzled me appreciatively while Chris loaded the tanks onto a tall outdoor rack.

"Did anyone else ever instruct Maggie in scuba besides you?" I asked, still petting his dog.

"No. She was a beginner when Alan asked me to work with her. She had this huge sinus issue, just couldn't equalize. She was a trooper, tried everything, but when it came down to it, it wasn't safe for her to dive."

He started back down the dock, and then stopped.

"You know, I just thought of something," Chris said. "At the end, I asked Chip to work with her. She wouldn't listen to me. She just wanted to keep at it, and so he came in. I wanted him to show her I was right. That's when she blew her eardrum."

"Do you think she might have told Chip something she didn't tell you?" I asked. "I mean, were they close?"

Chris snorted. "Hardly. Maggie didn't take to him at all, and Chip told me she was a real bitch—his words, not mine. I loved Maggie Culliver. But no, I don't see the two of them having a heart-to-heart."

"Then who else could it have been?" I asked, more to myself than Chris.

"Got me. Maybe the cops made it up, trying to get a rise out of him."

I didn't always agree with law enforcement, but it seemed unlikely they would have created a fictional witness in a murder case. I was about to go when another thought occurred to me.

"Don't you also work for I.U.S.?"

He picked up two more tanks and started back up the dock. "Yeah. You're probably wondering what I'm doing here. K.C., guy who runs this place, is a buddy of mine. We served together. I help him out once in a while when I can take the time off. When the water gets cold, he's always short of divemasters."

"What's it like working for I.U.S.? Josh has fond memories of going there with his uncle."

We were walking down to the dock again, talking as we went.

"It's a great company, but it's more than that. It saves lives," he said seriously.

"You mean the drones?"

"Well, yeah, they're important. The newest designs can search out and clear I.E.D.s and other explosives, a game changer for the Middle East, but that's not what I meant," Chris said, easing the tanks into the lowest racks and then straightening up. "I.U.S. hires mostly vets, guys who have PTSD or are struggling with physical disabilities when they come back. They provide counseling, job training, financial support. A lot of vets wouldn't have made it back into civilian life without Jack and Alan. They are the true patriots."

His deep belief in I.U.S. and its mission was unmistakable. I wondered how much this man personally owed I.U.S. for his own recovery.

"I didn't know all that."

"Not a lot of people do. If they did, maybe we wouldn't have to fight so hard to stay in business."

I looked at him questioningly.

"Military contracts aren't awarded on merit. It's all political. Bunch of pencil pushers and loud mouths who have never held a weapon trying to tell fighting men what they need. Makes me sick. It doesn't take much to lose a contract."

He paused, and his face clouded. Something, some thought, had disturbed him. He looked down at me impatiently. "Sorry, I need to finish this up. I promised Jack I'd check on something at the plant this afternoon."

I wasn't ready to let him go yet. I pretended I had not caught his meaning.

"You know most of the military contractors in this area, right?"

Chris nodded distractedly and glanced up at the sky, his way of communicating politely that I had taken up enough of his time. But there was always a chance he knew Dvorak's employer, and right now, he was my only source in the area.

"Do you know of any company in this area working with biological weapons?"

He looked at me like I had suddenly sprouted an extra head. "Jesus, no. Where'd you get that idea?"

"A scientist was found dead yesterday at Mallory's," I said. "He supposedly worked on bioweapons research for some company around here."

Chris's face grew pale.

"What was this scientist's name?"

"Everett Dvorak. He had a boat at Mallory's—the *Kathy Lee.*"

He wobbled on his feet for a second like a fighter who had taken a punch. Then he blinked, shook his head as if to clear it, and turned abruptly away.

"I've got to go," he muttered over his shoulder, untying Ripley. The dog was watching him intently, sensing his unrest. Chris pulled on the leash, and the two disappeared into a side door of the dive center.

Perhaps he didn't know anything about Alan's arrest, but Chris Holtz certainly appeared to know something about Dr. Dvorak.

I mused about the meeting on the way to the deli and all through my turkey club. What had spooked the former SEAL so badly? Was there some connection between I.U.S. and Everett Dvorak?

As soon as I got back to *Serenity*, I did an internet search on I.U.S. There were a lot of early articles about Alan's innovations in drone design, a few in North Carolina papers about the new plant, and some passing references in more recent pieces to the company's foray into the private sector in deals like the one with Atlantic Power. The energy company itself seemed to be routinely embroiled in controversy, accused of environmental mismanagement and a disregard for communities in the path of its projects. But I.U.S. was barely mentioned in these stories, and there was nothing to link Alan's company or Atlantic Power to either biological agents or Everett Dvorak.

I reconsidered my initial theory. What if Chris's sudden concern wasn't related to Dvorak's name at all? It could have been a delayed reaction to what I had said about Alan's arrest. Chris was preoccupied even before I mentioned the scientist. Maybe he was afraid the scandal of Alan's arrest and lingering suspicions could potentially affect the company's reputation in the minds of its clients. Or perhaps he was worried that Alan still believed Chris was the one who had made the accusations to police. How many companies would keep on an employee who suggested the founder and principal stockholder killed his wife?

The more I considered it, the more this seemed the plausible explanation.

One piece of our conversation had surprised me—Chip Holland and his alleged comment about Maggie. If he disliked her, did that animus include her husband? What other motivation might he have to slander the Cullivers' marriage? I knew nothing about the man except that he worked with Chris and was a partner in the Virginia Beach dive shop. This was a good time to find out more.

I Googled Holland's name and drew a blank. "Chip" was evidently not his given name. I tried a search on Adventure Diving and came up with a business registry site listing the store, its annual gross income, number of employees, and vested owners. There it was—Francis Michael Holland. With that information I quickly ascertained that Chip was thirty-four years old, too young to have done his twenty in the Navy and gotten out. He had almost no social media presence—no Facebook, Instagram, or Twitter accounts, just a single mention in a scuba site about the Virginia

Beach Commando Course. Then I came across a bombshell article in a Charleston newspaper. The pictures accompanying the article were grainy black-and-whites, but I vaguely recognized the face of the man from the dive shop photo.

Francis "Chip" Holland, former SEAL, had faced a court martial several years ago on two counts of assault against a commanding officer at the Naval base there. That explained his early departure from the military. He had made a deal and gotten out with no prison time but had received an "other-than-honorable" discharge, costing him his veteran's benefits and any chance of a high-level security clearance or opportunity to reenlist. I could understand Chris Holtz feeling sympathy for the man, but I wondered what in the world convinced I.U.S. executives to take him on. Holland was fortunate to have a subcontracted job with the company— why would he jeopardize it by providing evidence against Alan Culliver?

It made no sense.

I scrolled back through every hit on Holland's name, hoping for something more. An archived piece from ten years ago surfaced, a Mountain Valley News story from Grainsfield, Kentucky covering the local high school's Homecoming Hall of Fame. Several football players from the past were recognized during a Main Street Parade, including all-time high-scoring quarterback Chip Holland. I clicked on the photo, showing a man in his twenties, tall and well-built, accepting a plaque. I didn't recognize the face, but that wasn't what struck me. This was the second time I had seen it in a photograph, but the first time it registered with me.

Chip Holland had bright red hair.

Chapter 22

I KNEW THAT STATISTICALLY, only one to two percent of the general population was red-headed, and an even smaller number of those individuals had hair that could be described as bright in hue. Katya saw a broad-shouldered man with bright red hair visit Dvorak's boat on the day he drowned, a man who fit the description of Chip Holland. Based on what Chris Holtz said, Holland had to be the dive instructor who swore Maggie Culliver was afraid of her husband. I thought about Dave Burliss and his actuary tables and wondered what the chances were that a red-haired man would come forward to provide information about the drowning death of a former terrorism expert in Virginia Beach and a few months later appear at the scene of a drowning death of another former bioterrorism researcher in Morehead City.

My guess? Not good.

But what else could it be? From what Josh said, the police had no evidence Maggie's death was anything but an accident. It seemed the FBI had all but concluded Dvorak's death was accidental also. Even if there was a connection between Chip Holland and the two victims, it didn't prove anything.

But it must mean something.

I was sitting at my computer, still musing on this information, when my phone rang. I recognized the number as Kathy Dvorak's.

"Kathy, I tried to reach you. I'm so sorry about Everett," I said when I picked up the phone.

"I saw you called. I was going to call you back, but it's been...." Her voice trailed off.

"I understand."

"I had to drive down this morning to identify his body, and I thought, while I was here, I should see the boat. I'm over at Mallory's Yacht Basin now, but I just couldn't...I can't get on it by myself. I was wondering if you could come over and do it with me."

I felt a rush of sympathy. "Of course. I'm right across the highway. I'll be there in a couple of minutes."

"Thank you," she said gratefully. "This is all...harder than I thought it would be."

Kathy was sitting on a bench outside the marina office when I got there. The past twenty-four hours had shaken her existence, a fact advertised in the wrinkled blouse and skirt, the red-rimmed, swollen eyes, and the hand that shook as she reached for me. I grasped it gently and helped her up.

"I can't tell you how much I appreciate this. I just couldn't do it alone," she said, lip trembling. "When I saw the name...."

"It's all right. I'm glad I can help," I assured her, giving her a hug. She clung to me for a moment, then stepped away.

"It was horrible, seeing him like that," Kathy said, shuddering. They told me he had been...disfigured, but I almost couldn't recognize him. I was afraid I'd faint. It was all I could do to get out of the room."

I knew. I remembered. Standing by the cold metal table, looking down as the man in the white coat pulled back the sheet. Ryan but not Ryan. I had to look twice, to be sure, and even then, I had the irrational thought it was all a mistake. How much worse must it have been for Kathy Dvorak, whose husband had been in the water for weeks?

"I'm sorry," I said, because there was really nothing else to say.

She followed me down the dock and we stopped in front of *Kathy Lee*. She read the name on the transom and shook her head.

"I feel so ashamed for thinking he was unfaithful," she said softly. "I was blaming him, and he was here, all that time."

"It's not your fault," I said. "Everett never told you what he was doing."

"I know. But still, I wish I had trusted him more."

I helped her onto the boat. This time the glass doors were locked, but the office had given her one of the extra keys Everett left with them.

Everything looked exactly as it had when Josh and I boarded it a few days ago. Kathy walked through slowly, picking up the framed photograph and other objects. In the main stateroom, she lifted a pillow and buried her face in the cover.

"I can smell him," she whispered, and she started to cry.

We sat together on the edge of the bed, and I rubbed her back as she sobbed, her body shaken by convulsive waves of grief and remorse. When the worst of it subsided, I got up and found a box of tissues. I handed them to her, and she wiped her face."

"It's a beautiful boat," she said, looking up at me. "I'm glad he had it, even if was only for a day or two. I know it must have made him happy."

I murmured my agreement. These are the things we tell ourselves, so we can deal with the pain. He was doing what he loved. At least he was where he always wanted to be.

"What are you going to do now?" I asked.

She shrugged. "I don't know. Go back to Ocracoke, I guess. I'm burying Everett in the church cemetery there. I'll keep the shop and the house, but I can't keep a boat like this. You said he paid cash for it. Maybe I can sell it back to the company he bought it from or list it with another yacht broker."

"I can talk to the owner of Garrett's if you'd like. He seems like a reasonable man."

She nodded her thanks, then slowly rose off the bed and walked to the built-in nightstand, picking up the magazine on top.

"The Journal of Bacteriology," Kathy said with a wan smile. "Everett's idea of bedtime reading."

She began to leaf through it absently, and something fell out and dropped to the floor. She knelt and retrieved a thin leather-bound memo book.

"I haven't seen one of these for a while," she said, shaking her head. The book was about the size of an index card. "Everett kept his personal lab notes in books like this when he worked at Fort Detrick. They weren't official, and I'm not sure they knew he brought the books home. He kept them locked in his desk, but sometimes on the weekends he'd go back over them, especially when he was working on a problem he couldn't figure out."

She opened the cover and glanced at the first page, then looked over at me. "This is dated from almost two years ago."

That meant they might offer a clue as to what Dr. Dvorak had been doing. I put out my hand, and Kathy surrendered the booklet. The pages were covered with an indecipherable scribble of numbers and letters, the only intelligible writing being the dates. I checked the last page with an entry, and saw it was dated a little over four weeks ago.

"Can you read this?" I asked.

"No. I don't know if anyone could. Everett used a code. He didn't trust many people—he thought his colleagues might try to claim his research as their own."

I looked down at Dvorak's notes. "Do you mind if I keep this for a few days?"

Kathy didn't answer. She was staring off absently, her shoulders bowed, her face tired and drawn. "It doesn't matter, you know. Any of it. You don't need to look anymore. He's gone."

Kathy was not thinking of the implications of Dvorak's research, but of burying her husband. His life's work had never been more than a job to her. I did not think the federal government was going be as willing to let Dvorak's activities of the past two years go unexamined. But his widow was fragile, and this was not the time to discuss darker possibilities.

We spent another half hour on *Kathy Lee*. We found a cloth grocery bag and Kathy used it to collect a few personal items of Everett's she wanted to keep. She spoke very little, and once or twice her eyes filled with tears, but there were no more outbursts of emotion. In the end, she took one last long look at her name on the transom, then dropped the key at the office and carried the remains of her husband's dream back to the convertible he had bought her.

"I don't see the Subaru," she said, her eyes scanning the parking lot.

"No. It isn't here."

Kathy raised her brows. "I thought...you found Everett's body right here in the marina."

"Yes."

"Then why isn't his car here?"

My question exactly. "I don't know, Kathy. I told the FBI, and they're looking into it."

Her face froze. "The FBI?"

"Agent Neeman. He was here yesterday. Didn't anyone tell you they were investigating Everett's death?"

She shook her head, and the melancholy lifted, replaced by concern. "I talked to a police officer and medical examiner. Nobody said anything about the FBI. The only agent I ever spoke to was Mr. Culliver, and that was because Everett was missing. He's not missing now. The sheriff said he was sure Everett's death was an accident. What are they investigating?"

I chose my words carefully. "That's what they told me also. I think they started an informal investigation before I found…before we learned about your husband's death. With his skills and buying a boat like this—I imagine they would like to know what Everett was working on before he died."

Her face paled. "Then they'll see all that money. Oh, God. You know what they're going to think."

"We don't know if Everett was doing anything wrong," I said, trying to sound soothing.

Her shoulders sagged. "What else could it be? My husband was a good man, Sandi, but he didn't always see things the way other people do. I don't even know if he paid taxes on all that money. I could lose everything, couldn't I?"

"It's possible, yes," I said. There was no point in lying to her.

Kathy opened her purse and took out her wallet. Balancing her checkbook against the hood of the car, she wrote out a check and handed it to me. It was made out in my name for three thousand dollars.

I started to protest, but she shook her head.

"I don't know how much longer I'll be able to afford to pay you. Take it." She got in the car. "And see how quickly you can sell that boat."

Chapter 23

I CASHED THE CHECK at the Morehead City branch of Wells Fargo twenty minutes later, then borrowed the marina truck and drove to Garrett Bay. Greg Garrett ushered me into his office, happy to see me until I told him I was trying to return a boat rather than buy one. I explained Kathy Dvorak's situation as honestly as I could.

"This isn't Walmart," he said bluntly. "We don't take returns. That boat was customized for Everett Dvorak."

I pleaded with him for another ten minutes, but he held firm. He finally offered to broker the boat for a 10% commission as a "personal favor based on the unusual circumstances" with the understanding he was unlikely to get the original purchase price. I called Kathy and caught her sitting on the Cedar Island Ferry. I thought she might have second thoughts, but she agreed at once, without emotion.

"They made me pay for December's slip rent today. They said in the office Everett only paid for November. Every minute it sits there it's costing me money."

I relayed her answer to Mr. Garrett and gave him my contact information. He promised to be in touch. He must have had a buyer in mind because he was on the phone before I left the office.

By the time I got back to the marina it was after five. I pulled into the spot beside Josh's rental truck, then hurried to the office before they closed to drop off the keys.

"Your boyfriend's back," Ben Lancome called, looking up over the edge of some paperwork. "I told him where you'd gone. He said to tell you he'd be on the boat."

I ran down the dock to *Andromeda*. The companionway door was open, and I stuck my head inside. Josh was at the sink, rinsing out a glass. He smiled when he saw me and bounded up the ladder, engulfing me in a bear hug.

"Babe, it's so good to see you," he said, pressing his face into my hair.

I nuzzled his sweatshirt, reveling for the moment in the strength of his arms. He kissed the top of my head, then my cheek, before pulling back and cupping my face in his hand.

"You okay?"

I nodded, and he kissed my mouth.

I don't know how long we stood that way—minutes, no more, but all the doubts that had plagued me evaporated.

"You make me happy," I said when we finally pulled apart.

His green eyes radiated amusement. "You wait. I'm just warming up."

"Sounds like a promise."

He laughed. "You've gotten feisty since I left. I'll need to disappear more often."

Josh backed down the ladder and I climbed after him. "Hmm. You might not get such an enthusiastic welcome if you did."

"See? Feisty." He gestured around the cabin. "Thanks for straightening up. You did a great job."

"You're welcome."

He perched on the edge of a cushion and motioned for me to sit. "So I heard you went to Garrett's to sell a boat. Want to tell me about it?"

I described Kathy's visit to the boat and her concerns about the fallout from an investigation. Having just experienced what happened with his uncle, Josh understood how quickly an inquiry could move from allegations to action. When I finished, I handed him the booklet of Dvorak's notes.

"These were Everett's. Kathy found them on the boat. Can you make out anything?"

He bowed his head over the pages, perusing them slowly.

"You read some of his research, didn't you? Do you remember any specific bacteriology he was working on?'

I thought back to the articles Dvorak had published. "There was one piece about an antidote for chemical agents, but everything else I saw was food borne. He published some articles on E. coli. and a study of parasites. Why?"

Josh ran a hand through his hair.

"I can't say for sure, but I think I've seen some of these abbreviations before."

Just then my phone rang.

"It's Garrett. I hope he hasn't changed his mind."

Not only had Greg Garrett not changed his mind, he already had a prospective buyer for *Kathy Lee*. He wanted me to meet him there in ten minutes as Mrs. Dvorak's representative. "This guy's yacht was t-boned by a charter and the insurance company declared it a total loss. He's eager, and the Dvorak boat is close enough to be twins. It's a one-in-a-million opportunity."

I reluctantly agreed. Having just accepted a payment from Kathy Dvorak for my services, I didn't see what else I could do. Josh made an effort to hide his disappointment when I explained I needed to leave.

"It's no problem," he assured me. "It was a long drive. I'm going to kick back, drink a beer. I'll be here when you get back."

The potential buyer's name was Roger Kingsley, a lawyer from Raleigh who owned a place in Atlantic Beach. His insurance company had settled this morning, and Garrett was right—you could almost see the money smoking in his pocket.

"They all try to screw you," he advised me loudly. "You have to be tough. I told them, you don't know who you're dealing with!"

I had gotten the key from Brenda and we were making our way down the dock. Kingsley was one of those vertically challenged men who thought he could make up for his size with increased volume, and he positioned himself so he could shout directly in my ear. He regaled me with the play-by-play of his victory against the charter boat company's lawyers while Greg Garrett stayed three steps behind, pretending to look around.

I gave him a wide smile and handed him the key. "Why don't you go on up and see what you think?"

"You don't want to show me around?" Kingsley asked, winking suggestively.

"I wouldn't want to influence you one way or the other."

He laughed loudly. "Darlin', old Roger can't be influenced. Ask anybody."

Garrett stepped in and grabbed the key from my hand, and the two men climbed aboard. I waited a minute, then followed and took a seat on the stern. I listened as Kingsley belittled every inch of Everett Dvorak's pride and joy, but by now I was certain it was all bluster. He wanted the boat.

I laid my head back against the deck chair, looking out at the muted pinks and blues of sunset. Kingsley and Garrett were down in the engine room now, Kingsley poking and prodding parts while Greg identified each one and assured him that was exactly what it was supposed to look like. Then they were up in the tower, and I heard the beep of electronics turning on and off. Their voices faded into the background of seagull cries and traffic and the sounds of water....

"What are you doing here?"

I jolted awake. A man wearing dark shirt and slacks stood over me. I groaned. Agent Neeman.

"I'm showing the boat for Mrs. Dvorak. It's up for sale."

His face purpled, though he kept his voice controlled. "No. It is not up for sale."

"What the hell do you mean, it isn't for sale? What the hell's going on?" Robert Kingsley stomped down the stairs, having caught the FBI official's statement.

Neeman looked at him coldly. "And who are you?"

The lawyer puffed up his chest and raised his voice another ten decibels. "Robert Kingsley, Esquire, and I'm the one buyin' this boat!"

There was a sound of boots on wood, and we turned simultaneously to see a team of FBI agents carrying equipment down the dock.

"I'm sorry, but I'm afraid you're mistaken, Mr. Kingsley," said Neeman, though he did not sound sorry in the least. "This boat is a crime scene, part of a criminal investigation. Now I'll need to ask you to evacuate the premises."

The lawyer turned his abuse on Garrett. Amid Kingsley's tirade, I stood up and leaned closer to Neeman, keeping my voice low. "What crime?"

I didn't think he would answer, but the influence of Andrew Culliver must have still been at work. "Homicide," he replied, pitching his voice low. "We located Dvorak's Subaru."

"And?" I pressed.

"It contained an empty syringe with trace amounts of an unidentified substance and the victim's blood."

"You think Everett Dvorak was drugged and killed?"

I had gone a step too far. Neeman's eyes glinted.

"We are looking into all possibilities, including the victim's connections to the illicit drug trade," he said, adding with pointed contempt, "This is no longer amateur hour, Miss Beck. Your involvement is neither requested nor appreciated."

The other members of Neeman's team had surrounded the lawyer and yacht broker and were explaining the two men needed to provide fingerprints, a request that was met with a fresh round of indignation from Kingsley. I looked at Neeman.

"Do you want my fingerprints, too?"

His face cracked into a thin smile, neither warm nor friendly. More like a shark.

"No need. We already have them."

I got off *Kathy Lee* as quickly as I could, stepping around the irate Kingsley, Garrett, and the agents, and made my way up the dock. I jogged across the darkening highway, barely waiting for traffic, and ran all the way to *Andromeda*. Josh was on the bow, his back against the mast, watching the sunset through the space between buildings and trees.

"Did you make a sale?"

"Not at all." He lifted his arm and I sat beside him. He pulled me against his side and handed me his beer.

"Was the offer that bad?"

I took a long swallow and handed it back. "There was no offer. The FBI is there. They say it's a crime scene."

"The scientist?"

I nodded. "Yes. They're investigating his death as a homicide." I went on to detail my encounter with Agent Neeman and his suggestion Dvorak may have been involved in the illegal drug market. "I don't buy it, Josh. It's just too...."

"Too what?"

"Too cliché. Disgruntled scientist manufactures drugs to support lavish lifestyle. It's a bad T.V. movie."

"You know how clichés get to be clichés?"

"By being true. I know."

Josh hugged me closer, and I dropped my head to his shoulder. We sat that way while the last vestiges of daylight faded from view.

He rose and pulled me up. "You need a break. Let me take you out to dinner."

I went back to my cabin to find a decent-looking sweater. When I pulled off my old blue sweatjacket, Everett Dvorak's little memo booklet fell from the front pocket. I tossed it on the shelf, then thought the better of it.

Josh knocked on the deck.

"C'mon in for a minute," I called.

I noticed he had changed into clean blue jeans and a fresh sweater. He grabbed a seat on the settee, and I handed him the booklet.

"Can you take another look at this?"

"We're probably holding onto evidence," Josh said, but he didn't sound overly bothered by it. He motioned me to sit beside him. "I told you I thought I'd seen these abbreviations somewhere before. Like this one: Se-T. I remember it. When I was in the hospital in Germany, a doc there had just come from Pakistan. They had an outbreak of typhoid fever, super drug-resistant, high fatality rate. Anybody who was flown in from the Middle East was checked. He abbreviated that way on the charts, and I asked. He said it was a strain of salmonella."

"Which means Everett Dvorak was working on biological agents, not drugs."

"At least according to these notes." Josh handed the book back to me. "The question is why."

"Suppose Dvorak was telling the truth when he said his employer was a military contractor. Could they be experimenting with salmonella as a biological weapon?"

He sat back and drummed his fingers on the cushion, thinking. I waited.

"Yes and no," he said finally. "Salmonella could be used as a biological weapon, but the United States signed the BTWC back in 1975. That agreement prohibited nations from developing and using new biological weapons. No legitimate contractor could be conducting this research for offensive use."

"What about a drug company, contracted by the military, seeking some kind of antidote?"

"It's possible. If you look at the notes, Dvorak lists abbreviations with the numbers one, two, and three. I'm guessing those are batches, maybe different strains. There are time periods listed as well. But the thing is, would a legitimate drug company pay the kind of money Dvorak was getting? And if this was legitimate, why would they want him dead? And how do we explain the syringe in his car?"

I thought about Katya's story. "There's something else, Josh." I told him the waitress had seen a man going to Dvorak's boat on the day he was probably killed. "It could have been Chip Holland."

"Who's Chip Holland?"

"He does security work for I.U.S., and he's also a part-owner and instructor at the dive center where Maggie took lessons."

Josh's expression grew dark. "The same guy who told police Aunt Maggie was afraid of my uncle?"

"I don't know that for sure, but I don't see who else it could have been."

"I'd like to talk to him."

The way he said it, quietly and without emotion, was more frightening than if he had shouted.

"So would I." I thought about Chris Holtz's reaction when I mentioned the dead scientist. "Maybe Holland's doing some freelance security work for Dvorak's employer. Or maybe it wasn't Chip Holland on Dvorak's boat after all. Katya only saw the guy's back, so it could have been anybody." The more I talked, the more far-fetched all of it sounded. "I don't know what else to say. None of this makes any sense to me."

I rubbed my eyes tiredly. I was confused and frustrated and my head was starting to ache.

"Hey, that's enough for today." Josh's anger at Holland was replaced by concern for me. He pulled me up and hugged me to him. "I told you, you need a break. Take some time to clear your head."

I thought about Kathy. She might be home by now.

"I should call Dvorak's wife. She needs to know about the boat."

He sighed. "Okay. I'll be waiting for you on the dock. But San, five minutes. That's it. All these problems will still be here tomorrow."

Not exactly comforting words, but I knew he meant well.

I watched Josh climb out onto the deck, his broad shoulders filling the companionway. He was right. I was not good at compartmentalizing.

Once I set to work on a problem, it consumed me—I ate it, drank it, tossed and turned with it, dreamed it. Even when I purposely thought about other things, a part of me kept turning the issue over and over like a Rubik's cube, looking for a solution. This habit was not healthy for me or for my relationships, but thus far it had produced results, though not always the ones I intended.

I called Kathy Dvorak's cell, and getting no answer there, I tried her house. The answering machine picked up, still her husband's voice. I left a detailed message explaining what happened at the boat. It wasn't the best way to let a woman know her husband's death was being treated as a murder, but I thought it was better to get a message from me than an unexpected call from Agent Neeman. When I was finished, I left my phone on the table. I owed Josh a night without interruptions.

Chapter 24

I WOKE IN JOSH'S berth on *Andromeda*, the sun shining in my eyes.

I rose on my elbow and looked at the man beside me. Asleep, his face was smooth as a child's. I wondered that I had never noticed the dark lashes that lay against his cheeks, or the softness of his mouth, or the tiny scar that made a meandering trail from his chin to the edge of his jaw. I reached out a hand and laid it gently on his muscled chest, stroked the small patch of brown hair curled there, and he made a purring sound in his throat.

I thought back to last night. I couldn't tell you the moment I knew we would end up here, in this bed. Every moment was a link in a chain—his hand on my knee, a kiss on the cheek, the constant brushing of shoulders and legs, until our breath came a little faster and conversation was replaced by touch and look and the warm pressure of lips. The urgency propelled us here, past dark corners and empty benches, where we stripped off our clothes and our defenses. It was not making love, too fast and hard, too primal for that kind of name. It was a storm.

Later, when he held me, he told me about his time in combat, about his injuries and his regrets, and I told him about Ryan's accident, the terrible sadness that consumed me, and the times I almost welcomed my own death. We peeled back the layers of our pain, and in doing so I stepped through a mirror. I could see the person I had been, but she was a one-dimensional figure on the other side of the glass, and I was rounded and whole. It was the same, I think, for Josh. He told me he left the Army because he could not separate who he was from the things he did. He spoke now of missing the comfort of brotherhood and of his struggle to find meaning back home, in a fragmented society where everyone was both crowded together and alone. We fell asleep entwined, one creature out of two, and my last thought was a prayer that we might be enough for each other.

Now, watching him sleep, I wanted nothing more than to make this last. This ache, this is love.

Josh's eyes fluttered open as if in response to my thoughts.

"Hey," he said, voice rough with sleep.

"Hey."

"You know this is my boyhood fantasy—waking up on a sailboat with a beautiful woman." His tone was teasing, but his green eyes were warm.

"Just waking up?" I asked, laughing.

"No, there's more," he said, and he pulled me to him and kissed me.

It wasn't until much later, when he was making coffee, that I remembered my cell phone still sitting in *Serenity*'s cabin.

"I need to get some clean clothes from my boat."

He looked at me knowingly. "You mean you need to check your phone. It's okay, I understand. Just promise to be back in ten minutes. I'm making eggs and bacon."

My mouth watered at the sound of real food. "I promise."

The phone was right where I left it. There were two missed calls from Kathy and one from Wayne Kremm at the Post. His was the only message.

"San, Wayne. Are you still in Morehead City? Story just came out on Buzzfeed about the murder of a scientist named Everett Dvorak. According to the report, an unnamed female diver found the body. Knowing you, I'm guessing you're involved. Give me a call."

I cringed. If the news about Dvorak's death included a reference to me, it was only a matter of time before other reporters tracked me down. I used to write for a small Virginia paper, but my experience with the media in my position as an advocate had been mixed. I trusted Wayne to verify his sources, but I knew him. He would never intentionally hurt me in pursuit of a story. I couldn't say the same for every journalist I'd met. I had learned the best way to head off unwanted publicity was to create your own because at least then you controlled the direction of the attention. However, eggs and bacon wouldn't wait, so I grabbed a quick

The Lies Beneath - 179

shower and changed, making a mental note to return both calls after breakfast.

The smell from *Andromeda*'s cabin was wafting up from the open companionway door when I got back on board. Josh looked at the clock in mock surprise, noting I had reappeared with two minutes to spare.

"I have to admit, I didn't expect you back so soon," he said, shoveling a pile of bacon and two fried eggs onto my plate. "Now that I know how to get your attention, I'll fry bacon more often."

I would have made a witty retort, but my mouth was full.

He sat down across from me and dug in his fork. We ate in comfortable silence, and when we finished, I cleared away the dishes. "You cooked, I'll clean."

He leaned back on the dinette bench and sipped his coffee. "Any news from Kathy Dvorak?"

"Two missed calls, no messages. I'll call her when I'm done." I filled the sink with hot, soapy water. "I did have a voicemail from Wayne Kremm. Dvorak's murder made the online news."

"Why would he call you?"

"He knew we were here. The report mentions a female diver, and—"

"And Wayne believes you're a magnet for trouble?" His voice was joking, but he knew enough about me now to understand it wasn't far from the truth.

"He knows there are fewer female than male divers, so he made an educated guess," I said, channeling Dave Burliss.

Josh looked at me thoughtfully. "I'm not trying to tell you what to do. But if this is in the news, it won't be long before someone looks into Dvorak's background and brings up biological weapons. That booklet probably needs to go to the Bureau."

I had already thought the same thing. "I don't suppose I can just slip it back on *Kathy Lee*."

"Probably not, but you haven't done anything wrong. His wife gave it to you before the FBI showed up. It just slipped your mind."

I doubted Agent Neeman would see it that way.

"Uncle Alan called while you were over on *Serenity*. He's coming down tonight instead of tomorrow. Jack Gardner invited him out deep sea fishing on Friday."

I hid my disappointment. That meant I would be back on *Serenity*, alone.

"Gardner lives around here?"

"It's closer to the end of Emerald Isle. That's one of the reasons he opened the plant here. He has a place near Bogue Inlet with a big fishing boat—sounds like it's bigger than *Kathy Lee*. He invited us to go along."

I love sailing, but I can't handle powerboats in the ocean. I've gone on two offshore dive trips, and both times I spent the day bent over the rail losing my lunch. I outlined my seasickness to Josh, adding, "You go ahead. It will be fun."

He nodded, though I could see he didn't like the thought of going without me. "So what's the plan for today?"

I shrugged. "I don't have one. I need to call Kathy back, but there's nothing more I can do for her except offer moral support. With the FBI involved and this much money at stake, she needs a lawyer."

"And the notebook?"

I had conveniently forgotten about it. I groaned.

"I'll call Agent Neeman and arrange a drop-off as soon as I finish the dishes."

Josh gave me an encouraging smile. "How bad can it be?"

Very. I must have caught Neeman at an inopportune moment, because he sounded more unpleasant than usual. When I explained I had a notebook belonging to Dr. Dvorak, I was chilled by the iciness in his voice.

"Do you intend to continue withholding evidence, Miss Beck?"

"I'm not withholding anything. I called you," I protested. "And Kathy gave it to me before we knew there was a homicide investigation."

He didn't bother to acknowledge my argument. "Meet me at Mallory's at ten," he growled, and the line went dead.

It was just before nine now. Josh wanted to remove his foresail and get the canvas cover re-stitched. While I was talking to Neeman, he found a woman in a New Bern sail loft who said she could do it while he waited. I had time to help him lower the sail and haul it to the truck, where he gave me a quick goodbye kiss and agreed to meet at Captain Tom's for lunch. With a half-hour to spare, I called Kathy Dvorak, again getting no answer. My next call went to Wayne.

"So was it you?" he asked by way of greeting.

"Is this on or off the record?"

"I knew it!" he yelped. "Go on, tell me the whole story. I won't print anything you don't want me to."

I told him how I had come to bump into Dr. Dvorak's body. "I didn't find out until yesterday they were looking into his death as a murder."

"From what I've heard, this guy worked at Fort Detrick. Top secret. Maybe some kind of an anthrax expert."

"No, salmonella," I said without thinking.

"How do you know that?"

I would have lied but I could use Wayne's take on the scientist and the drug allegations. I told him about meeting Kathy Dvorak in Ocracoke, the mysterious employer, the huge payments, the fishing boat, and the syringe and blood found in Dvorak's car. Only the last bit of information had been in the overnight reporting.

"You amaze me. How do you do it? Most people go on vacation and end up with a sunburn and a hangover. You get Breaking Bad."

I ignored the humor. "The thing is, I don't think it has anything to do with illegal drugs." I described the notebook and Josh's theory that the abbreviations stood for salmonella strains. I added what I knew about Chip Holland and how he might have been on Dvorak's boat the day he died. "I can't shake the feeling this is related to Everett's past government work. There are a lot of military contractors in this area. Josh's uncle is coming down tonight, and maybe he or Jack Gardner will know where else Holland could be working, or who might have hired Dvorak."

"We signed a disarmament treaty on biologics decades ago," Wayne pointed out, echoing what Josh had said. "The only people who would be paying Dvorak that kind of dough to work with lethal bacteria are terrorists. Salmonella and other food-borne bacteria are on Homeland's list of potential terrorist weapons. No better way to panic a country than screw with its food supply."

"I never met him, but based on what I've seen, there's no way Everett Dvorak would knowingly do that. According to his wife, he was a little paranoid about academic competition, but otherwise he worked for the U.S. government faithfully for years."

"You said he had money problems. You and I both know what people will do for money. You know...." Wayne's voice drifted off.

"What?"

He sounded pensive. "Something about this reminds me of a story I

182 - Ann Eichenmuller

worked on a long time ago. I want to go back and take a look."

"You aren't going to use anything I said in print, are you?"

"No. There's nothing concrete there. But I agree with you—I've got the same feeling. I'll get back to you, San."

After he hung up, I caught a glimpse of the clock. Five minutes till ten. The last thing I needed was to be late for Agent Neeman.

I was tempted at this point to tell the FBI agent everything, to give him not only the notebook but also Josh's theory, Katya's eyewitness account, and Chip Holland. Then it would be out of my hands. But I had promised Katya no police, and Agent Neeman hadn't exactly been endearing. And with no real proof of the red-haired man's identity, I couldn't start throwing out names and accusations. Twice in my short career I had laid blame for a death on the wrong person, and in the process set in motion a chain of events that cost people their lives.

Wayne once told me an old folktale about a man who sees Death on his street. Sure he is the target, the man buys a plane ticket to Istanbul, where he is certain Death will not find him. A week goes by, when one day he is in the market, and Death appears at his elbow. "This is impossible!" he cries. "I left the country so you wouldn't find me." Death looks at him in a puzzled way. "What do you mean? Our appointment has always been for right here, today."

I was a believer in free will, but the point of the story was clear—regardless of what we do, we cannot escape our fate.

Despite my best efforts, was I going to cost another man his life?

Chapter 25

MY MEETING WITH AGENT Neeman went exactly as I guessed it would. He was sitting alone in the front seat of his dark sedan when I walked into the parking lot. He rolled down the window, not even bothering to get out of the car, and held out his hand.

"Good morning, Agent."

He looked at me woodenly. I pulled the notebook from my backpack and passed it to him.

"Have you altered or removed any pages from this book?"

"No."

"Have you shared this book or the information it contains with anyone?"

"Well…."

He clenched his jaw.

"Have you let anyone else see this notebook, Miss Beck?"

"Joshua Culliver. He's the only one besides Mrs. Dvorak who has seen it." Which was true. Wayne Kremm had not seen the notebook—I just told him about it.

"And is there anything else—and please consider carefully—any other piece of evidence you have in your possession or any other information which could be pertinent to this investigation?"

Neeman was glaring at me with such focus I nearly blurted out Chip Holland's name, but I bit my lip instead.

"Miss Beck—"

"No," I muttered.

He stared at me a minute more, than rolled up his window. I backed up a few steps, just in case he was considering running me over, but he drove away slowly as if to prove he hadn't let me get under his skin.

I walked back to *Serenity*, unable to shake the ominous feeling I was still missing something.

Josh called around eleven-thirty to say the sailmaker's industrial sewing machine had seized up and she was on Facetime with the manufacturer's service department. It looked like they'd be able to get it fixed within the hour, but she wasn't going to be able to finish the repair until after lunch. It was another hour's drive back from New Bern, and he wanted to wait for the sail, if I didn't mind having lunch alone.

I had seen a gourmet market on the corner of Tenth Street and Arendell where I could grab a bite to eat and buy wine and cheese, then cut across to the waterfront and pick up shrimp for dinner. Although the road was always busy and railroad tracks ran in a median down the center, there was a sidewalk, and the street was lined with shops and houses. The day was cool and cloudy, perfect for a walk, and after the encounter with Agent Neeman, I could use a little exercise to work off my angst. I picked up my backpack and headed out.

Perhaps it was the weather, or living on a boat, but the Christmas season had come without my noticing. For the first time I was conscious of green wreaths on doors and lampposts and holiday displays in windows. It felt wrong somehow, to be wearing only a light jacket and hear "Jingle Bells" play on gas station speakers. If I had been in Irvington, there would have been a Christmas party at the museum and a Festival of Trees at the gym. Debbie would have hung lights along the ceiling of the Back Porch Café so it looked like a thousand stars were twinkling in the middle of the day. I would have sat on the bow with a mug of hot cider and watched the boats parade along Carter's Creek, each more elaborately decorated than the last. After Ryan's death I tried to ignore the season as much as my mother would let me, but slowly, insidiously, new traditions crept in to replace the old ones. Now, a traveler in a strange place, I found myself craving the rituals of a familiar life.

Perhaps that explains why I bought a three-foot Christmas tree made of crab pots, complete with lights, on my way back to the marina. The shop clerk, a sweet elderly lady, looked at me uncertainly as I balanced it in my arms, my full backpack weighing me down from behind.

"Honey, do you want me to help you get this to your car?"

I smiled. "I don't have one. I'm up at Dockside Marina."

"Bless your heart. You can't walk all that way carrying a Christmas tree. Give me a minute and I'll lock up and drive you."

I protested, but the woman was adamant. She scrawled a quick sign on a sheet of paper and taped it to the door. Minutes later I was regally ensconced in the front seat of a spotless white Cadillac. In no time at all I was back on *Serenity*, my crab pot tree on the shelf blinking merrily, the blues of the morning chased away by the kindness of a stranger.

Josh got back a little after four, and his wide grin when he saw my cabin, vindicated my purchase. He downloaded a mix of Christmas albums on his iPod, and I prepared dinner to the joyous sounds of John Denver and the Muppets.

Alan got to Morehead City an hour after the sun went down, coming in with the smell of a weather change. A cold wind was blowing from the northwest, pushing the salt air out to sea and giving us a dry, crisp night. Josh and I were inside *Serenity* when he came, the propane fireplace burning. Shrimp Alfredo simmered on the stove, a rich concoction of butter and garlic and white wine.

Alan Culliver should have shown the stress of the past week, but he looked better than I expected. Thinner, yes, and there were worry lines I did not remember around his eyes and across his forehead. But he seemed relaxed and in good spirits when he embraced me and gave me a kiss on the cheek.

"Sandi, you look wonderful as always," he said, handing me a bottle of wine. "Thank you so much for letting me barge in on the two of you."

I assured him he was more than welcome and poured him a drink while he chatted with Josh about the drive.

"Are you hungry yet? Dinner's ready, so we can eat whenever you'd like."

Alan looked at me gratefully. "That sounds wonderful. To be honest, I haven't eaten since breakfast. I'm starving."

I put the food on the table, family style, and Josh slid to the middle of the L-shaped seat. As we ate, I marveled again at their identical foreheads and jaw lines, chiseled and strong, and the deep, genuine laugh they shared. I wondered if it ever bothered Alan that Josh was his brother's son and not his own.

"I heard you had a bad experience this week," Alan said to me as we were clearing away the plates. "How are you doing?"

I thought perhaps Josh wouldn't tell him about finding the body, given Maggie's drowning death and all he had been through. "I'm fine," I answered.

"Do you know what happened? Josh just said a retired man had fallen overboard."

I hesitated and Josh and I exchanged glances. This wasn't festive after-dinner conversation. I decided to gloss over the details and change the subject.

"I believe they're still not quite sure how Dr. Dvorak died. Would you like coffee with your cheesecake?"

Alan Culliver didn't answer. All the color had drained from his face.

"Alan? Are you all right?"

He didn't seem to hear me. His hand shook as he laid it on my arm. "Did you say Dvorak? Everett Dvorak?"

"Yes."

"That's...that's not possible."

He turned from me and felt his way to the table like a blind man. Josh rushed over, supporting his uncle as he fell into the seat, his eyes searching Alan's face.

"What is it? What's wrong?"

He looked from Josh to me, his expression a mixture of horror and disbelief.

"That's the man Maggie met in Ocracoke."

Chapter 26

ALAN DRANK THE COFFEE I gave him with shaking hands. He had recovered somewhat and sat at the table now, both elbows on the top, his head bowed over the cup. He spoke to his reflection in the glossy wood surface.

"I told you I thought she was seeing someone. There were things that didn't add up…saying she was going one place but ending up in another. Maggie always did the bills, but over the summer I looked at the statements, and there were charges for places in North Carolina when she was supposed to be visiting her mother. I should have asked her, but I didn't want to accuse her. We've always gone our own way, never had to answer to each other.…"

Alan's coffee sloshed over the edge and splashed on the table. He looked at it as if surprised, then pushed the liquid around with his napkin until it finally disappeared. Josh and I both waited, unwilling to press him.

"One evening in August she was on the back porch talking on her cell phone. She thought I was in the shower. I heard her ask how long the flight to Ocracoke would be, and what time she could expect to get there. When I came outside she told me she was meeting a friend in Richmond the next day for lunch and shopping. She planned to leave at nine-thirty in the morning and be back around seven that night. I didn't know what to do, so I followed her."

"You went to the airport?"

"No," he said, looking embarrassed, "I went to Ocracoke. I told Maggie

I was going out fishing with some friends, and I left at six a.m. I stopped at Enterprise and rented a car so she wouldn't know it was me. Then I drove down to Hatteras and took the ferry."

"You looked at a boat," I said. "On Ocracoke. A little runabout named *Lorelai*."

Alan's eyes widened. "How do you know that?"

"When we were walking on the island, the owner thought I was you," Josh explained.

His uncle's mouth twisted into a wry grin. "I had forgotten all about that. It was a beautiful boat. I got to Ocracoke early and talked to a guy working on his plane. He said he had a friend who was a pilot out of Williamsburg-Norfolk due in with a charter around one-forty-five, so I had time to kill. I parked down by the water, got some lunch, took a walk, tried to figure out what I was going to do. Now that I was there...I just didn't know."

He closed his eyes a moment, then took a breath and went on. "I went back to the airport at one-thirty and pulled behind the building. A man was waiting in his car in the parking lot. A single engine plane landed, and Maggie came right off and got in his car. I stayed way back, but I followed them. They didn't go into town. They went to the National Park and drove out on the off-road beach access. My rental was a little Hyundai, and there was no way I could drive on the sand, so I waited.

"They were gone a long time. Hours. When they came back out on the road they went straight to the airport. The plane was already on the taxiway, and there was no chance to talk to her then. I decided to follow the man she was...the man she had met. He drove into town, got gas, then went into the ABC store. I went down a street and turned around, and when I got back, he was gone."

What he had seen matched perfectly with Kathy's tale of a woman flying in to see her husband. Yet the idea of the two of them together seemed so unlikely. How had they met? What was the attraction between them?

"Uncle Alan, how do you know the man was Everett Dvorak?" Josh asked.

"Because I went in the liquor store and told them the man with the glasses in the Subaru dropped something in the parking lot. The clerk said I must mean Everett Dvorak." Alan looked up at me. "I didn't know he was a doctor. All I had was a name."

I did not correct him. I was too busy thinking Everett Dvorak was the last person Maggie Culliver would find attractive. "What did you do when Maggie got home?"

Alan smiled sadly. "Nothing. I did nothing." He turned his attention to Josh. "I had a long time to think on the way back. At first I was angry. I even called Jack Gardner and asked for the name of his personal attorney. But fifty, sixty miles in, I started thinking. For most of our marriage, I was either in the lab or coming up with new designs in my head. I haven't always been the best husband. But I loved your aunt, Josh. I didn't want to face the rest of my life without her. By the time I got back to the house, I decided I would try harder. And it worked. Within a couple of weeks, the calls and the trips stopped. She seemed more relaxed, happier—like she'd made a choice."

Exactly the words Kathy Dvorak had used. Perhaps Maggie and Everett had agreed to end their affair. Had that been the impetus for Dvorak to leave his new job and name a boat after his wife?

Josh was rubbing his uncle's shoulder. "You did the right thing. Whatever was going on, Aunt Maggie loved you."

Alan stood and hugged his nephew. "Thank you, Josh." He turned to me. "Sandi, I'm sorry. It wasn't something I planned on telling anyone. It's just that hearing Dvorak had drowned, so soon after Maggie…do you think he took his own life?"

It was a question I hadn't considered, and I doubted the FBI had either. The used syringe found in the Subaru could have delivered a lethal injection. If the substance didn't take effect immediately, Dvorak could have returned to the boat. Unfortunately, that scenario did not explain how the Subaru left the marina parking lot without its owner, and it didn't line up with Everett's reported good spirits at the prospect of bringing down his wife. If anything, what Alan said made me more confident Everett Dvorak had been murdered. But as Agent Neeman stated so succinctly, this wasn't amateur hour. Dvorak's death was now the purview of the FBI.

I shrugged. "I don't know, Alan. It's under investigation."

"You don't think the thing about Maggie will come out, do you? I don't want people to remember her for that."

"She saw him months ago, Uncle Alan. I don't think it has anything to do with what happened this week," Josh assured him.

The widower seemed mollified. In an attempt to salvage the evening, I cut the cheesecake and passed out plates, but the mood did not lighten. Alan excused himself and Josh went with him to *Andromeda*, giving me an apologetic kiss as he left.

"I'll try to come back in an hour," he said softly, his lips against my ear as Alan went up the steps to the deck.

I shook my head. "It's okay. I'll see you when you get back tomorrow."

The plan was for both men to get up early and go to Jack Gardner's. They were headed offshore to the warm waters of the Gulf Stream and wouldn't be back till late afternoon.

He kissed me again. "Thanks for tonight. I owe you."

I smiled. "I'll collect."

I tried turning up the holiday music after they left, but the bells sounded tinny and the crab pot tree looked spindly and forlorn. Peace and goodwill seemed pale ghosts to jealousy and deceit. I finished my wine and rinsed out the glass.

"Merry Christmas," I whispered as I turned out the lights.

Chapter 27

I JOLTED AWAKE JUST after midnight, my heart racing, my body wet with sweat.

It took me a minute to remember where I was. The dream had been incredibly vivid, realistic despite its impossibilities. I was walking alone down a city street I didn't recognize, and people began pouring out of restaurants and shops, clutching at their throats, stumbling blindly, moaning and screaming. I went to each one to try to help, but there were so many, their hands reaching for me, their faces purpled and twisted with pain, that I panicked. I began to run, pushing and shoving my way through the bodies, when a small freckled woman grabbed my arm. I looked down and saw I was holding a sandwich wrapped in paper. "Don't eat the food," she whispered, and then she screamed as her face melted into nothingness.

I took several deep breaths. Just a dream. Given the conversation of the evening, I understood why Maggie Culliver might haunt my sleep.

I turned on the light and got a glass of water. Sitting at the table, I replayed Alan's confession. Maggie, however improbable, involved with Dvorak. The phone calls and meetings both her husband and his wife had shared with me. The scientist's body, floating beneath the pier. The little notebook I had surrendered to Neeman, filled with scribbled abbreviations for salmonella.

People dying in my dream…don't eat the food….

I groaned at my own blindness.

Maggie Culliver wasn't having an affair with the scientist—she was investigating him.

I ran this new scenario through. Wayne had heard a rumor about a bioterrorism threat. That's when the calls to Maggie started. Let's assume she was helping him, and they found something worth pursuing, but then Jansen died. Maggie Culliver was the kind of woman who would continue to investigate on her own. She contacted Dr. Dvorak, either because he was an expert in the field or because she had reason to suspect he was involved. They met several times.

I pulled a file box out of the side cabinet and found the hard copies of some documents I printed while researching Dvorak's disappearance. I pulled out the ad for *Kathy Lee*, torn from Southern Boater magazine. The date at the top was August of this year, the same month Alan had followed Maggie to Ocracoke. That was when Kathy noticed a change in her husband.

Perhaps Dvorak told Maggie about his new employer, or perhaps she uncovered the information on her own. Either way, soon after, Dvorak must have decided to get out. He bought the boat, and on his next visit to the lab, he resigned. There was only one problem with this version of events: if Maggie had information on the illegal production of a potential biological weapon, why didn't she report it?

I was positive the FBI knew nothing about Dvorak until I called Josh's father. Why had Maggie kept it a secret? She had dedicated her life to defend this country. Who or what could be important enough to make her betray her oath to protect the United States?

In the end, there was only one plausible answer—Alan.

Katya's description of one of Dvorak's visitors matched Chip Holland, and he was a contract worker for I.U.S. Alan's company had opened a plant nearby, near the time when Dvorak was approached and offered a job. I shivered. I hoped I was wrong, but it was possible Dvorak's employer, the one involved in working illegally with biological agents, was I.U.S. No wonder Maggie tried to pressure Alan to cut his ties to the company.

But why was I.U.S. involved? What use did a drone manufacturer have with food-borne bacteria?

Neeman was right. I was out of my league. I opened the junk drawer, pulled out the FBI agent's business card, and reached for my phone.

I was halfway through punching in the number when I put it down again. Making the call could lead to an investigation that would bankrupt Alan's company, harm hundreds of the veterans who were employed there, and hurt Kathy Dvorak. So far, I had nothing but conjecture. Maggie must have believed it was more important to protect Alan and I.U.S. than to tell anyone, even her brother-in-law, what she had found. Until I knew more, I would do the same.

At that moment, my cell began to vibrate in my hand. I didn't recognize the number.

"Hello?"

"I'm getting on a plane to Jacksonville. I'll be there in an hour." It was Wayne, sounding tense and grim.

"What—where are you?" I fished around for my watch. It was nine-thirty-seven.

"At Reagan International. I'm calling you from a pay phone."

"They still have those?"

He lowered his voice. "I don't have time to explain. I'm on a story. It involves you. Meet me at the Jacksonville airport at eleven." There was a pause while he answered someone in the background. "I mean it, Sandi. This is important."

He hung up.

Wayne was not given to histrionics. He was a man who had covered everything from mob bosses and drug kingpins to violent dictators. He also hated to fly. If he thought a story was serious enough to leave D.C. by plane, I had to take him at his word. I showered and dressed in ten minutes, only then remembering I had no car. I stood on the dock, squinting at the parking lot in the bright sun. Alan's car was gone, but the rental truck was still there. I just had no idea where the keys might be.

I tried the companionway door on *Andromeda* and was relieved to find it unlocked. Even better, the keys were left out on the kitchen counter in plain sight—a good thing, because otherwise I never would have found them. Josh's cabin, normally bare of clutter, looked like a college dorm room after a frat party. Clothes and blankets were strewn on the floor, empty beer bottles covered the table, and the sink was full of dirty dishes. It appeared they had eaten breakfast and gotten out in a hurry. I checked my watch—nine-fifty-three. According to Google Maps, the airport was a little less than an hour away.

It is a rule of life that whenever you are in a hurry you get behind a tractor or a little old lady with thick glasses and an "I Love Cats" bumper sticker. Today must have been my lucky day, because I got behind both at the same time, one in the right lane and one in the left, effectively reducing the speed of traffic to a fast walk on the only highway to Jacksonville. I occupied myself by looking for a radio station while I waited for one of them to inch past the other. There was nothing on but news, and I might have switched it off except the word salmonella caught my attention. I turned up the volume.

"The CDC has released a statement this morning confirming the cause of the food poisoning in Charleston as an antibiotic-resistant strain of the bacteria salmonella enterica, the same strain found previously in the outbreak in Bald Head Island. Several people in this latest incident were confirmed dead, including Naval officer Captain Brooks Reed and his wife, Alicia. Investigators are still trying to determine how the virulent strain infected salad greens in the two states."

I stared at the radio in disbelief. I knew that name—Captain Reed was the officer who had pressed charges against Chip Holland.

There it was, a definitive link between Dvorak's research and Holland, one even Dave Burliss should concede was not a coincidence. Yet this attack was a personal vendetta—why would Dvorak or I.U.S. be involved? Unless Holland stole the bacteria....

I bit my lip in frustration. Even if there was a link between Holland and the Charleston attack, it only fit one outbreak, not both. As far as I could see, there was no link between Holland or I.U.S. and the victims in Bald Head Island. I was missing something, something crucial.

The tractor in front of me turned off onto a dirt road, and I increased my speed. I was still turning the problem over in my mind when I pulled into the Ellis Airport entrance. As I was parking, I got a text from Wayne telling me to meet him inside at the Carolina's Finest Lounge, with no directions whatsoever on how to find it. As soon as I stepped inside the terminal, however, I realized there had been no need. Besides a small coffee shop, the Lounge was the only restaurant in the facility. The terminal was nearly empty, and only a few travelers, looking haggard and jet-lagged, sat in booths. Wayne waved at me from his seat in a darkened corner farthest from the door, his laptop open on the table.

I noticed at once he had lost weight in the two weeks since I'd last seen him. Wayne was never fat, but he was under five-and-a-half feet and even a few extra pounds give the illusion of heaviness.

He rose and I bent down just a bit to hug him. "Hasn't anybody been feeding you?"

"Just pining away for you," he responded, but his voice lacked the usual mocking edge. "Sit down. I've only got a half-hour."

My first reaction was irritation—it had taken me longer than an hour to get here—but something in his face made me stop. I took a chair next to his as a waitress came over.

"She'll have an iced tea, unsweet," Wayne said before I could open my mouth. "I'll take another Coke, and you can bring the sampler whenever it comes up. We won't be ordering lunch."

The server nodded and left.

"That's okay, I'm not really hungry, but thanks for asking."

He shrugged unapologetically. "I ordered appetizers to save time. You can get something later. I have an appointment with General Hellerman at the marine base this afternoon, and it was hard enough to get him to see me."

"What's going on, Wayne?"

He dropped his voice. "What I'm going to tell you, most of it has not been confirmed, but it will be. I've never been so sure about a story. If I'm right, there will be collateral damage—no question. I want you as far away from this as possible."

"Away from what?" I asked, impatience creeping into my voice.

"The Cullivers. I.U.S. And before you jump on your high horse and tell me what you will and will not do, you need to listen."

I knew then he had somehow arrived at the same conclusions I had. It might be impossible to protect Alan after all.

"I'm listening," I said.

"Okay." He took a last sip of his Coke just as our server brought the drinks, waiting until she left to continue.

"I told you Dvorak's notes reminded me of something. After I got off the phone with you, I remembered. Back in 1984, a group of followers of this Indian mystic named Rajneeshee deliberately contaminated salad bars at ten local restaurants in Oregon. They used salmonella. They were hoping to incapacitate the voting population in specific parts of the city so their own candidates would win the Wasco County elections. It was the largest bioterrorist attack on American soil, and it was done to influence local government."

The parallel was obvious. "You believe the salmonella poisonings in the Carolinas were political?"

Wayne looked around us, but the closest customer was at least fifty feet away, talking on her cell phone.

"Bald Island, yes, and another attack before that," he said in a low voice. "But not Charleston, at least not yet. I haven't figured that one out."

I have. But I didn't say it aloud.

"I have a source at the CDC, a microbiologist. She was responsible for testing the salad from the North Carolina food poisoning. She noticed right away the salmonella bacteria had some unusual properties. I don't pretend to understand the specifics, but she said it had been engineered—her words—to produce severe symptoms and to spread more quickly within the human body. She was doing some additional tests when the FBI came yesterday and took everything: the specimens, her notes, even her hard drive. They told her it was part of a highly classified investigation."

It looked like the notebook had gotten some attention.

"Everett Dvorak's research," I said.

"Yes. And I am convinced your boyfriend's uncle's company is involved, but you've got to go back a few years to see the whole picture."

"Go on," I said, sitting back and crossing my arms. Wayne took in the stubborn pose, and a faint smile flitted across his lips.

"Try to keep an open mind," he said. "When Alan Culliver brought in Jack Gardner to I.U.S., it was a small company with a tiny fraction of military drone contracts. By the time he stepped down from an active role, Gardner had more than tripled its contracts, but they were still a small fish in a very big pond. Everybody was getting into unmanned vehicles, and Gardner was pouring money into research to stay competitive. He made a lot of big promises, but his margins were thin. Anything went wrong, he wouldn't have the resources to continue, so he decided to sell off the older technology to foreign governments—a lot of red tape there. You can set up the deal, but it gets funneled through the Department of Defense, and they take their cut as the middleman.

"Around two years ago, Gardner landed a billion-dollar contract with

Pakistan to supply drones. He got tentative DOD approval, built two new plants, hired nothing but vets, made the paper. Then last year two generals raised red flags, said they wouldn't sign off on the deal because the weapons could be a threat to U.S. forces. Here's the interesting part—both of them got food poisoning and were hospitalized before the final decision was handed down. Traces of E. Coli were found on their water glasses. This was inside the Pentagon. Everybody figured poor hygiene on the part of the cafeteria staff, end of story, but just to be on the safe side someone in Homeland asked a retired intelligence official to review the report."

"Bart Jansen," I guessed.

"Right. Apparently, this guy wanted to rule out the possibility of terrorism. One of the cafeteria workers reported a refrigeration repairman had been hanging around the kitchen that morning, and no one could find a record of who he was or who he worked for. It wasn't enough to warrant a full-scale inquiry—both men recovered within forty-eight hours. But someone in Homeland still had concerns, so he called in Jansen to investigate unofficially, and Jansen must have called in Maggie. Coincidentally, I.U.S. still lost the project.

"Gardner had to find a cash source, and soon. That's when he realized his military drones had civilian application monitoring and repairing gas pipelines, solar, and wind farms. He sold the idea to Atlantic Power. They had a gas pipeline project already under construction in western North Carolina and a solar farm going in on some swamp land along the coast. It was a huge deal—we're talking billions, more than Gardner would have gotten from Pakistan."

What was it Jack Gardner said at Maggie's memorial service? "We were fortunate. The referendum on the ballot could have killed the whole deal, but Atlantic just squeaked by with the votes to defeat it."

"You think Gardner poisoned those people on Bald Head Island."

There was glint of admiration in Wayne's eyes as he continued. "Not by himself, but yeah, I do. There was a bill in the North Carolina Assembly to put a stay on pipeline construction and also conduct further environmental impact studies on the solar farms. It was scheduled for a vote in the Senate, and it looked like it might just pass. I think Gardner panicked. That could have cost him the company. Look at the facts, San—four of the senators who supported the bill were at that dinner.

Three of them were hospitalized. The bill died on the Senate floor."

"If this is true, then Dvorak was working directly for I.U.S." I said, more to myself than to Wayne.

"Yes."

"How much of this can you prove?"

"Conclusively? Not much. But look."

He turned the computer to face me. It showed a grainy black-and-white video clip.

"This is the camera in the country club parking lot on Bald Head Island. Watch and tell me what you see."

I hit play. A white van pulled in and parked near the service entrance. There was a magnetic sign on the side for Peabody Refrigeration. A man in a uniform got out, a hat obscuring his hair and face, and took a small tool case out of the back of the van. He disappeared inside the building.

"Fast forward ten minutes," Wayne directed.

I did, and the man returned to the van. He loaded the tool case, then removed a pair of latex gloves and tossed them in the back as well. As he turned, there was the loud screech of a seagull landing on the roof near the camera. The man looked up, and I saw his face.

Francis Michael Holland.

"I called the country club. They have a full-time kitchen staff, and the manager said yeah, she remembered a man coming in to check on the walk-in fridge that morning—the same one where the salad was kept. I'm still looking for surveillance footage from Charleston. Then maybe I can get a buddy of mine in the police department to run facial recognition."

"You don't need it," I said. "I know who it is."

I told him about Chip Holland's checkered past, his role at I.U.S., and his connection to the Charleston victims. He pulled out his notebook, jotting down the basic facts, and I made no move to stop him. It was too late.

"The Charleston attack is different. It was definitely personal," I ended. "I think Holland was working on his own."

Wayne whistled.

"I can't imagine Gardner being very happy about Holland freelancing. I've got to hand it to you—this fills in all pieces, San. You are in the wrong line of work. You'd make a hell of a reporter."

"None of this is Alan's fault, Wayne," I said, and I didn't care if it sounded like I was pleading. "You can't run this story. It will destroy everything he has worked for."

"I'm sorry, San," he said, shaking his head, "but you're being naïve. Alan Culliver has the controlling interest in I.U.S. If he didn't know what was going on, he should have."

"He didn't," I insisted. "He didn't know Everett Dvorak worked for I.U.S. He didn't even know the man was a scientist until last night, and he definitely didn't know he had been killed."

He held his hand up. "Hang on a minute. Alan Culliver didn't know Dvorak was a scientist—but he did know him?"

I hesitated. "Not exactly. Alan followed his wife to a meeting with Dvorak. He thought she was having an affair. But I'm pretty sure she was continuing Jansen's investigation."

Wayne reopened up his notebook. "Maggie Culliver met with Dvorak? When was this?"

"You can put that down. None of this is on the record," I said angrily. He closed the pad and placed it on the table, raising both hands in mock surrender. I told him what Alan had seen and compared it to what I had gotten from Kathy Dvorak. "But it doesn't matter."

He shook his head. "Don't you get it? Jansen investigated, he died. Maggie investigated, and what happened? She found out about Dvorak, and that's probably what got her killed."

"She wasn't killed. The police—"

"The police dropped the charges against Alan. That doesn't mean she wasn't killed," Wayne asserted. "Who else knew about Maggie meeting Dvorak?"

"No one...." I began, but the words died on my lips. Alan Culliver told one person about that meeting—Jack Gardner.

"Alan called Gardner after he followed Maggie to Ocracoke, but it isn't what you think. He didn't know what Gardner was up to. He called for advice about a divorce lawyer. Maggie's death was an accident."

"Okay, it was an accident," Wayne repeated, but he was clearly unconvinced. "Look, San, I admit I could be wrong about Culliver. For all I know, he had no clue what was going on. But Dvorak—I'm sure Gardner gave him some cock-and-bull story about the purpose of his research, but any idiot would know you don't get that kind of dough for legitimate science. And Everett Dvorak was nobody's idiot. He might have lied to himself about it, but from what you've said, it sounds like he was considering getting out after his last meeting with Maggie. Maybe she convinced him. Or maybe he found out what Holland did, and that was the last straw."

The timeline fit. He resigned from I.U.S. shortly after the Charleston poisoning.

"Alan had nothing to do with it. I'm positive," I maintained.

"Fine. He's a choir boy. But if he really was clueless, he's in trouble. Jack Gardner is too smart to go down for this. I would bet he set up a contingency plan, someone else to take the blame. Whether Alan Culliver knew anything or not wouldn't matter. Either he takes the fall, or it gets pinned on Holland. Then Gardner can play the victim, take what's left of I.U.S., and start over."

"How can he blame Alan? He's retired. He hasn't had anything to do with daily operations for years."

Wayne gave me a pitying look. "Think about it—if Holland is the one who gave the police dirt about the Cullivers' marriage, Gardner was probably behind Alan's arrest. He could doctor up some memos, pin it all on Alan, and even if Alan denies it, who's going to believe an accused murderer?"

"But Alan was cleared."

"True. Which is what I meant about this being dangerous. If Alan knows about everything, he's been playing you. If he doesn't, he is a threat to Gardner's plan."

I froze. "You think Jack Gardner would try to kill Josh's uncle?"

"If he isn't in on it, yeah. Why not? He hasn't shown any hesitation about eliminating threats so far."

I rose abruptly, nearly knocking over my glass of tea.

"I've got to go."

"Whoa, hold on! You can't tell this to anyone," he said, getting up to block my exit. "If Gardner finds out anyone is on to him, he'll disappear, and he'll probably take all I.U.S.'s pennies with him."

I stared Wayne down. "Alan and Josh are out on Jack Gardner's fishing boat right now. I am not going to sit here while something happens to them."

"What do you think you're going to do? I told you, I don't have enough to go to the police. That's why I'm here to see the general. He was one of the men poisoned with E. coli at the Pentagon. I'm hoping he'll grease the wheels so I can get access to the reports from the North Carolina attack."

"This isn't about your story, Wayne. It's about the safety of people I care for. Are you going to help me or not?"

Wayne sighed. "I can give you Gardner's address. But San, I'm asking you not to say anything. Right now, it's in Gardner's best interest to wait and see if he can get away clean and keep doing business as usual. He won't make a move unless he thinks the walls are closing in. Alan is safe as long as Gardner thinks he's safe. Do you understand?"

His words were reasonable, the logic sound, but I chafed under the constraint.

"I understand. Now let me go."

Wayne broke the stand-off by stepping aside. He tore a page from his notebook and handed it to me.

"Here. Be careful. And call me."

"I will."

Wayne looked at me with troubled eyes. "You know, I asked you to meet me because I wanted to protect you, not throw you to the wolves."

"I know." I put my arms around him. He hugged me once, hard, then let me go.

"You always have been a pain in the ass," he said, but he smiled.

Chapter 28

I HADN'T COUNTED ON the gate.

Jack Gardner's house was on the sound side of Emerald Drive out on the coast. While most of the houses there were three-story beach homes, built side by side on tiny lots, there was a stretch of dense pine at the north end of the road with a few long driveways set far apart. Most had tall iron gates, including Gardner's.

I got out of the truck and looked down the gravel drive. It twisted to the left and disappeared into the trees. There was no house to be seen. I tried the gate, but it was locked. There was a keypad with a call button. I pushed it.

No one answered.

I had called Josh twice on the way here. Both times it had gone straight to voicemail. Remembering Wayne's warning, I left a message saying I was taking a drive and would try to meet up with them at Jack's house. I tried to keep the fear from my voice. But I had not gotten anything back, and panic threatened to overwhelm me. I wanted to be there when the boat came in. I had to know Josh was all right.

I backed up and parked the truck on the sand and gravel shoulder between Gardner's entrance and his neighbor's and got out. There was new growth on either side of Gardner's gate, short bushy pines crowded close enough to form a natural fence, but where they met the older trees there was enough space to squeeze through. I shouldered my purse, then maneuvered between the branches and onto Jack Gardner's property.

I walked along the edge of the driveway, torn between the hope someone would see me and the fear of what they might do to an unannounced and uninvited guest. It was perhaps a quarter-mile long with two sharp turns before it ended at a clearing. While the long driveway gave the property a feeling of seclusion, it was just an illusion. Once I reached the opening, I could look up and down the shore at homes in both directions, no more than a hundred yards apart. In front of me stretched Gardner's house, a sprawling modern Mediterranean built of sand-colored brick with a tile roof. Unlike its neighbors, it was not elevated on wooden stilts, but rather had concrete arches underneath that formed a sort of bridge-like platform on which the house perched. In the space between the arches a Porsche convertible and a Jeep Wrangler were parked.

The house itself was only one level, but it must have been two hundred feet long, with a huge brick staircase leading from the yard up to massive stained wooden doors. It looked generically European, like an Americanized copy of something you might see in Italy, cheapened by the giant concrete mermaids that stood looking painfully whimsical on either side of the entrance.

I walked up the steps slowly. There was a brass knocker shaped like a starfish which I let rise and fall. It made a loud, low sound, but no answering movement could be discerned within. I waited a few minutes, looking around me. The arched concrete foundation was larger than the house itself, allowing for a walled brick patio that stretched to the ends. When no one came, I took the walkway to the left and found it circled the building. Every wall included floor-to-ceiling windows, but the blinds were drawn so I could not make out anything inside.

When I reached the back of the house, the wind caught me, whipping the hair into my face. Here the patio opened to a much wider veranda, its floor patterned with tile, brick, and glass, containing tables, chairs, and lounges, all artfully placed around a tiled swimming pool/Jacuzzi. In the center, another concrete mermaid was pouring water from a giant shell she held above her head.

My eyes were drawn west, to Bogue Sound. Brick spiral stairs led from the veranda down to a paved path that ran along the riprapped seawall. Whitecaps rushed forward in angry lines, their tops torn violently by a relentless northerly wind, sending spray over the jagged gray rocks. Farther from shore they broke against a wooden dock, the yacht tied there bouncing back and forth like a child's tub toy against the rubber bumpers.

They were already back.

A man on board struggled to keep his footing as he hosed off the foredeck, his face and body obscured by a yellow slicker, but I could see from the way he moved he wasn't Josh or Alan.

"Sandi?"

The voice startled me, and I jumped.

"I'm sorry to sneak up on you like that," Jack Gardner said, smiling. "I saw someone on the patio, but I couldn't tell who it was."

His shaved head was still wet, and he wore a thick white terrycloth robe with a gold monogram. I tried to keep my face neutral and my voice light.

"I hope you don't mind. I called Josh to say I was taking a drive and thought I'd come by. I wanted to see your house. Alan said it was amazing, and I can see why. I buzzed in at the gate, and I knocked on the front door, but no one answered."

"My apologies. The call button isn't working, and I was in the shower," he said, but I caught him looking at me oddly. "We got back early. It was rough today and the fishing was less than spectacular. I'm afraid you missed Josh and Alan. They left about twenty minutes ago."

"Oh, then I'm sorry for bothering you. I'll go ahead and catch up with them back at the marina." I started to turn away, but Gardner put his hand on my forearm.

"No need to rush off. You wanted to see the house. I have to admit it is, as you say, amazing. I designed it myself. I won't let you leave without taking the tour and joining me for a drink."

He steered me inside two French doors to the living room, furnished with leather couches and a mix of pieces, some blonde wood, some iron and glass. The walls were hung with cubist artwork, all in tans and browns with an occasional jarring splash of red. It reminded me of an expensive business hotel, a place built for a purpose, without any aspirations to happiness or warmth or soul.

"What can I get you? Gin and tonic? Bourbon? Wine?"

He stood behind a dark brown granite bar, its surface reflecting the room and my host in a collage of disembodied images.

"Wine, thank you."

He poured a glass of red and poured himself some liquor from an engraved glass decanter.

"Cheers," he said, handing it to me.

I looked at the glass in my hand, and an icy dread gripped at my throat. I imagined microscopic creatures swimming in the dark liquid, multiplying and feeding....

"Is something wrong?" Jack asked.

I shivered. "No. I'm fine," I said, and sipped my wine.

"Do you like it? A merlot, Napa Valley, 2013. I'm told it's excellent, though I'm not a wine drinker myself."

"It's very good."

We drank for a few moments while the silence widened. I pretended to study the room, but I could feel him watching me.

"Please excuse me while I get on some clothes," he said. "Feel free to look around. I'll just be a minute."

I dropped my purse on a table by the couch and then walked back and forth awkwardly, not sure whether to sit or stand, finally choosing to lean on a high-backed chair near the window. Even through the triple-paned glass, I could hear the shriek of the wind. The water was a riot of waves, their foam crests spilling over the long pier as they broke. Darker clouds were rushing in, bringing with them the steely gray of twilight at mid-afternoon. A light flickered in the yacht's portholes, though the presence of another stranger did little to quiet my unease.

Men have told me my face is transparent. I could only hope Jack Gardner did not decipher what was written there.

As if he heard my thoughts, Alan Culliver's partner appeared again at my shoulder.

"Beautiful, isn't it? The unbound power of nature," he said, touching his glass to mine.

"But dangerous," I added.

Gardner smiled. "Indeed. Beauty is often dangerous. More wine?"

I declined, since I had barely touched the merlot he poured for me. He finished his own liquor in a single swallow, then went to the bar to refill his glass.

"You say you were out taking a drive?" he asked blandly. "It doesn't seem much of a day for that."

"I was bored. Not much else to do," I said, but it lacked the ring of truth.

"Hmm. Boredom can also be dangerous," Gardner observed, pouring from the decanter. "You know, Sandi, I've heard some interesting things about you," he added, and I was grateful he was not looking at me.

"Really? Like what?"

He lifted his drink slowly, eyes on the glass. "You are something of a private investigator."

I waited till he looked up and then shrugged, forcing a casual tone. "Not really. I prefer the term personal advocate. If someone has a problem, I try to help them. I'm not a detective."

"Then Chris must have been mistaken. Chris Holtz—I'm sure you know he works for me. He told me you were asking questions about Francis Holland. He got the impression you were doing some investigation of your own into Maggie's death."

I paused a moment before answering.

"I wouldn't call it an investigation. I was told a diving instructor gave the police information about Maggie. I knew Chris was her teacher, so naturally I assumed it was him. But he said it wasn't, so that would only leave Mr. Holland."

Gardner took a sip of his drink and made a satisfied sound. Then he moved toward me, motioning to the leather couch. I sat down and he took the chair opposite me.

"I take it you believe Francis provided evidence to support the district attorney's case."

"I can't think of anyone else in the position to do it," I answered, glancing out the window, chilled by a sudden thought. Could that be Holland I saw on the boat?

Jack caught my look and a small, amused smile played across his lips. He took another drink and leaned back comfortably. "Chip is no longer employed at I.U.S. He did some security work on the new plant through Chris's firm, but we were never what you would call close, so I'm afraid I can't speak to his motives. Since the charges were dropped, I assume you are comfortable the information he provided was false."

"Yes," I said, nodding. I sensed he was probing, testing to see what I knew or suspected.

"Of course, I'm sure you're aware by now Alan and Maggie were having problems. Did you know Alan even called me at one point to ask about my divorce attorney? Sad, isn't it, how people will deceive each other?"

His voice was smooth and pleasant, but there was a derisive glint in his eye. I didn't answer.

"But then, let's face it, Alan is no saint either. I'm sure you've realized that. He is, in fact, a man of many faults."

"Well, we all have faults," I said. His tone was starting to get under my skin. "But Alan did build I.U.S. from the ground up."

Gardner snorted. "Quite the opposite. He would have run I.U.S. into the ground if not for me."

I feigned surprise. "But wasn't the company in some trouble just this year? Some rumors about being on the verge of bankruptcy. It was a close call, wasn't it—your contract with Atlantic Power?"

Gardener waved his hand at me dismissively. "I don't know where you're getting your information, but that's a lie. Alan poured money into research projects that didn't bring in a dime, thousands of hours on failed models no one wanted. Because of him, Atlantic Power was our only way out, and he knew it."

This is where I should have told Gardner he was a genius, thanked him for the drink, and walked out the door. But my instinctive dislike of Jack Gardner had only deepened with every minute I spent in his presence, and I wanted nothing more than to wipe the smug expression from his face.

"But the contract was in trouble," I observed. "There was a concerted effort by environmental groups in North Carolina to put a stay on Atlantic's gas pipeline. The state legislature was considering a bill to shut the whole thing down."

"Irrelevant. It was defeated, as I'm sure you know."

"Yes. It was convenient the state senators who opposed the project didn't make it out of the hospital to vote."

Gardner's jaw tightened, but his voice remained smooth. "A fortunate coincidence."

"Like the death of Everett Dvorak?"

I couldn't believe I said it. The words electrified the air between us. Gardner tensed and leaned forward, as if to push himself toward me, but the moment passed. He sat back against the cushions, the smile once again pasted on his face.

"Interesting you should bring him up. Did Alan tell you he was the one who recommended we employ Everett Dvorak?"

"Alan didn't even know who Dvorak was," I argued.

"Really?" his lip curled. "Are you sure about that?"

I didn't answer. Gardner stood.

"It does make one wonder, doesn't it?" Jack Gardner said, moving toward me. "You know, Sandi, I have a confession to make. Alan and I are not particularly fond of each other. We don't call each other on a regular basis. We don't Snapchat or send each other photos on Instagram. We don't even text. In fact, there are only a few times in the past year or so I have heard from Alan directly. And do you know what those were?"

I shook my head.

"One was last winter, when Alan went to see Bart Jansen. If the visit were only about Bart's relationship with Maggie, why would I have been included? Do you suppose he called me because he just needed a buddy to talk to, given that has never been my role in Alan's life? Another call came when Alan followed Maggie to Ocracoke. Do you suppose he just wanted advice about attorneys? Or was he telling me these pieces of information for another reason?"

"How should I know?" I retorted, but the seed had been sown.

"Oh, I think you might guess. I.U.S. is a private company, you know, owned by Alan and myself and our employees. We pay a percentage of our profits in dividends at the end of each year, but beyond that and salaries, the money we make is reinvested in the company. The worth of shares has grown exponentially. The company could not buy back Alan's interest at anything near its appraised value. And if the Atlantic Power contract didn't go through, the net worth of all of our shareholders would have dropped significantly."

"But it didn't."

"No. And the person who benefited most from that was Alan Culliver. You can understand why it might have concerned him, his wife meeting Everett Dvorak. Food for thought, isn't it?"

Wayne was right. Gardner was poised to lay the blame for everything on Alan, and he was hoping I might be just naïve enough to help him do it. And while I was certain Jack Gardner was the one responsible for the food poisonings and for orchestrating the deaths of Dvorak and Jansen, a tinge of suspicion seeped in to color my feelings about Alan. Had he warned Gardner about the investigation? If I could not dismiss Gardner's veiled accusations, what chance did Josh's uncle have when Wayne's story broke?

"Thank you for the drink," I said, hoping he did not see the tremor in my hand as I placed my glass on the table. "I'm sorry to have interrupted your afternoon."

I rose and Gardner stepped back slightly, once again smiling.

"Not at all. It has been…instructional, I think, for both of us. Let me walk you to the door."

He gestured toward the hallway, and I walked in front of him. We stopped in the foyer and he unlocked a deadbolt and swung one of the massive doors open.

"It is up to you, of course, but it might be better for everyone if we kept this conversation private," Gardner suggested smoothly.

"I'll have to think about it," I answered. "The FBI has already been to see me about Dr. Dvorak's death."

That was a piece of information he did not know.

"If you don't mind me asking, why would they have come to you?"

I studied his face.

"Because I'm the one who found the body."

He raised an eyebrow. It was only the slightest reaction, but enough to say he was surprised by the information. He had no way of knowing I worked for Kathy Dvorak.

"Thank you for the heads up," he said. "Drive safely."

I stepped onto the front veranda, and the door shut solidly behind me. This side of the house was sheltered from the wind, but the sky had grown darker and was spitting rain. I made my way slowly down the long brick stairs, lost in thought as I replayed our conversation, ignoring the drops as they fell on my shoulders and dampened my short hair. Had Alan lied about the reasons behind his phone calls to Gardner?

If he lied about one thing, who's to say he did not lie about everything?

I started down the driveway, the rain and the waves behind me all but drowning out the sound of gravel crunching under my feet, so I was not aware of footsteps behind me until a deep voice spoke in my ear.

"Come with me," it said.

I whirled around and stared into the eyes of Chris Holtz. Hat, yellow slicker, blue jeans—the figure I saw on the boat. Beside him trotted Ripley.

"Sorry, I thought you heard me," he said, reading my look. "Jack told me you parked outside the gate and asked me to give you a ride out. It's starting to rain."

My first instinct was to decline. I liked Holtz, but he was sub-contracted to I.U.S., and as much as he seemed to be an upright guy, there was no way to be sure how deeply he was involved in Gardner's plans. He had obviously reported our conversation on the dock to Jack. On the other hand, he might let slip information about I.U.S. I didn't already know. Besides, the dog was wagging her tail, and the rain was picking up.

"Thank you. I'd appreciate that."

I followed him to the Jeep under the house. He held open the passenger door and we both waited while Ripley jumped in and took her place on the back seat. Then I climbed in and he shut the door behind me. Ripley put her head next to mine, and I petted her while Chris got in. I noticed he seemed uncomfortable, avoiding looking at me and Ripley as he started the car. He put it in gear, eased backward, and then stopped.

"I want to apologize. I'm sorry about the other day," he said. "You probably thought I was being rude, but what you said about Doc, it kind of threw me."

"Doc? You mean Everett Dvorak?"

He nodded. "I guess it doesn't matter now, with him being dead, but he did some research for I.U.S., something classified. He was a little, you know, fussy, but he was basically a nice old guy. He decided to leave the company, and Jack sent me to talk to him. I don't know what went on between him and Jack. Doc wouldn't tell me. But he wouldn't even consider going back. It upset him to even talk about it." Chris hesitated and ran a hand across his face. "He told me the past was the past, and he was going to enjoy what was left of his life. So, you can understand why it kinda' shook me when you told me about the accident."

I fit this into what Katya and Brenda saw. Chris Holtz was the first visitor on the day Dvorak died.

When I didn't respond, he gave the Jeep a little gas and we backed into the driveway. I waited until he turned the wheel and headed toward the gate before I spoke.

"Chris, it wasn't an accident."

He looked over at me sharply. "What wasn't?"

Ripley's ears stood up at his tone.

"Everett Dvorak's death. It wasn't an accident. The FBI is investigating it as a homicide."

His hands clenched the wheel tightly.

"They think he was killed the same day you went to see him. A neighbor saw a second man go down to the boat that afternoon."

We were at the gate. The Jeep must have triggered a sensor, because it slowly opened in front of us. Chris stared out the front windshield. "The other man—did your friend say what he looked like?"

I hesitated.

"I need to know," he said, voice tight. In the back seat, Ripley moved nervously.

"He had red hair," I said.

Chris pressed his lips together as if to suppress a sound. This was no act—he really didn't know what had been happening around him. I made the decision without thinking.

"There is a reason the FBI is investigating instead of the local police. Everett Dvorak was an expert in biological agents." Chris turned toward me, face clouded. I softened my voice and continued. "He wasn't working on drone technology for I.U.S. He was working on a biological weapon, a salmonella strain. It was used to poison people who opposed the Atlantic Power contract."

A strong hand gripped my arm, fingers biting into the flesh beneath my sweater. "How do you know this?" he asked.

My throat tightened.

"I can't tell you. But I know."

He released me and raised his fist once, smashing it into the dashboard. I jumped back and Ripley whined. A minute passed while Holtz's breath came in heavy gasps, the struggle for control evident, and then Ripley made a low, keening sound and nuzzled his shoulder. He turned to her at once.

"It's okay, girl," he whispered, softly cradling Ripley's head in his hands. When her tail began to wag, he reached across my lap and opened the passenger door.

"Thank you," he said quietly.

I got out of the car and walked through the gate as the ex-SEAL swung the Jeep around and headed back toward the house. The last thing I saw was Ripley's head still turned toward me, watching me through the back window. Then the rain started to fall in sheets, and I ran for the truck. I had left the doors unlocked, so it wasn't until I clambered inside and reached for the keys that I realized what was missing.

I left my purse, along with the truck keys and my cell phone, in Jack Gardner's house.

Chapter 29

I LISTENED TO THE rain drumming on the roof and hood, disgusted with my carelessness. The last thing I wanted to do was walk back to that house. It wasn't the weather that frightened me, nor was it Gardner—it was the look in Chris Holtz's eyes when I got out of his car. I knew from our conversation on the dock he believed wholeheartedly in I.U.S., in its mission and its support for veterans, and that idealistic view had just been shattered. If Holtz was an honorable man—and I believed he was— he would not be able to look the other way. Gardner had lied to him and used him, and these were violations of a moral code Chris had spent a military career upholding.

I would not want to be Jack Gardner right now.

I was still trying to decide what to do thirty minutes later when headlights flashed in front of me. A black Escalade pulled in front, and through the fogged windshield I watched as Josh jumped out and came around to the passenger door.

"What's wrong?" he asked as he slid into the seat beside me.

For a moment I vacillated between pouring out everything and saying nothing at all. There were things Josh needed to know, but this was not the time or place. It was a long and complicated story, and Alan was sitting in the car just a few feet away.

"Nothing's wrong," I assured him. "I drove here to meet you when you came back from fishing, and the gate wasn't working. You were already gone, so Chris Holtz gave me a ride back out. That's when I realized I left my purse with my keys and phone inside the house."

Josh gave a sigh of relief. "Man, I thought something had happened to you. My phone got wet and died when we were out on the boat. I took it apart to dry out, and we were just about home when I put it back together and got your message. I tried to call, but you didn't answer, and finally Alan called Jack. He said you'd stopped by but had already left. I was afraid you'd gotten in an accident or the truck broke down or something. We backtracked thinking we'd find you."

"I'm sorry I scared you," I said, giving his hand a squeeze.

"That's okay. I'm just glad you're all right."

"I'm fine. I was just waiting for the rain to slow down so I could walk back in and get my purse."

"Alan got the gate code this morning. He'll drive us back in," he said. "Are you sure everything is okay? You still seem kind of frazzled."

I flushed under his scrutiny.

"Sandi, what's going on?"

Just then the Escalade's lights went off and the driver's door opened. While we were talking the rain had slackened to a light mist.

"I need you to trust me," I said hurriedly. "There's a lot going on you don't know, and I can't go into it now. When we get back to *Serenity*, I'll tell you everything. Please, Josh."

He glanced up at Alan, moving toward us, then back at me.

"Must be some story," he said. "Let's go get your purse."

If Alan thought there was anything odd about my visit to Gardner's, he didn't show it. He was relaxed and pleasant, and as soon as Josh explained I had left my keys inside, he offered to take me back to the house. The three of us returned to the Escalade as the rain ended.

"Jack said the call button is corroded," he explained, punching in the numbers as he pulled to the gate. "He's got a repairman coming out next week to work on it. What did you think of the house?"

"It's incredible," I answered.

"That's a good word for it. Kind of much for my taste," Alan said with a laugh. "But I guess to each his own."

As we neared the house, I saw Holtz's Jeep was again parked underneath. Alan pulled around the side to the paved walkway, and the three of us got out. The wind had already begun to die down, the waves no longer sending spray over the seawall. My eyes were drawn to a shape silhouetted against the riprap. I thought at first a cover had blown off the veranda furniture, but as we drew closer, it took on a more definitive outline.

Alan, who had been saying something about the morning fishing trip, suddenly froze, his gaze following mine.

"Oh, my God," he said.

Jack Gardener's body lay grotesquely twisted on the jagged rocks.

Josh started forward, but his movement was arrested by Chris Holtz's voice above us.

"There's nothing you can do. He's already dead."

Chapter 30

CHRIS HOLTZ SAT ON the sofa in Jack Gardner's living room, Ripley at his feet. Her body was alert, her eyes on her master. I could overhear Alan in the kitchen, talking to Josh's father on the phone. Josh carried in a glass of water, placing it on the coffee table in front of the former SEAL, then pulled a chair next to Holtz.

"Tell me again what happened."

The former head of I.U.S. security shrugged his shoulders tiredly. "It's just what I said. We had some words, and I told him I quit. He got in front of me, started yelling that I couldn't go, that I owed him, and I wouldn't make it without him. I tried to get past, and he shoved me. Ripley bit his arm. It wasn't her fault—she thought she was protecting me, it's what she's trained to do. He was backing up, trying to shake her off, and when she let go, he fell over the porch wall."

"And then what?" Josh prompted.

"I went down, looked for a pulse, didn't get anything. I did CPR for maybe four, five minutes, but I knew it wouldn't do any good. He was gone. His neck was broken."

It was the same story he told us on the veranda, and it fit with Gardner's torn shirt sleeve and the tooth marks on his arm. Josh homed in on the one thing Chris had not said.

"What was the argument about?"

Holtz shot a glance at me, then looked back at Josh.

"I heard about some things Jack did. He admitted he'd done them. I couldn't work for him after that."

Josh's gaze flicked from Chris to me. I looked down at my hands.

"What things?"

This was from Alan, standing in the doorway. He was still holding his cell phone.

Chris hesitated.

"If it has to do with I.U.S., Chris, I have a right to know," Josh's uncle said firmly. "I just got off the phone with my brother at the FBI. He told me they found Chip Holland's body last night in a hotel room in Atlantic Beach."

"He's dead?" Chris asked, and again he darted a look at my face.

"The preliminary report is calling it a suicide, but there is an ongoing investigation."

The big man seemed to shrink against the cushions. "I think I need a lawyer."

"And we'll get you one, but right now you need to tell us exactly what Jack did."

Chris reached for the water and took a swallow, then carefully placed the glass back on the table. For all his distress, I noticed his hand did not shake. He focused his attention on Alan.

"I don't know much. Jack hired me for I.U.S. when he built his new plants. He was my first real contract, so I pulled Chip in to assist. Everything was up and running, no problems. Then one day last winter, I don't know the exact date, Jack called us in and said some CIA bureaucrat had a beef with you and Maggie, and he was retaliating by pulling I.U.S.'s security clearance. That would shut down the R and D and all the military contracts, and a lot of vets were going to lose their jobs. He said you were going to try and smooth things over with the guy, but if that didn't work, he wanted us to handle it."

I moved in my seat.

"Not anything physical," he added hastily, turning to me, "more like pressure. I didn't like it, but I've done worse under orders, and this didn't seem like that big a deal."

Josh looked at his uncle. "I thought you went to see Jansen about Aunt Maggie?"

"I did," Alan insisted. "I didn't know anything about pulling our security clearance."

"Go on," I said to Chris.

"Anyway, Jack gave Chip some dirt on Jansen—I don't know what, I didn't ask—and we headed up to Maryland as back up." He looked directly at Alan. "I figured you called Jack to say you didn't have any luck, so he told us to pay Jansen a visit. Chip told me to give him ten minutes, said he thought the two of us might spook the guy too much. He said the dirt he had was something really personal, and it might be better if he talked to Jansen alone. Next thing I know, Chip's back in the car, says we need to move, guy had a heart attack and dropped dead while Chip was talking to him. I wanted to go back in, call 911, but Chip said there would be questions and it would end up hurting the company. I went along. At the time, it made sense to me, but now...."

Josh was grim. "You think Chip Holland killed Bart Jansen."

"I don't know. Chris had... skills. He was into the history of warfare, you know, ancient tribal stuff. He told me once about this poison, curare—I think it was South American—that Indians used on arrows to paralyze their victims. He knew how to make it, told me he'd used it once on a mission and his CO never found out. It could have been bullshit, but with Chip you couldn't tell."

Another piece locked into place. Jansen basically drowned in three feet of water. There was no indication of a struggle, no defensive wounds, no tracks on the shoreline. Because there was no need. Holland must have injected Jansen with curare before he pushed him off the dock. I would bet the same poison was in the empty syringe found in Dvorak's car.

"Anyway, Chip was pretty screwed up after his last tour, got kicked out of the service, and I knew he could be a loose cannon," Chris continued. "I could see him getting in a fight, you know, but I never really believed he'd kill a guy outside of combat."

He glanced at me again, and I knew he was thinking of Everett Dvorak.

"Is that what the fight with Jack was about? Chip Holland?" Josh asked.

Chris nodded. "More or less. One of my jobs at I.U.S. was to oversee protection for classified employees. One of them quit, and Jack asked me to go talk to him. Today I found out Chip Holland went to see him after I left, and then the guy drowned, just like Jansen."

Alan Culliver's mouth opened soundlessly as he made the connection between the man Holtz described and the body I found.

"Who did Chip Holland go to see?" he asked haltingly.

"The Doc. Everett Dvorak."

Alan collapsed.

Chris and Josh were both on their feet and eased Culliver back on the seat. His eyes fluttered and opened, and Chris pressed water to his lips. Alan pushed him away and struggled to sit up.

"What...what was Dvorak doing for I.U.S.?" he whispered.

Chris hesitated. "It was above my pay grade. His lab was high security, sterile, and he worked alone, no one but him in or out. He came for three weeks at a time. I met him at the gate when he arrived, secured his personal items, and escorted him out when his time was up. But I never went in the lab."

"Sandi?" Josh asked. He had seen the look I exchanged with Chris. "This is what was in the notebook?"

I nodded. "Yes. You were right. The abbreviation was for salmonella enterica. Dvorak was working on a new strain. It was a biological weapon."

Alan buried his face in his hands.

Chris went on, this time talking to Josh. "Sandi told me about Doc's work, that it was used to poison people. She said Chip had been at Doc's boat the day he was killed. I had to know if she was telling the truth."

Josh frowned at me. "When did you find all this out?"

"I wasn't sure until today," I said, which was true. Josh turned back to Chris.

"So, you told Jack Gardner what Sandi said."

"Not at first. I asked Jack if he knew about Doc's work, and he said I wouldn't understand, it was too complicated. The way he said it got to me, talking down to me like I was some kind of idiot. I asked if he knew Chip Holland killed Jansen and the doc—there wasn't anything complicated about that."

He took a painful breath. "I expected him to deny it, but he just laughed and said it was the cost of doing business, and a soldier should understand. I guess that was what pissed me off the most. I told him I quit, and he started screaming I wasn't allowed to leave, I was in too deep to walk away, and that's when he shoved me, and Ripley attacked him."

Spent, Chris sat down heavily on the sofa. Alan, who had not looked up once during this part of Holtz's story, raised his head.

"I'm sorry, Alan," he said, looking over at I.U.S.'s surviving partner. "I didn't mean for him to die, but I'm not sorry he's dead."

There was a long pause before Alan spoke.

"If this gets out, we're finished."

Josh looked at his uncle with a mix of worry and shame. I understood what he was thinking: After all he had heard, Alan's first thought was for his business, not the people who had been hurt.

Chris looked up in alarm. "But that's not fair. It wasn't the company—it was Jack."

"It doesn't matter," Alan said, shaking his head. "The company is legally liable for the actions of its CEO. We're going to be crucified."

"I'll take the blame," Holtz began.

In the distance, I heard a siren. Andrew Culliver must have alerted local law enforcement after Alan's call. There wasn't much time, and I did not want Chris Holtz to become a scapegoat to save I.U.S. Not when I knew it would accomplish nothing.

"It won't matter, Chris. The Washington Post is going to print a story linking I.U.S. to an E. coli poisoning and two salmonella outbreaks, including one that helped Atlantic Power," I said.

Alan turned on me, panicked. "What do you mean? How can you know that?"

I didn't answer him, but instead walked over to Josh. "That's why I called you. I met Wayne in Jacksonville this morning. He's got most of this already, and what he doesn't know, Chris just filled in. Wayne said Jack might lay the blame for everything on your uncle. I was afraid Jack might try to hurt both of you."

Josh looked at me as if he didn't quite know who I was.

"I can't believe this," Alan muttered to himself. "This is a nightmare. What am I supposed to do? We have to think of some way to fix this."

Josh knelt beside his uncle. "Don't try to fix anything. You have to tell the truth," he entreated. "You can't cover this up. You and Chris and the veterans who work for I.U.S. are Gardner's victims, and you need to make that part of the story. There's nothing else to do."

The sirens were close now, and Ripley was becoming agitated. Chris held the dog to her, murmuring in her ear. Josh walked toward the front door as we heard car doors opening.

Chapter 31

THE STORY NEVER BROKE.

The police who arrived at Gardner's house were told the scene was under the jurisdiction of the FBI. Neeman and his agents arrived shortly after, and Chris was taken to the resident agency field office in Wilmington for questioning. Alan insisted on accompanying him, though he was still shaken and in no condition to drive the ninety miles from Emerald Isle. Josh offered to take Alan's Escalade to Wilmington, saying I could drive the truck home. He avoided looking at me when he spoke.

I started for the door, but Neeman pulled me to a corner and gestured for two of his agents to stand nearby. It is an understatement to say he was surprised to find me at the site of yet another homicide—and by surprised, I don't mean in a wow, what a coincidence kind of way. My presence clearly irritated him.

"I am going to ask you this one time, Miss Beck. Do you have, on your person or elsewhere, any material—?" I opened my mouth, but he raised a hand. "Not yet. We've played this game before. By material I mean anything, Miss Beck, down to the smallest scrap of paper. Do you have material or information pertinent to this investigation? Consider carefully before you speak."

"I don't have anything," I answered truthfully. "Sorry."

The agent dismissed me with a scornful nod and motioned for the two officers to drive me out to my vehicle. Alan was on the phone with the I.U.S. legal counsel, and Josh walked with us to the officers' car. I knew he had questions, but there wasn't much I could say—not with FBI agents a foot away. He bent down and gave me a kiss goodbye. It was barely a brush of his lips.

"I don't know when I'll be home," he said, but there was not much warmth in it.

"Text me," I said. "Let me know what's going on."

He half-smiled, his green eyes troubled.

"It sounds like you know more about it than I do."

I watched as he walked away.

I went back to the boat and waited, but an hour went by, then two, and I did not hear from Josh. I lay down on the V-berth, closed my eyes, and fell into a coma-like sleep. When I awoke it was dark, and my phone was ringing.

"I don't know what's going on, but all hell broke loose after I went to see the general," Wayne said when I answered. "They took my phone and I got locked in a room for hours. When they brought it back, my editor was on it. It's the first time I've ever heard him sound intimidated. He told me we have a command appearance at FBI headquarters tomorrow morning. They're putting me on a military transport tonight."

I told him what had happened at Gardner's house. When I finished, he groaned.

"What about don't tell anyone didn't you understand? For God's sake, San. Everything I told you this morning was supposed to be a secret."

"Are you blaming me?" I asked sharply.

"Blaming you? No. I'm blaming myself for telling you anything. It's just in your nature to interfere in people's lives. It's like a gift. At least now I know what's going on. I've gotta' go—they say the plane is ready. I'll call you after the meeting tomorrow. Try to stay out of trouble till then."

I stared into the darkness, my mind on Wayne's words. He was right. If I had listened to him, I never would have gone to Jack Gardner's. If I had kept my mouth shut, Jack Gardner wouldn't be lying on a slab in some morgue, Chris Holtz wouldn't be sitting in an interrogation room, and Josh would not be ninety miles away.

I was sorry for at least two out of three.

My screen lit with a single tone—a text from Josh. Chris was still being held for questioning, and now Neeman wanted Alan to come in and answer questions in the morning. The attorney for I.U.S. was also on the way. Because of the distance, Josh and Alan were getting a hotel room for the night.

A text, not a phone call, cold and impersonal. I tried not to read too much into it.

I lay back down and tried to close my eyes, but my sleep was fitful at best. I finally gave up at 6 a.m. and dressed, spent my morning cleaning the already-clean cabin of *Serenity*, and checked my phone every ten minutes. I took a walk and got some lunch, then took another walk along the waterfront. Finally, with nothing left to do, I sat in the cabin and stared at the Christmas tree, my mind too restless to focus on a book.

Around 4:00 p.m. I heard a knock on the hull. I stuck my head out of the hatch eagerly, sure it was Josh, only to find Neeman standing there, minus his signature dark suit. He was wearing jeans and a navy windbreaker and looked painfully uncomfortable.

"Would you take a walk with me, Miss Beck?"

I was going to ask if I had any choice but decided against it. I grabbed a jacket and joined him on the dock. I noticed there were dark circles beneath his sunglasses. It looked like neither of us had gotten much sleep.

"What's going to happen to Chris?" I asked.

Neeman ignored the question and instead strode purposefully toward the end of the pier. I followed alongside, waiting for an answer. He stopped in front of an empty slip.

"I want you to understand, if it were up to me, you would be charged with obstructing an investigation," he began, looking out over the water. "But it is not up to me. I am here to remind you that everything involving this case is classified, and you will be held criminally liable if you so much as breathe a word about it to any other individual, now or at any point in the future. Do you understand?"

It just didn't come off as well without the suit.

"Tell me what's happening with Chris Holtz."

"This isn't a negotiation."

I waited.

"He is being released. Mr. Gardner's death was an accident," he said finally, voice clipped.

"And what about the rest of it? Dvorak, Holland, the salmonella?" I pressed.

"Miss Beck, you will not be receiving any further information, nor will you seek any further information. Your involvement is at a conclusion. If you do not agree to those terms, I will place you under arrest."

"You know, you really need to work on your people skills."

The barb had no effect. Neeman removed his sunglasses and trained his coal black eyes on me.

"I need to hear you say the words, Miss Beck. Now."

I sighed. "Fine. I understand. I'll carry the secret to my grave."

"That is an encouraging thought. Take care of yourself, Miss Beck," he said, and he turned on his heel and walked away.

"You, too, Agent," I called after him, but he didn't look back.

I didn't hear from Josh until eight that night, and again it was a text. Josh and his uncle were stopping for dinner on the way back to *Andromeda* but did not expect to get in until at least eleven.

He told me not to wait up.

This was too much. Any guilt I felt was replaced by anger. What had I done that was so wrong? I did not create this mess, despite what Wayne said. My involvement came as a result of doing the job Kathy Dvorak hired me to do, and I could not have foreseen it would intersect with Alan Culliver's company. As for Jack Gardner, his death was an accident, and I wasn't going to waste any tears over him.

Wayne called me a half-hour later to tell me about his meeting.

"It was the carrot and stick approach," he said acerbically, "though more stick than carrot. Big Brother told us he was appealing to our sense of patriotism, and if we didn't drop the story, they'd bury us."

After that initial threat, the government offered an olive branch in the form of exclusive information on an alternate story. Then the director of the FBI came in, and Wayne was sent to a waiting room while the man spoke privately to Wayne's editor for another twenty minutes. The Post is known for its support of journalistic freedom, but whatever leverage the government brought to bear worked this time. Wayne's editor killed the story and agreed to run a sanitized, Justice Department-dictated version instead.

"I had a visit from the FBI, too," I said, telling him what had happened. "I guess that's the end of it."

Wayne didn't sound as upset as I would have expected. "San, as much as I hate to admit it, Big Brother might be right. Writing about these attacks would be giving a blueprint to copycats and terrorists. The intelligence services need to figure out where the cracks are in the system and plug them up before anybody knows about this."

"That's unusually altruistic of you," I said.

"The thing is, I wasn't ready to run it. I didn't have enough evidence yet, and I wasn't going to get any cooperation from the government. With almost everybody involved already dead, I was running out of sources. Besides," he laughed, "the FBI gave me some front-page stuff instead, enough for a series. I'm working on it now. I can almost smell a Pulitzer."

At least some things never changed.

I watched an old movie on Netflix and went to bed, never hearing Josh and Alan come home. When I woke at 8 a.m., it was raining, both the truck and the Escalade were gone, and *Andromeda*'s companionway door was locked from the outside. It was the only way I knew they had been there at all.

Another day of waiting, with nothing to do.

I dressed and put on a slicker, then walked in the rain to a coffee shop a few blocks away. There was a paper rack with local papers, along with a few national dailies like the New York Times and the Washington Post. I paid for the Post and a cappuccino and sat down to read the front page. As expected, there was nothing about I.U.S., though there was a column with Wayne's byline. It was the government-sanctioned version of events, tying the recent salmonella outbreaks to contaminated water at an unnamed processing facility. According to the FDA, the problem had been remedied and the public could safely eat salad greens again. It was a good cover, and less messy than the truth.

I flipped through the pages. On page A eighteen there was a brief piece about the accidental death of I.U.S. CEO Jack Gardner. He reportedly fell from the balcony of his Emerald Isle home during severe weather. No other names were included in the article. I combed through the rest of the paper.

Francis Holland's death was never mentioned. Perhaps he killed himself, as Alan said. Or perhaps Gardner killed him. It didn't matter. He was effectively erased.

All the loose ends neatly tied up. Except for one thing.

I was still bothered by something Jack Gardner said.

It had been lingering at the back of my mind for the past two days. Yes,

Gardner was a liar. Yes, he had wanted to manipulate me. But I couldn't shake the feeling that when he talked about Alan Culliver, at least some of what he said was the truth.

Gardner was I.U.S.'s fixer; Alan said as much himself. He knew the man as well as anyone. Gardner claimed Alan called him about Jansen. That, at least, must have been accurate; how else could he have known to send Chris and Chip to Jansen's house that day? Yet Alan had lied about it, and I thought I knew why.

There was only one reason to call your fixer, and that was to have him fix your problems.

That made Alan Culliver responsible for Bart Jansen's murder.

Chapter 32

WHEN I GOT BACK to *Serenity*, Josh was sitting in my cabin. He waited until I hung up the wet slicker, then motioned me to the seat across from him.

"Sit down. We need to talk."

There was no tenderness in his voice. He sounded worn-out.

"I want you to tell me everything. I don't care if I've heard some of it before. I feel like there are things you've been keeping from me since you met me in Norfolk. Am I right?"

I thought about Sallie Hathaway.

"Yes."

"Then I want you to start there, at the very beginning. Are you willing to do that?"

I heard the unspoken alternative.

I told him everything: Sallie Hathaway's suggestion of an affair, his mother's confession, every piece of information I had put together, many of them already known to him, my belief Maggie had been investigating Dvorak, and every conversation I had with Wayne, including the one in the Jacksonville airport. Everything… except what Jack Gardner said about Alan.

Josh listened closely, without comment. I couldn't read his expression when I finished.

"Thank you for telling me," he said.

"But?" I asked, because the word was there, even if was unspoken.

232 - Ann Eichenmuller

"But I wish you had shared this sooner."

The cold way he said it frightened me.

"This is not an excuse, Josh, but I didn't know most of it until recently. And you haven't been around."

I waited, but he didn't respond, his gaze fixed on the floor.

"Do you want to call off our trip?" I asked finally.

He looked at me in surprise. "No. Do you?"

"I don't know. I feel like we're broken."

He rose and came to stand in front of me.

"You need to give me a minute, Sandi. I'm still trying to figure this whole thing out. But it hasn't changed how I feel about you."

He reached out his hand and pulled me up, and I relaxed in his arms.

Over the next few days our relationship returned to what it had been before his uncle came, but we were cautious with each other, and several times I caught him staring at me thoughtfully, then quickly looking away. We were supposed to start the next leg of our journey on the twenty-first to be in Myrtle Beach for Christmas, yet we still had not discussed whether we were taking one boat or two. We avoided the topic, the state of our relationship too fragile for an argument. That, and the doubts I harbored about Josh's uncle, made me jittery and nervous, and the more I tried to hide how I felt, the worse it became. I lost five pounds in four days without even trying.

"Your mother's going to think I don't feed you," Josh said one evening, watching as I rolled out dough for appetizers. He had invited Alan for dinner that night. It was the sixteenth, my birthday, but that was a fact I kept to myself.

"Believe me, she'll take care of it. I gain ten pounds every time I visit."

"I hope you're right," he said. "I'm going to go pick up the food. I'll be back in a half hour."

He gave me a quick kiss on the forehead as he left.

I filled the dough with brie, put the cookie sheet in the oven, and set the timer for twenty minutes. We had ordered steamed shrimp and clams for dinner, so there was little preparation left to do. I pulled out my laptop to check my email and noticed I still had the Dvorak folder on the desktop. There was no point in keeping it any longer. The FBI had released all of Everett's assets, wisely avoiding a public battle with his widow, and Kathy no longer needed my help.

I opened the folder to be certain I hadn't accidentally saved something unrelated there before deleting. My eye was caught by the row of PDF articles I downloaded while researching the scientist's background. More out of boredom than anything else, I clicked on the first one. It was a five-year-old front page from the Military Times, with the headline "New Antidote Will Make Chemical Weapon Obsolete." I had never read it, only scanned the headline and first paragraph, since it covered the work of a team of researchers rather than focusing on Dr. Dvorak. They had perfected a gas capable of counteracting several deadly nerve agents that, though banned internationally, had recently been used against civilians in the Middle East. Now I read through the rest of the article, which went on to talk about the necessity of better delivery systems for antidotes like this one. The team was working with the military and private companies to develop a drone capable of tactically delivering and dispersing the airborne antidote during a chemical weapons attack. Beneath was a group photo of men and women standing behind a table which held a three-foot unmanned aerial vehicle. I glanced at it and was about to close the document when my mind registered what I had seen.

In the center of the photo stood Alan Culliver, his arm draped around the shoulder of a white-coated scientist standing next to him.

The scientist was Everett Dvorak.

I heard noise on the deck, and Alan slid back the hatch, calling out a hello and brandishing two bottles of wine. I closed the laptop and jumped up.

"Can you grab these, Sandi? I don't think I can make it down the ladder holding them."

I took the bottles and busied myself in opening one as Alan came down into the cabin. I didn't trust myself to look at him.

"Something smells good."

"Those are hors d'oeuvres," I said, struggling for a normal tone. "Josh went to pick up the shrimp and clams. He should be back in few minutes."

"Great. I'm going to take a seat, if you don't mind. It's been a long day. I've been at the plant since six this morning, and I have to fly up to our Maryland lab for some meetings tomorrow. I'm afraid I'm going to have to make it an early night."

I handed him a glass of wine. I tried to smile, but the muscles in my face were frozen.

"What about the two of you? What are your plans? Can you stick around for Christmas?"

"No," I said, turning away and moving back to the galley. "We're leaving in four days."

I pulled out the cutting board, got vegetables out of the fridge, and began chopping them for a salad I hadn't planned on making. A few minutes passed in silence, then Alan cleared his throat. I raised my eyes and found he was staring at me.

"Is something wrong?" he asked.

"No," I responded quickly, resuming my chopping. The sharp staccato sound of the knife as it hit the plastic cutting board seemed to echo in the cabin. Alan moved on the settee, and I heard my laptop slide to the floor.

"Oh, Sandi, I'm sorry," he said, reaching for it. I watched in horror as he pulled it up by the corner and the computer opened. The screen lit up at once.

I put down the knife as Alan looked at the photo and then over at me. "Ah," he said.

He rose and started toward me.

"I can explain."

I held up my hand as if to ward him off. "No. Don't. You lied, Alan. About everything."

"Sandi, you can't believe that. Just because I once met Dr. Dvorak—"

I cut him off. "Did you lie about the reason for your visit to Jansen?"

His lips thinned. "Is that what Jack Gardner told you?"

"Answer the question."

He sighed. "It's complicated."

"It's a yes or no question."

He smiled tiredly. "Nothing is really a yes or no question, Sandi. It was what I told you before—Bart was calling Maggie all the time. She was behaving strangely, asked me what I knew about any problems between the Pentagon and I.U.S. I thought it was Jansen's influence, that he knew something negative about the company. I wanted to know what was going on."

"So, you told Gardner."

"Yes. I thought maybe there was some issue he hadn't told me about. It was his idea for me to go. He suggested I talk to Jansen myself, find out if the phone calls had anything to do with the way Maggie was behaving."

"Why didn't you just ask your wife?"

He twisted his mouth in a painful smile.

"You should understand. You were married. I didn't want to make an accusation…I didn't want to bring up something when I didn't know where it would lead. We were already on shaky ground. I was afraid of losing her."

But you did lose her, I wanted to say.

"Did Jansen tell you what you wanted to know?"

"No. He just said I should cut my ties with I.U.S."

"And when you left you called Jack Gardner."

"What would you have done? It was my company—I wanted to know what the hell he'd done to make Jansen say that. He swore he had no idea."

I shook my head in disbelief. "And you didn't think it was strange Bart Jansen died the same day?"

"I wondered, yes," he admitted. "But the police said it was an accident. There was no proof Jack was involved. I mean, for God's sake, he was in North Carolina at the time."

It sounded rehearsed, like an answer he had ready for an occasion like this one. We had perhaps fifteen more minutes before Josh came back, and I needed to know the truth.

"You must have recognized Dvorak when you followed Maggie."

"No. Not at first. He looked familiar, but I wasn't sure until I heard the name. You've got to understand, I have worked with a lot of people on designs, and most of it is via email. I only met Everett Dvorak the one time."

"Did you honestly believe he was Maggie's lover?"

Alan colored. "Not after I saw him. But I couldn't think of any other reason Maggie would lie to me, unless…."

"Unless she was investigating I.U.S."

He sat back on the settee, rubbing the back of his neck. "I didn't know what else to do. I was upset. I called Jack and told him what I saw and asked if there was any connection between Dvorak and the company. He said there wasn't, and he gave me the number for his divorce lawyer."

In that moment, the horrible reality of what Alan had done became clear. When he called Gardner, the Bald Head Island attack would have already been planned. Once he learned Maggie tracked the Pentagon attack to Dvorak, Gardner knew Maggie would eventually link the North Carolina poisonings to I.U.S. Yet he couldn't call them off or the company would go bankrupt. I flashed back to the dive shop, the rebreather tanks belonging to Chip Holland and his "commando friends," brought in to be refilled right after Maggie Culliver died. Diving without bubbles, undetectable from the surface.

"Gardner killed your wife," I said.

Alan shook his head emphatically. "No. You're wrong. Maggie's death was an accident."

I told him about the rebreather tanks. It was the first crack I saw in his façade.

"You think it was my fault...my fault Maggie was killed," he said, his voice breaking on his wife's name.

I didn't answer.

We both started at the sound of footsteps on the deck. Alan looked up, stricken with shame and fear.

"Are you going to tell Josh?" he choked out.

I bit my lip, torn between pity and anger. Whatever excuses he might tell himself, Alan Culliver had put himself and his company above the interests of anyone else, even his wife. In doing so he had lied—to Maggie, to his nephew, to me. Those lies had cost three people their lives and led to the suffering of hundreds more. It wasn't a secret I could keep.

"No," I said. "You are."

Epilogue

THE DROPS OF WATER fall like diamonds from *Serenity*'s hull as she is hoisted from the ramp in the late December sun. Josh squeezes my hand, and I sense his concern for me, but he is wrong. I have no regrets, though I will miss her. But there is a season for all things, and it is my time to move on.

We watch as the boatlift powers its way into the yard, the sailboat swinging gently in its cradle. Here she will sleep away the winter, nestled between her sisters on dry land, while the rivers carry me southward. I do not know if I will ever stand behind her wheel again.

I turn to look at the man beside me. I know his eyes, the curve of his face, the feel of his hair between my fingers, but his thoughts are still a mystery to me. He has said little about his uncle since that night, when I left the two of them alone. I took a long walk in the moonlight, and when I returned, Alan was gone. I do not know exactly what passed between them, though Josh said his uncle took responsibility for what he had done, and Josh forgave him. But we did not see Alan again, and I knew he would never again look at his uncle with the same eyes.

Yet Josh is unchanged—still seeking the good in people, still looking to the future. It is not in his nature to dwell on the past. It is a trait I am trying to learn, and why I told him I would move aboard his boat and leave *Serenity* here. *Andromeda* is better equipped, and she is free of memories. It is not that I want to forget Ryan and the life we shared, but rather that I am finally able to step away and remember them. Like sea glass, the edges of those memories have worn to smoothness. They cut no more.

We watch as the workers carefully place jack stands under *Serenity*'s hull, and Josh rubs his finger absently over the single diamond I wear on my right hand, his birthday gift to me. He knew the date after all. It is not an engagement ring—not yet—but in time he hopes it could be. Like us, he said, it is not a finished product. It is becoming.

I lean against him and he smiles. I do not know for certain what kind of relationship we will build between us, or how our story will end, but I know how it begins: with hope and love, and no lies beneath.

Other Books by Ann Eichenmuller

Fiction:

Kind Lies (Book 1 - The Lies Murder Mystery Series) The

Lies We Are (Book 2 - The Lies Murder Mystery Series)

Non-Fiction

The Writing Rx: Using the Power of Writing for a Happier, Healthier Life

The Writing Rx Workbook: Guided Activities in Expressive Writing

About the Author

Ann Eichenmuller has always had a love affair with words. Born in Baltimore, Maryland in 1960, she created stories before she could read or write. Her family was her captive audience, a role they did not always relish.

"My grandmother once offered me 25 cents if I would keep quiet for five minutes," she laughs.

She spent her childhood scribbling fiction, and in high school created "Search for Sanity, "a serial soap opera written to entertain her friends. Ann went on to attend St. Mary's College of Maryland, where she was inspired by Dr. Michael Glaser (Maryland's Poet Laureate) to take on the editorship of the school's literary magazine. It was at St. Mary's that she also met and married fellow student Eric Eichenmuller, a musician and songwriter with whom she later co-wrote the musical All *Good Gifts* based on O. Henry's "The Gift of the Magi." After graduating with a B.A. in English in 1982, Ann accepted a teaching position with St. Mary's County Schools.

"I wanted share the taste of words, the smell of them, the way they feel as they roll off of your tongue," she says, adding she also wanted her students to realize "that words have incredible power."

Her efforts earned her two Teacher of the Year Awards as well as the prestigious Washington Post's Agnes Meyer Award for Excellence in 1999. Despite long hours developing lesson plans and editing papers, Ann still found a creative outlet in writing plays for her students to perform. In these she explored the serious issues facing adolescents in modern society.

When they weren't working, Ann and Eric spent their time camping and sailing with their three children. In 1996 the couple purchased a cruising sailboat, and less than a year later, they set sail from Cobb Island, Maryland for the Bahamas. Ann celebrated their adventure in her first-ever non-fiction piece, "A Life Less Ordinary" published in Spin Sheet magazine in 1997.

In the next few years Ann found the time to publish two short stories. She and Eric also became certified divers, licensed private pilots, and proud owners of their Piper Cherokee airplane. Then in 2007, with their children grown, they came up with a new life plan.

"Our saying became, 'How long do you live?' It's an answer you can't know. It propelled us to do what we really wanted," Ann says.

That meant selling their house, moving aboard their boat, and buying an 1886 farmhouse on Virginia's Northern Neck. Their goal? An early retirement and a second chance to pursue their dreams. They spent seven years of weekends renovating the house, and meanwhile Ann also completed her M.A. in Humanities. In 2014 the plan was completed, and Ann returned to her writing.

With Eric's encouragement, she responded to an ad in All at Sea for "inkslingers" and pitched her first essay. She still remembers the thrill of that acceptance–and that first check.

"I was just so excited that someone was willing to pay me for what I wrote!" she laughs.

Encouraged by her success, she pitched article ideas to other magazines, eventually landing regular spots in Chesapeake Bay and Motorhome. She also joined a local writers' group, whose members she credits with getting her beyond the "20,000 word barrier." In 2017 her first novel, *Kind Lies*, was published by High Tide Publications. Now she hopes to finish one of the other three unfinished manuscripts she's working on, but her main focus is to continue growing both as a writer and a person.

"Then I know I'll have no regrets."

CPSIA information can be obtained
at www.ICGtesting.com
Printed in the USA
LVHW031510290719
625730LV00002B/398